When Love Heals

A Novel

S. J. Greene

Book Two of the Fresh Start Series

To everyone I'm lucky enough to have in my life, related or not.

You are my *family*.

Contents

A Note to Readers vii

Part I: Jessica 1

Prologue 2

Chapter 1.. 9

Chapter 2... 13

Chapter 3... 16

Chapter 4... 21

Chapter 5... 26

Chapter 6... 31

Chapter 7... 34

Chapter 8... 47

Chapter 9... 53

Chapter 10.. 57

Chapter 11.. 67

Chapter 12.. 77

Chapter 13.. 81

Chapter 14.. 85

Chapter 15.. 89

Chapter 16.. 99

Chapter 17... 107

Part II: Avery.......................................**112**

Chapter 18... 113

Chapter 19... 124

Chapter 20... 131

Chapter 21... 145

Chapter 22...151

Chapter 23...156

Chapter 24...164

Chapter 25...174

Chapter 26...181

Part III: Jessica **186**

Chapter 27...187

Chapter 28...192

Chapter 29...198

Chapter 30...202

Chapter 31...215

Chapter 32...224

Chapter 33...228

Chapter 34...234

Chapter 35...246

Chapter 36...259

Part IV: We only have Now **263**

Chapter 37- Avery...264

Chapter 38- Jessica.......................................268

Chapter 39- Avery...271

Chapter 40- Jessica.......................................274

Chapter 41- Avery...278

Chapter 42- Jessica.......................................281

Chapter 43- Avery...287

Epilogue - Jessica..291

Acknowledgments..**297**

About the Author **299**

A Note to Readers

Although many of the characters in this book were introduced in *When Love Hurts: Book One of the Fresh Start Series*, this novel is a standalone story, written in a different style. Readers who have not yet read the first book will have no problem following along. That said, a huge **thank-you** to all who are continuing the series!

This novel was inspired by a combination of people in my life, as well as independent research and my own overactive imagination. To be honest, I struggled while writing this story. The characters' personalities and experiences are so drastically different from my own that I often considered scrapping the whole thing, out of fear of not getting the representation correct. I have stressed over this endlessly but landed on the following conclusion: all I can do is my best.

It seems impossible to perfectly represent any group of people, given each individual's personal experience is unique, and therefore not necessarily representative of others in similar, yet different, circumstances. If any of this sounds cryptic or confusing, it's because I don't want to share any spoilers. (You'll have to read the story!) However, I do believe in providing trigger warnings. This novel touches on several potentially sensitive topics or triggers, including: body shaming/ image issues, religion, infertility, infidelity, child with a syndrome, homophobia, sexual abuse of a minor (not graphic), abortion, and animal cruelty. There are lots of positive, uplifting things, too!

Lastly, thank you for giving me the opportunity to do what I love: write emotional stories with entertainment value. I hope all readers—new and returning—enjoy this book!

XOXO,
S. J. Greene

Part I: Jessica

"Love is patient, love is kind. It does not envy, it does not boast, it is not proud… Love never fails."

—The Bible (NIV), 1 Cor. 13:4,8

Prologue

Twenty years ago

Sometimes, the hardest person to love is yourself. I always try my best. And when I make mistakes, I show myself grace, as God would. I try to fit in, and to be friendly and likable. But I never feel good enough… except here.

Here, I belong. Here, I am seen and heard. Nothing else matters. Preparing to begin, I clear my throat, steady my breath, and take a step forward. My heart is pounding, more from excitement than nerves.

"Today, I will be reciting a dramatic monologue from *The Diary of Anne Frank* by Frances Goodrich and Albert Hackett." After a curt nod from Mrs. Beckett, I proceed without hesitation.

> "The sun is shining, the sky is a deep blue, there's
> a magnificent breeze, and I'm longing—so
> longing—for everything! I walk from room to
> room, breathe through the crack in the window
> frame, feel my heart beating as if to say, 'Can't
> you fulfill this longing at last?'… I feel spring
> within me, I feel spring awakening, I feel it in my
> entire body and soul."

Faint giggles from the back of the room are muted by the continued drumming of my heart, even louder now, as I move off center stage to rejoin my classmates in the audience. Their applause echoes throughout my entire body, warming it from the inside out with an emotion even stronger than joy: self-confidence. A confidence so intense it borders on, but never crosses into, the realm of pride—arguably the worst of the seven deadly sins.

After sending silent praise to God for the strength I was given during my performance, I search for signs of approval, but not from Mrs. Beckett. No, my eyes scan the dimly lit auditorium for someone whose opinion matters much more.

"Great job, Jessica. Very well done," I hear Mrs. Beckett say in her British accent that sounds as forced as it is real. Our prim and proper high school drama teacher moved to San Diego from London over a decade ago, but I'm pretty sure she practices her *Received Pronunciation* in the mirror before bed each night to retain it.

Ignoring her praise, I search the rows of faces for *the one, the only*, Avery Emerald. The smile in my heart fades once my gaze lands on her. She's neither smiling nor frowning. Her lips are drawn tight; her face, stoic and unreadable. It knots my insides. Did she not like it?

Avery started here as a new student a month into the school year. We have two classes together: fourth period Brit Lit with Mr. Johnson, who ironically has a strong southern accent, and this sixth period drama class with the somewhat-still-British Mrs. Beckett.

I knew there was something special about Avery as soon as she walked into Mr. Johnson's class and got introduced. She had seemed terrified when standing in front of the room, but once our eyes met, she'd relaxed. That was the moment I realized she had come to Clairemont High—and into my life—for a reason. All I have to do is figure out what that is.

Looking at her now, I can't help but compare myself. Her height and weight are average, same as mine. Her hair and eyes are both brown, like mine. Our complexions are similar, but her cheeks are dusted with cute freckles, while the only spots on my face are acne and one large beauty mark to the right of my mouth.

Avery and I are both freshmen girls with more commonalities than differences. And yet, she is better than me in every way. She's a mirror in one of those fancy department stores, where you see an ideal version of yourself reflected. It keeps you shopping there, or in my case, keeps me compulsively wanting to be in her presence.

"Avery, you're up next," Mrs. Beckett says.

A slight grimace flashes on Avery's previously expressionless face, and then it disappears as quickly as it came when she ascends the stairs to the right of the stage. She appears as composed and confident as ever when she steps up to the microphone and says, "Today, I will also be reciting a dramatic monologue from *The Diary of Anne Frank* by Frances Goodrich and Albert Hackett."

My heart sinks into my stomach at those words. *Please don't tell me she selected the same monologue for today's audition.* No, I'm sure that's not the case. There are plenty of other options she could have chosen from that play. Waiting for her to start, I squeeze my eyes tight and tell myself I'm overreacting.

My eyes pop open at the words, "Sometimes I see myself alone in a dungeon…"

Air rushes out of my lungs in relief. It's a different monologue. No longer worried about the awkwardness of us performing the same lines, I'm entranced listening to hers. I watch and listen in awe as she emotes each word, each syllable. Realization quickly sets in, though… Her monologue is better than mine. *Of course, it is.*

But as I watch her performance, there are no feelings of envy— *another deadly sin*, I remind myself. I'm not jealous of her. I feel nothing but admiration, like that of being star-struck by your favorite celebrity. Though the entire stage is lit, I imagine a bright spotlight haloed over her, and above that, her name in large block letters outlined in lights. AVERY EMERALD. Even her name is perfect for the stage.

As Avery nears the end of her powerful delivery, I hear snickering behind me and attempt to block it out—almost successfully—until I feel something hit my hair. I swat at it, still trying to focus on Avery's every word, and something drops to the floor. I ignore it. Seconds later, a small but jagged object hits my bare shoulder and then also falls to the ground.

Glancing down, I notice two crumbled pieces of paper near my feet. I roll my eyes and finally turn around to see Bradley Clark grinning at me from two rows back. He is beyond immature, but also annoyingly cute, with blond hair, blue eyes, and dimples that rival those of Mario Lopez. I think it's the dimples that get me, because I find myself uncontrollably smiling back at him.

He motions toward the paper at my feet, and like a puppet on strings, my hand reaches down to grab them. Heat rises to my face and chest, causing me to panic. *Do not let him see you blush, Jessica.* The voice I hear in my head is not my own. It belongs to my best friend, Natalya Petrova. Ever since the *one time* I chased and kissed a boy on the kindergarten playground—causing him to cry, and me to get sent home early—Nat has been constantly reminding me to play it cool around boys.

I face away from Brad and his friends right as Avery is exiting the stage. All the heat vanishes and my heart drops once more. *I missed the end of her monologue.* What were her final words? What was Mrs. Beckett's reaction? Anger replaces whatever I was feeling toward Brad moments earlier. How could I let him distract me like that?

I put on my best smile and clap and cheer for Avery, but her dark eyes never meet mine as she takes her seat in front of me. Is she mad at me? Did she notice I hadn't been paying attention? I mentally kick myself. This is not the way to befriend her.

I should probably mention that I've never actually spoken with Avery. Every time I try to strike up a conversation, I either lose the nerve or get interrupted. As more time passes, it grows increasingly awkward to try. Still, I imagine us becoming great friends one day. We're only three months into the school year, and we'll be on winter break soon. Worst case, I can ask her about her holiday in the new year and get on talking terms that way.

A third note flies over my shoulder, hits the back of Avery's head, and bounces into my lap. Avery turns around but says nothing. My mortification causes me to shrug my shoulders as if I have no idea what happened. Her eyes drift down to the crumpled note in my lap, and I squeeze the other two in my hand to further conceal them.

"I think someone wants your attention" is all she says before turning back around.

Dumbfounded, I stare between the note in my lap and the back of Avery's head. Jason Peters is on stage reciting a monologue from *Lord of the Flies*, but it's only background noise to the boisterous thoughts in my head. They are clamoring over each other like my family at dinnertime.

Avery spoke to me, one thought says. Another asks, *what's in the note?* Yet another wonders if I should have said something back, but if so, what? Endless questions continue to flood my mind: Why is Brad throwing notes at me? Does he like me? Did Avery seem upset that he was trying to get my attention? Does Avery like Brad? Would that hurt our chance of becoming friends? Why have I still not opened the notes?

At that last thought, I roll open the crumbled paper from my fist, revealing the messages of the first two notes.

One simply reads: *Hey.*

The second one reads: *Wanna hang out?*

I look over my shoulder to see if Brad is watching me, and he absolutely is. The dimples strike again, and I find myself nodding and smiling like… well, like the teenage girl I am. The third note is still on my lap, so I discreetly roll that one open as well, glancing to read it while attempting to look like I'm not.

The third note reads: *Yours was better.*

I'm glad my back is to Brad right now, because my smile grows three Grinch-heart sizes and my cheeks burn from blushing.

"Miss Serrano, is there something you'd like to share with the class?" The now perfect British accent belongs to Mrs. Beckett.

My cheeks drop, and I shake my head. "No, nothing to share."

Mrs. Beckett eyes me wearily and then calls the next student onto the stage. The school play, a modern-day retelling of *Romeo and Juliet*, is expected to be cast by the end of the week. Our monologues are our auditions, but we weren't allowed to choose anything by Shakespeare. A weird rule, if you ask me, but Mrs. Beckett had stressed that half the test was seeing "the choices we make in the face of adversity." Whatever that means.

My purple backpack sits near my feet, covered in various patches I proudly ironed-on myself. One, to my slight embarrassment, says "Bye Bye Bye" beneath all five faces of NSYNC. Another is a black-and-white ball encircled in text that reads, "Soccer Rules!" because, obviously, it does. My favorite patch, however, is a large golden sunflower that reads, "Sunflowers Kick Butt."

Sunflowers are the prettiest flowers, after all. They're happy flowers. Nat has the same patch on her backpack. I had given it to her as a gift after she had gotten us matching friendship necklaces. Her half of the sunflower charm says, "Best." Mine says, "Friends."

I shove all three notes into my backpack and then smile again at the memory of Brad's third message. *Yours was better.*

Once the bell rings, I gather my belongings and head for the door. Brad jogs up next to me. "Hey. Wanna hang out?"

Wasn't that the point of the notes?

"Sure," I say. "What did you have in mind?"

"A bunch of us are headed to the mall. We could get Dairy Queen or something."

No sweeter words have been uttered than *mall* and *Dairy Queen.* I follow Brad toward a group of his friends gathered near the gate that leads off school property. I slow when I see Avery Emerald among them. Is Brad friends with Avery? Or is she dating one of his friends? If she is, maybe we could double-date sometime. I'm excited by that prospect, possibly more than I am about dating Bradley Clark, but then I remind myself of the third note. *Yours was better.*

Chapter 1

Now

"How about tonight?" I blurt, after my physical therapist, Kevin, mentions getting dinner sometime. "Not that I'm overeager or anything. It's just that my kids are with their father tonight… who I'm no longer with, by the way. We're separated, and it's complicated, but the point is… I have a sitter tonight."

My cheeks burn with embarrassment. "Wow, after saying all that out loud, I realize it's probably too complicated. Men don't like complicated, right? You can take back your dinner offer. I promise I won't judge you if you do… I might even judge you a little if you don't. Better yet, let's pretend this conversation never happened. I'm rambling. Please stop me."

Kevin touches my non-injured arm, setting my already overheated skin on fire with his warm hand. "I don't mind a little complication… for the right woman."

All I can hear after that is the *thud, thud, thud* of my pounding heart. How am I supposed to interpret that? Am I the right woman? Or was it his way of letting me down gently? Flirting with him the past few weeks has been fun, but my life has more than a *little* complication.

"How about I pick you up at six?" he says with a smile. "I'll make us a seven o'clock reservation somewhere near the harbor. We can take a walk around the water before we eat."

Shock washes over me. All I have to do is get ready, and he'll take care of the rest? *He's a planner*, I realize. Brad had never planned a single date or meal during our entire relationship. "That sounds perfect! Should I give you my number? Or my address?"

"I already have both in your file here." He wiggles the folder in his hand. "I also know your full name is Jessica Marie Serrano-Clark, and that you broke this arm once before when you were a kid."

"Right," I say.

"See, not too complicated. And since today is my last day as a PT here, we won't have to worry about you being my patient." He winks at me, and I gulp.

"Um, it's your last day?"

"Oh, yeah. Sorry, I thought the front office had told all my patients already. I'm taking an opportunity at another rehab center downtown, but you'll be in good hands with my replacement. I hear she has lots of great experience. She's even worked for some pro sports teams. Tell me when this hurts," he says while lifting my left arm.

Stabbing pain shoots through my shoulder and down my upper back almost immediately. "Ow," I say, wincing and sucking in air through my teeth.

"Your range of motion is not where I'd hoped it would be yet. Have you been keeping up on your exercises at home?"

Busted. *But when is there time?* Between shuttling two kids around to endless doctor appointments and activities, working at the hotel, doing everyone's laundry, cooking, cleaning, and trying my best not to fall apart, I'm lucky if I even have time to bathe most days. Despite the hot weather, I had to throw on yoga pants this morning to cover the fur coat growing on my legs, thanks to my lack of life's most precious commodity: Time.

I'll definitely be bathing before my date tonight, though. And shaving my legs. Oh goodness… Is Kevin expecting sex tonight?

Maybe I shouldn't shave my legs. If I do, I'll be more tempted to do things I shouldn't. I am *not* the type of girl to sleep with someone on the first date.

Or am I? It occurs to me I haven't been on a first date since high school. I also realize I'm not technically single or even divorced yet, just separated. The idea of going out on a date suddenly feels all kinds of wrong.

I'm still married to Brad. Although… being married didn't stop Brad from sleeping with a woman named Susan. *In my kitchen. On my birthday.* A date tonight no longer sounds like a bad idea. I dwell on the prospect of sex with Kevin until he clears his throat, reminding me I have yet to answer his question.

"Oh, I try to do a few of the exercises each night before bed, but I know I should do more." Just saying the word *bed* around him has me feeling flustered.

"Well, compliance is key to a full recovery. Shoulder injuries can be limiting, but now that the cast is off your arm, you should be pushing yourself with the exercises to regain strength and mobility. Here's another set I recommend working into your routine." He hands me a piece of paper with illustrated instructions, and I feel like I'm back in school. And hot for teacher.

I stand to leave and wonder how I got here. Not literally… I mean, I know how I got to the rehab center this morning. I drove myself—with great care—in a pre-owned SUV, which was all I could afford with the scant insurance money. My older model Camry had been totaled after the jerk texting while driving plowed into the back of it in stopped traffic two months ago.

The worst part was that I saw it coming but couldn't do anything about it. My tense arms bore the brunt of the damage, since I had instinctively gripped the steering wheel while waiting for impact. It left me with two fractures in my left wrist and forearm, a dislocated left shoulder, and horrible pain from whiplash in my neck and back. I just thank the Lord that my kids, Lucas and Chloe, weren't in the car with me. They are my entire world.

Their safety is part of the reason I upsized my vehicle after the crash, even though it guzzles gas like no other. I would love to drive a fancy electric car like my bestie, Natalie, but they're out of my price range. My finances have been especially tight since Brad moved out—correction, since I kicked him out—almost a year ago. Natalie has offered to help me manage my budget, but the idea of opening the spreadsheet she emailed me turns my stomach in knots. We all have our strengths; budgets and spreadsheets are not mine.

After saying "see you later" to Kevin, I cross the rehab center's lobby and head toward the exit. I fish for my car keys in my purse before heading outside and bump shoulders—my good one, luckily—with another person who is entering the building. Silky skin brushes against mine a split second before my keys fling from my right hand and land outside the door.

"Sorry! I wasn't paying attention," I say without looking up. I then step outside and bend over to grab my keys off the ground. *Oh, my aching back.* My teeth grind at the sudden sensation of pain.

"No, I'm sorry. I should have been more careful," a female voice says.

As soon as I stand back up, which takes painfully longer than it should, all I see are pretty, dark curls bouncing away at a fast pace—almost like she's running away from me. *That's weird.*

Chapter 2

Kevin grew up in the Bay Area but moved here almost twenty years ago to play college football at San Diego State. In a city of transplants, that makes him practically a native. A knee injury during his first season as an Aztec had prompted his interest in becoming a physical therapist. He is also close with his family—a big plus in my book.

His parents are still happily married, same as mine. He has an older brother named Kyle and a first-cousin named Kylie, who is like a sister to him. Kyle and Kylie were born only months apart, and Kevin's mother and aunt apparently both liked baby names that started with "K." Kevin came along two years later and dutifully played his role as the baby of the family, getting spoiled by the grandparents he adores.

I learned all this over dinner and yet, somehow, still don't know his last name. I also learned that Kevin likes to talk about himself. *A lot.* So much that I don't recall him asking me a single question about my life during dinner. But I suppose that's for the best.

My disaster of a life doesn't make for interesting conversation these days. Though, to be fair, neither did hearing about his top picks for the next fantasy football draft or the self-touted number of touchdowns he once scored in a single game. It was five—same as the number of times he mentioned it during our date.

"Well, thank you again for dinner," I say as we approach the front door of my pink house. "I had a fun time tonight."

But did I? The food had certainly been delicious. He had treated me to Ruth's Chris, a fancy steak house near the harbor. The Filet Mignon had literally melted in my mouth. Kevin couldn't possibly know the special place red meat holds in my heart, but as we stand on the front porch, I wonder if he thinks it might get him lucky tonight.

I fumble with my keys while considering my options. On the one hand, this is a first date, and I wouldn't want him getting the wrong impression about me. Being promiscuous would go against the core values long instilled by my faith, which he would know if he had bothered to get to know me at all.

On the other hand, the kids aren't home, and it's been way too long since I've had sex. Ten months, to be exact. Ten long months since Brad had surprised me in the shower, knowing full well it would be our last time. My best friend would soon drop the bomb that she had caught him in the act with another woman.

Then there's the fact that I shaved my legs for tonight. After a lifetime playing soccer, my legs are my best assets. They're shapely and lean, unlike the rest of my top-heavy body. Despite the many frustrating diets and programs I've tried over the years, I can't seem to shed the extra twenty pounds or so in my boobs and belly.

Shifting my focus from my keys to Kevin, I notice his eyes are glued to my chest. He's a boob guy, apparently, just like Brad. Heat rushes to my face as I realize I'm showing more cleavage than usual, thanks to my baby sister telling me not to wear a cami under the V-shaped neckline of my dress. Why I ever listen to her is beyond me.

Hoping to conceal more of myself, I tug up the straps of my dress. "Maybe we can do this again sometime."

I'm also hoping he'll take the hint and leave, but he just stands there, looking at me expectantly with deep blue eyes that remind me far too much of Brad's. Then it hits me. Although Kevin is tall, muscular, and objectively handsome, I feel nothing for him. Nothing good, at least. *I won't be sleeping with him tonight.*

Resolute in my decision, I lean in to peck him on the cheek, only to have him turn and catch my lips with his. The kiss is brief, but it confirms what I already sensed. There isn't any chemistry between us. No heart flutters. No *fizzle, pop, boom, pow.* Nothing.

"Good night, Kevin. Thanks again for a nice time." Turning to insert my key in the lock, I hear a loud scoff.

"That's it?" he asks. "You're not going to invite me in?"

His harsh tone spins me on my heels. "What do you mean?" I ask with equal parts offense and disbelief.

"Don't play coy. You know exactly what I mean. Or did you think I asked you out for the mere pleasure of your company?"

Is he seriously saying this to me right now? My jaw drops, but then the look in his eyes has it snap shut. My stomach does flips under his glare. I'm alone at night with this a-hole, my front door is unlocked, and he could easily push me inside. Fear for my personal safety swells inside me, and I clench my fists.

"My best friend is on her way over," I lie, nerves boiling over. "We had a girls' night planned for tonight before you asked me out to dinner."

He laughs almost manically. "So, you wore that dress and ran up the tab at dinner already knowing you weren't going to put out tonight? Classic. Word of advice…" He takes a step closer and points his finger at my stomach. "If you want a second date from a guy next time, try skipping dessert."

He turns and walks away after the low blow that might as well have been a punch. Tears fill my eyes. When he's almost to his shiny BMW, he hollers over his shoulder, "And don't forget to do your PT exercises."

Chapter 3

Three years ago

It's almost ten o'clock. Ten means I can finally eat breakfast. Lucas had a bad dream last night and crawled into bed with Brad and me at two o'clock in the morning. It's not that I mind having my sweet baby boy sleep with us, but between his kicking, Brad's snoring, and the periodic chirp from one of the smoke detectors I've been nagging Brad to change the batteries in all week, I wasn't able to fall back asleep. That means I've already been awake for eight hours, and this bacon needs to hurry and crisp already.

My mouth salivates as I flip each of the eight thick-cut strips sizzling on the electric griddle. As a bonus, there will be fewer pans to clean, since I had used this griddle earlier to make pancakes in the shape of Mickey Mouse for the kids. That was at seven o'clock, and it had been sheer torture not to sample them.

"Mmm, smells delicious, babe. Can you remind me again why we're not allowed to eat until now?" Brad asks, walking into the kitchen and opening the refrigerator door. He peers inside as if looking for something that's not there and then shuts it.

"Intermittent fasting," I say and then point in his direction. "Since you're here, can you please hand me the eggs from the fridge? The bacon is almost ready."

He grabs the carton of eggs and sets them down next to the griddle. "Yeah, but *why* are we fasting?"

"Eating for only eight hours of the day is supposed to boost our metabolism and burn more fat. Plus, I've started a keto diet this week, where I'm cutting out all carbs except a few high-fiber vegetables. I'm finally going to get rid of this stupid belly fat." I move the bacon to a plate lined with paper towels and then crack open several eggs on top of the bacon grease.

Brad stands behind me and wraps his arms around my waist. "You're perfect just the way you are, babe." He then leans over my shoulder and kisses my cheek as I carefully flip the fried eggs. His body is firm against the back of mine, and unless I'm imagining things, he's in the mood for more than breakfast. This is confirmed as one of his hands travels from my waist to cup my left breast.

It feels good to be wanted. So good that I allow the ache to build between my thighs for several moments before looking up to check on Lucas and Chloe, who are watching *Sesame Street* in the adjacent family room. The beauty of an open floor plan is that I can see them from the kitchen, but it also means they could see Brad and me right now, if they were to look. I debate swatting Brad's hand away, even though what he's doing with his thumb forces me to bite back a moan.

The kids are distracted by Elmo, who is saying something I can't understand in that trademark high-pitched voice of his, so I lean back into Brad. His hardness complements my softness in all the right places as he towers over me. I'm thinking about grabbing Brad's other hand—and guiding it beneath the waistband of my pajama pants—when I realize it's no longer on my waist. In my peripheral vision, I see it reaching toward the plate of bacon.

With a forced laugh, I playfully slap his hand away from the plate. "Nice try! Go sit down, and I'll bring you your eggs and bacon in a minute."

Much to my delight, he instead wraps both arms around me again from behind. He rests his chin on my shoulder and plants soft kisses on the side of my neck. "Seriously, though… you don't need all these crazy diets, babe. You're beautiful at any size. And if anyone ever says differently, I'll kick their ass."

"Language," I mutter, motioning to where the kids luckily, and somewhat miraculously, are still focused on the television. *God bless PBS.* "And thank you, my love, but it's not all about looks. You know diabetes runs in my family. I want to make sure I stay healthy for you and the kids."

"Well, I'll always support that… and anything you want to do, you know that, right?"

After putting the eggs onto two separate plates, I add four slices of bacon to each and then turn to face my husband. "Yes, I know, and I love you for that," I say, leaning in for a kiss.

"Ew! Mommy and daddy are kissing!" The declaration by Lucas is followed by squeals and giggles from both children.

Brad breaks our kiss. "Okay, okay. That's enough TV for this morning. Bud, why don't you help your sister up and go play in the backyard while your mommy and I eat our breakfast."

A groan from Lucas is followed with, "We don't want to go outside. We wanna play Mario Kart!"

I suppress a laugh, unsure if Lucas is using the royal "we" here or if he truly believes his two-year-old sister would also prefer to play video games. Never mind that she lacks the necessary motor skills. In either case, the word "we" has replaced "I" in his vocabulary whenever she's in the same room, and sometimes even when she's not.

Brad and I exchange a brief glance, silently discussing whether we should cave to keep them occupied or stand our ground. *When did kids stop wanting to play outside anyway?* Natalie and I would spend hours on end in my parents' backyard as kids. We'd use our imaginations to turn an assortment of plants into either potions for casting spells, medicines to heal each other, or various food dishes when playing restaurant. My favorite memories are from all the times we'd pretend we were filming a movie, acting out various dramatic scenes and often involving our siblings as extras. *All outside.*

The glimmer in Brad's baby blue eyes tells me he's thinking the same thing. I nod at him, put on my biggest smile, and then enthusiastically say, "Look how beautiful it is outside! Oh, I wish we could play out there all day, but we have chores to do." Turning toward the family room, I ask, "What do you think we should do first, Lucas? Clean our rooms or organize the garage?"

"But daddy said we can play outside! Chores are boring." Lucas groans even louder this time and tucks his chin into his chest with a pout on his adorable face.

With my arms crossed, I tilt my head like I'm thinking. "Hmm… Your daddy did say that, but I don't know if there's enough time to play outside with everything that needs to get done. What do you think, honey?" I ask Brad.

"Well, you're right that there's a lot to do, but since the kids have been so well-behaved… could we maybe spare at least an hour for some outdoor fun?"

My head tilts on cue. "I guess an hour would be okay, I mean, if the kids even *want* to go outside."

"We do! We do!" Lucas shouts, as Chloe scribbles on a coloring book.

"Okay, then. I'll set a timer for one hour exactly." I fiddle with my phone, doing nothing in particular. "I'll let you know when time is up. Have fun!"

"Yay!" More squeals, and then Lucas holds Chloe's hand as they walk outside to play. The sight of her wobbly legs in forward motion fills me with the same gratitude and joy as when witnessing her first steps.

"And scene," I say with a small bow once they're outside.

"You always were an amazing actress," Brad says, gripping my hips.

"You weren't bad yourself, Romeo." I take a bite of bacon and then lean in to kiss Brad again.

The salty, savory taste has me lingering longer this time. His hips press into mine, and a fresh surge of longing shoots straight through my core. My hand reaches down to trace the wondrously solid bulge between us through the thin fabric of his warm-up shorts.

"Somebody's happy to see me."

"We have an hour," he whispers into my ear with a voice full of need.

Though the heat of his breath sends tingles down my body, I force myself to reply, "They're only two and five. They still need supervision, unfortunately. Let's go eat our breakfast on the patio, and I promise we'll pick this up later tonight."

He groans as I pull away, and I get another surge of pleasure from knowing how much he wants me. Bradley Clark has always done this for me. He's a drug that makes me high whenever I'm feeling low. *You're beautiful at any size* repeats in my brain as I grab my plate and head outside.

Chapter 4

Now

"I still can't believe the bastard said that to you!" Natalie says after looking over her shoulder. "I say we find out which rehab center he works at now and send Derek to go kick his ass!"

I look outside to confirm Lucas and Chloe are still playing in my parents' backyard and well out of earshot. My dad is standing at the grill, waving the spatula in his hand in his usual animated fashion as he talks with Derek, Natalie's sweetheart of a boyfriend.

Lucas catches a Nerf football tossed by Derek and then runs to the opposite end of the yard, throwing the ball down into the grass triumphantly before performing a crazed end-zone dance. Chloe is sitting cross-legged on the patio in the pink ballerina skirt and leggings she had insisted on wearing this morning, pouring what appears to be imaginary tea for three of her dolls. My heart swells at the sight of them both. *I have the best kids.*

Sunday barbecues with my parents after church have been a weekly tradition for as long as I can remember. Brad had stopped coming a full year before I found out about his affair. I suppose that should have been a warning sign, but I'd believed him when he'd said he was tired and needed to rest.

Being in construction, Brad had been insanely busy due to the booming housing and remodeling markets. But not too busy, apparently. I guess men are never too busy for sex. Or at least that's true for men like Brad… and jerks like Kevin.

"I'm sure the SDPD would frown on Derek beating some guy up," I say. "But thanks for the offer."

"And *I'm sure* Derek would agree that any trouble he'd get into would be worth it," Natalie says, not letting it go. "His detective gig here is temporary anyway, and once he becomes a lawyer, he can get himself out of any silly legal mess." Natalie flicks her wrist with a grin that lets me know she's joking about siccing Derek on Kevin. It's also impossible to miss all the pride and love beaming from her eyes when she talks about him.

"I'm so happy for you two." My eyes fill with joyful tears, which are much better than all the tears spilled on Friday night. These tears warm my soul, because I want nothing but the best for her, and it seems she may finally have what she's always deserved.

"Thanks, Jess. I'm happy, too. Derek is excited to start applying to law schools, and even though he missed the fall admission deadline at Cal Western, he can still apply to be admitted next spring."

"That's great." I wipe away my tears, as well as all thoughts of stupid Kevin. There's too much to be grateful for in this world.

My mom's voice travels from the kitchen. Her words are indiscernible, but I hear laughter from Natalie's mom, Linda, and it reminds me of the last time we were all together like this.

We had all gone out the night Derek received his LSAT score a few weeks back. It was a great night of eating, drinking, laughing, and, overall, enjoying each other's company. We hadn't gone anywhere fancy, and it was only dinner—a commonplace event easy to take for granted—but after the past year, everyone at the table knew exactly how precious such a moment was.

"How are things going at the women's center?" I ask, right before Lucas bursts into the living room.

"Mom! Mom! Guess what?"

The look I shoot Natalie carries two silent messages: *Sorry for the interruption,* and *it figures.* "What buddy?"

"Uncle Derek said he'll get me a dog for my birthday, if it's okay with you!"

All the love and gratitude I have for the man who saved my best friend's life fades.

"He said what?" I ask, gritting my teeth to avoid yelling.

Derek's hazel eyes widen at my tone. Is he surprised I'm upset? I know he and Natalie don't have children, but anyone should know you don't go around offering dogs to other people's kids. Now, I'll either be the bad guy who tells them no, as usual, or I'll be stuck taking care of a dog I don't have time for. Lucas and Chloe are both jumping up and down shrieking "doggie, doggie!" when Derek cuts in with an apologetic look on his face.

"I asked Lucas what he wants for his upcoming birthday. He said a dog, but I told him we'd have to talk to you first."

My anger abates after learning Derek didn't initiate the idea of a dog, but I'm still in the predicament of having to either crush my sweet boy's excitement or say yes to something I'm not sure I can handle. All eyes are on me as Lucas continues pleading with his own set of puppy eyes. A classic parenting technique would be to delay this conversation by saying something like, *we'll see* or *let's discuss later.* I suppose the *ask your father* card is off the table now.

And that's when Lucas hits me with, "I thought since dad doesn't live with us anymore, we could get a dog now." *Again, with the puppy eyes.*

The lie comes screaming back to me. When Lucas had first raised the topic of getting a dog a couple of years back, Brad had taken one for the team by saying he was allergic to dogs. His fictitious allergies were the perfect cover for the fact that neither of us had wanted the additional responsibility. I suppose I could say I'm allergic too, but it doesn't feel right.

Perhaps it's the memory of how heartbroken the kids had been when we told them the news of our separation, or maybe it's the guilt of my indecision over whether it's permanent, but something inside bends so far it almost breaks.

"Okay," I say. "We can get a dog. But not a puppy. We'll get a rescue dog from the shelter. It has to be housebroken already, and you're going to have to help feed it and take it on walks."

"I will! I will!" Lucas jumps around in a circle, holding his sister's hands as if playing *Ring around the Rosie*. "I'll help pick up the poop, too. Because everything poops!"

Chloe giggles while clapping, and the smile on Lucas' face is the biggest I've seen since Brad moved out. Peace settles in over my decision. I am truly blessed with these kids.

"Yes, Lucas. Everything poops," I parrot back.

"On that note, dinner's ready," my dad says, walking into the house with a large platter of hamburgers and hot dogs fresh off the grill.

After the delicious meal and hours of card games—Uno with the kids, followed by poker for the adults—I am standing in my parents' kitchen, washing dishes with Natalie by my side. Derek had to leave before the poker game to investigate an attempted mugging at the trolley station. Lucas and Chloe are both sleeping in the spare room furnished specifically for them, and my parents are most likely asleep in front of the television.

If there were ever a right time to tell Natalie what I've been putting off all night, it would be now. Still, I'm nervous. *She will not approve.* I finish loading the last plate into the dishwasher and then dry my hands, running the dish towel through my fingers one too many times, because Natalie asks, "Is everything okay, Jess?"

My chest involuntarily heaves all the air from my lungs. I don't want to tell her, but I can't *not* tell her. So, I figure I might as well rip off the Band-Aid. "I did a thing last night… after you left."

She eyes me warily. "What kind of thing?"

"Well, you know how Brad has been asking me—begging me, really—to try marriage counseling before I file for a divorce?"

"Yeah… but I don't like where this is headed."

"I know, and you're not going to be happy about this, but I texted him last night. I told him if he makes the appointment, I'll go."

Natalie doesn't say anything; she doesn't need to. When you are best friends with someone for thirty years, words aren't necessary to know what they're thinking.

"I'm not committing to anything," I say in my defense. "But he's the father of my children, Nat. I can't throw our marriage away without at least trying."

Natalie sighs. "I'd argue that he threw it away when he slept with another woman, but you obviously feel differently. It's your life, Jess. I'm not here to judge."

Except that she was. As much as I love Natalie, she's always been the most judgmental person I've ever known. Everything is right or wrong, black or white, with no gray area in between. But she doesn't know the full story, and I can't tell her. Some things are too awful to ever be shared, so I suppose I shouldn't be mad at her for not understanding.

"It's just a few counseling sessions," I say, partially to convince myself. "It doesn't mean I'm taking him back."

But as the words escape my lips, even I don't believe them.

Chapter 5

"I gotta poop," Lucas says matter-of-factly, before pausing his video game and disappearing down the hall the next day.

I laugh from the kitchen, wondering if everyone's Monday morning is as entertaining as mine while stuffing celery, baby carrots, apple wedges, and multi-grain crackers into small reusable pouches for today's outing. Having healthy snacks on hand is always important, but especially on days like today. We're going to the San Diego Humane Society to pick out the newest member of our family, and it's possible we'll need to visit several of their shelter locations to find *the one*.

"I'm hungry, Mommy."

My insides cringe and my heart cracks at those three words—my absolute least favorite. They take me back to the first time Chloe had said them almost a year ago. Even though we had been warned, it didn't lessen the shock and panic that followed those words. It was the day everything had changed.

"It's not snack time yet, baby," I say with a forced smile. "I'm packing these so we'll have snacks for later… after we pick out our new doggie!"

Chloe is looking up at me with the saddest eyes I think I've ever seen. She's at the edge of the family room, where the carpet meets the tiled floor of the kitchen, knowing she is not supposed to enter unless given permission.

Our kitchen is the center of our older but newly renovated home and has two entry points. One is an arched entryway that leads in from the formal living and dining areas, which are the only rooms visible when entering our front door. I had loved how perfect that was for entertaining when Brad and I first bought this home nearly eight years ago.

The other entry point to the kitchen is where Chloe is standing, with the family room at her back and the sliding glass door to the backyard beyond that. To her left, or my right, is a long hall that leads to all three bedrooms and the second bathroom. The hall is not visible from the kitchen, but sound travels through it well.

It's as if Lucas is yelling directly in my ear when I hear him holler from the bathroom. "Mom! We're out of toilet paper!"

"Check under the sink!" I holler back.

"I did! There isn't any. Hurry!"

"Just a minute!" I sigh and wipe my hands on the towel hanging from the center island.

"Apples, Mommy. Please!" Chloe hasn't budged from her spot at the edge of the kitchen, and there are tears forming in her eyes. She is pointing at the pouch of apple slices on the counter. *Dear Lord, please give me the strength I'm going to need to get through this day.*

Hoping to distract her, I crank my enthusiasm level to fifteen on a ten-point-scale and ask, "Aren't you excited we're getting a doggie today, Chloe?"

The tears are now rolling down her face as she stomps her smaller than average foot. "Apples! Apples!"

"Mom!" Lucas' voice travels down the hall again. "I need to wipe my butt! Hurry! Please!"

For a brief second, I consider placating Chloe with an apple slice so I can go help Lucas. Then I remind myself that her BMI is already in the eighty-fifth percentile. She's overweight, but not yet obese. *I will not let her become obese.* "Baby, you already had breakfast.

I'm sorry, but please go sit back down with your dollies while I help your brother."

I scoot her backward, toward her toys in the family room, as I exit the kitchen and head down the hall. She's in full meltdown mode, sobbing and writhing on the floor when I glance back over my shoulder. But I can't deal with that right now. Darting into the master bedroom, the first one off the long hall, I head toward my bathroom and rummage under the sink once there. "Hangnail," I mutter. *We're out of toilet paper.*

To avoid swearing in front of our kids, Brad and I had long ago developed a list of alternative curse words. Well, I created the list and Brad adopted it, mostly. It had started out as simple modifications, like saying *shirt* or *puck*, but we quickly discovered those words sounded much too similar to the actual curses when coming out of little mouths. I have since made a game out of coming up with new expletives from ordinary things I dislike, steering clear of anything food-related for Chloe's benefit.

Acceptable curses range from minor annoyances, such as *broken pencil* or *missing sock*, to more offensive items, like *stinky diapers* or *dirty dishes*. When things get especially bad, I drop the t-word: *taxes.* Running out of toilet paper doesn't warrant a t-bomb, but it's one heck of a *bloody hangnail.*

After pulling the partial roll off the holder in my bathroom, I jog farther down the hall to where Lucas is sitting on the toilet. "Here you go, bud."

He grabs the roll I hand him and unravels far more than should be needed for his little tush.

"That's our last roll," I say while looking under the sink in his bathroom to confirm. "Save a square, will ya?"

He's giggling as I close the door and make my way back toward the kitchen. Chloe seems to have calmed down and is sitting with her back to me while brushing her doll's hair. *Thank you, Jesus.* I reach into the cupboard for an insulated lunch bag and begin to fill it with the previously prepared snacks. That's when I notice the pouch of apple slices isn't as full.

One, two, three, four, five, six, seven, eight. Eight wedges remain out of ten. I'm certain there were ten, because I have a tool that both cores and slices the apple in a single press. It makes ten wedges. My throat constricts. Tears pool behind my eyes, but I fight them back. This is not the time to be emotional.

Deep breaths. My chest rises and falls repeatedly as I think about my next steps. Chloe's back is to me, and the guilt I'm sure she feels breaks my heart. Stealing food is not okay, but it's also not her fault. It's one hundred percent *my fault* for creating the opportunity.

I need to say something to help her understand that, but I'm not sure I can speak right now. My breath is shaky as I reach for my phone and debate texting Brad. He's better at handling these situations. I'm not sure I can do this on my own.

Despite our marital challenges, Brad and I were the perfect parenting team. We presented a unified front on most issues and a flawless *good cop, bad cop* routine when needed. More importantly, whenever one of us felt like we were failing, the other seamlessly stepped in without question.

Now, I'm tight-rope walking without a safety net—one I had assumed would always be there. The realization hits me hard. There's no longer anyone to catch me when I fall. My thoughts are interrupted by Lucas bursting back into the family room.

"Can we go get my dog now, Mom?"

I clear my throat and speak with confidence. "Yes, after a quick stop at Target to get some toilet paper and pet supplies. Turn off your video game and grab your shoes, bud."

Lucas runs back down the hall shouting "yippee!" at the top of his lungs, and I add, "Chloe, baby, go get your shoes on as well. You can have the rest of your apple slices after we find a doggie, okay?"

Her chubby cheeks are streaked with tears when she slowly turns and nods, and it takes everything in my power to hold back my own emotions. The understanding in her eyes helps. She knows I'm aware of the stolen apple slices, but she also needs to know I'm not angry at her. *A safety net isn't needed*, I tell myself. *I've got this.*

I give her a wide smile, zip the lunch bag closed, and head out of the kitchen. "Come on. Let's go have some fun today!"

Chapter 6

Five years ago

There aren't enough words to describe the amount of love flooding my heart and spilling over my entire soul right now. Brad's pale eyes reflect the same as he stares down at our little miracle in his arms. Although I've been here every single day for the last month, touching her tiny hand through the incubator, nothing compares to today. Today is heavenly. Today, we finally held our sweet baby girl.

She'd decided to come out a few weeks early while still in a breech position, forcing an unplanned cesarean. After the delivery, they had whisked her away to the NICU, citing concerns of poor muscle tone and a weak cry. Two weeks and several blood tests later, we had a diagnosis: Prader-Willi syndrome.

We're told it's a genetic disorder that occurs in about one out of every fifteen thousand births—which is not as rare as one would hope, given there are lots of complications and no cure. We're still reeling from the surprise of her syndrome and what that will mean, but none of it matters in this moment. She is with us now, and all five pounds ten ounces of her are perfect. Even the small feeding tube in her nose cannot take away from her beauty. *Brad and I have a daughter.*

As much as I enjoy witnessing the bond she's forming with her father, I miss her too much already. I motion from my seat next to the incubator for Brad to hand her over to me, and he stands from the chair by my side.

My arm instinctively cradles my baby girl when she's placed on my chest. Her body is as limp as it had been the first time I held her—a whole ten minutes ago—but the gravity of her weakened condition hits me afresh. I'm reminded that poor muscle tone is only the beginning of what will be a lifetime of challenges. My heart swells and aches at once.

I've always had big emotions. My mom used to say my "emotional range" was one of my many gifts—perfect for an aspiring actress. It unfortunately doesn't feel like a gift when every emotion in my "range" crashes over me like a tidal wave. I'm grateful my precious daughter is alive, but I'm also worried sick about her future.

As I hold her fragile body in my arms, I'm afraid she will break. Am I hurting her? Can she sense my fear? And how is Lucas going to feel? If this past month is any indication, the additional needs of his little sister will certainly take attention away from him. Will he act out? What if he resents her... or me?

I take a few deep breaths, watching her rise and fall atop my chest. The warmth of her permeates my heart, and all my worries melt away as quickly as they came.

"What should we name her?" Brad asks.

"Chloe," I say without hesitation.

I've known my daughter's name long before she was born. I had chosen it the same day I'd learned I might never get pregnant. Since my entire being had wanted nothing more, the words "blooming" and "fertility" stood out next to the name Chloe as I'd scrolled through the baby book at the doctor's office. I'd vowed it would be my daughter's name if I were ever so blessed to have one.

"That's pretty," he says, peering down into Chloe's angelic face. "How'd you think of it?"

I shrug, not wanting him to know how broken I had been—and what I had done to mend the shattered pieces. "I saw it in a baby book and liked it."

"I like it, too. She looks like a Chloe." Brad delicately strokes the side of Chloe's face with his knuckles and then kisses my forehead. "And you look beautiful but exhausted, my love. Why don't I hold her again while you get some rest?"

Part of me knows he's only saying that to get extra time with her, which makes me love him more; the other part realizes how right he is. I don't remember the last time I've slept. After over a month of twelve-hour days at the hospital with Chloe, frequent pumping to keep up milk production, and daily trips to my parents' house to see Lucas—all while still recovering from a C-section—I am emotionally and physically drained. Since it's taking all of my strength to even hold her, I nod, and Brad gently lifts Chloe away.

There's an immediate ache, both from missing her and from fatigue, but it subsides when I again witness the overwhelming love in Brad's eyes as he gazes at Chloe. I sit observing their father-daughter connection a moment longer before my eyelids feel heavy. Then everything fades to black.

Chapter 7

Now

Careful not to step on the warm ball of fluff at my feet, I finish placing eight candles on the strawberry birthday cake, cover it, and walk toward the fridge. The medium-sized, off-white poodle mix we brought home earlier this week is my new shadow. When I move, Prince Petey follows.

I'm removing the child-proof lock from the fridge when Noelle sticks her head in from outside. "Is there anything else I can help with?"

It's a genuine offer, and while I'm grateful to her and my parents for coming over early to help decorate, I know my baby sister well enough to decipher the hidden message in her question. It reads: *If you don't need me anymore, please let me leave. Now.*

Noelle has always been a bit flighty—with jobs, boyfriends, apartments, you name it—but her loyalty to me and this family has never wavered. She's there when it matters, and I couldn't ask for a better sister.

True to her name, Noelle was born on Christmas day. Our parents had been trying for a second child for years, and after my own fertility challenges, I now understand why they regarded her as the only gift our family needed that year. Still, actual presents would have been nice. After all, Noelle constantly reminds us that she expects both a Christmas *and* birthday gift each year. Doubling up with one big gift is not acceptable in her book.

"Thanks, Sissy." I scan the room, pretending to look for additional tasks. "I think we should be all set. See you in a few hours for the party?"

"Of course!" Noelle grabs her purse from the sofa, her radiant smile brightening the room as it always does. "Who's all coming today?"

I count the guests on my fingers. "You, Mom, and Dad, of course. Natalie, Linda, and Derek. Abuela. Tia Rosa. All our San Diego primos and their kids," I say, running out of fingers to list them all. "Then there's mom's side of the family, with Aunt Cece, Uncle Phillip, Brenda and her three kids. Also, two friends from Lucas' class are supposed to be dropped off. Oh, and… Carole and Kent are coming too."

"Ugh. You invited KFC?"

"Lucas loves his uncle. And it's Kent, not KFC. Be nice, Noelle."

"It's not my fault he has unfortunate initials. Don't you think that's weird, though? Inviting Brad's brother but not Brad?"

I sigh, thinking back to how I had struggled with the decision myself. "It was a tough call. After Carole said she was coming, I *almost* invited Brad."

"Ew! I wasn't suggesting to invite Brad. He's a dirt ball! I'm just saying his brother shouldn't come either."

I make sure the kids are still occupied outside and then glare at my sister. "Please keep your voice down. Brad is many things, one of which is a great father. He also gave up his Saturday with the kids so I could have this party today. The only reason I decided not to invite him is because I didn't want any of the awkwardness between adults to spoil Lucas' special day."

"Ha! I would pay good money to see Natalie's reaction if he showed up here."

"Yes, that's a good example of the awkwardness I'm referring to, but it's more than that. Brad picks the kids up after school every Thursday and drops them off at church on Sundays. It's been convenient for avoiding each other, but it also means I haven't seen Brad in almost a year. I wouldn't want our first interaction to be today."

"Good point… and I get why Brad's mother will be here. But, seriously…" Noelle glances anxiously at the hall that leads to the front door. "Why Kent? You don't have a thing for him, do you?"

"What? No! He's like a little brother to me. And I already explained that I invited him because Lucas loves his Uncle Kent. I don't understand why he bothers you so much. He's a nice person."

"Maybe to you," she mutters under her breath.

"Plus, he helps with the kids whenever I'm in a jam."

"I help!" Noelle places her fists on her hips and huffs.

"I never said you didn't. It's not a competition, Noelle. The kids need you *and* their uncle. Actually… I've always thought it would be cute if you two ended up together."

"Ugh. Gag me now! He's the worst, and apparently, so are you." She grips the purse straps on her shoulder. "On that note, I've got to go. This hot guy I recently met wants to take me out. He works nights, so we're doing a brunch date."

"How come I haven't heard about this guy before now? Where'd you meet him?" I ask.

"Don't get all judgy, but he works in a bar—like you used to when you were younger, by the way—and did I mention he's hot?"

"You might have mentioned that. Yes. And I wasn't going to get *judgy*. Does this hot guy have a name?"

"Yes," she says with mock annoyance. "It's Hayden, and it's tattooed on the inside of his bicep—his very large, very hot bicep."

I laugh at her dreamy expression. "Don't let me keep you, then."

Prince Petey follows closely behind as I walk from the kitchen to the family room to give Noelle a hug goodbye. Once she leaves, my hands busy themselves, fluffing pillows and straightening the throw on the sofa. From where I stand, I can see Lucas and Chloe playing in the backyard with my parents, and I'm reminded for the millionth time how blessed I am with my incredible family. As I give the adorable fluff ball near my feet a quick pat on the head, my mind travels back to the day our family grew by four paws and a tail.

The dog formerly known as Petey—before his ascent to royalty—was lying in an enclosure full of other dogs that jumped and whined when we approached. But Petey simply stared up from the ground with big brown eyes. With his chin rested atop his paws, he sighed heavily as if saying, "Why bother getting up? No one wants me anyway." Being the sweet boy he is, Lucas immediately set his heart on Petey, saying we had to rescue "the sad white dog" so we could cheer him up.

God works in mysterious ways sometimes. Whether it was His will or dumb luck, we never made it to the animal shelter that day. We instead stumbled upon an adoption event held by a local dog rescue after a quick stop at Target. *All because we had run out of toilet paper.*

I was prepared to get a dog that day. I wasn't prepared for the person volunteering at the event. There was recognition in her brown eyes when they locked with mine for three full seconds— easily six or seven rapid heartbeats. Once my initial shock faded, panic set in over what I should say. But as I worked up the courage to at least smile and wave, she looked away, never to glance in my direction again.

Dwelling on the memory feels like ripping off a scab too soon. What's left is raw and unprotected, but it can't be undone. If you don't count Facebook stalking, I hadn't seen Avery Emerald since the night of our high school graduation party. So, why did being ignored by her seventeen years later still hurt?

After feeling dismissed, I'd quickly filled out the paperwork, wrote a check, and hurried away with our new pet in tow. In hindsight, I might have been more focused on fleeing the situation than selecting the right dog, but it would have been impossible to argue with Lucas' benevolent intentions anyway. Petey truly was the saddest dog I think I've ever seen.

Lucas also insisted we add "Prince" to the four-year-old dog's name, because he said Petey deserved to feel special. My son's infinite kindness is how I know I'm not entirely failing as a mother.

As if summoned by thoughts of motherhood, my mom pokes her head inside as I finish organizing a caddy full of remotes. *What they each control remains a mystery.*

"Is it Chloe's snack time yet?" she asks.

I glance at the wall clock, which reads a quarter to ten. "Almost. How's she doing?"

Mom holds her hand parallel to the ground and tilts it back and forth. "It's touch and go."

"Okay. I'll start prepping her snack now, so it'll be ready."

Chloe materializes out of nowhere and clings to my mother's leg. "Snack, Gigi?"

"Your mommy is going to get it ready for you, but it's not time yet. Soon, baby girl," my mom says.

Brad's mother claimed the title of *nana* early on, so my mom happily became the kids' *gigi*. It's easier to say than grandma and, coincidently, rhymes with her first name: Deedee.

Most people assume Deedee is a nickname, but her full given name is Deedee Eloise Dion, now Dion-Serrano. I suppose her decision to hyphenate had inspired my own when marrying Brad. There was something about giving up the Serrano family name, even back then, that didn't sit right with me. Now, I couldn't be more grateful I kept it.

It's like she's reading my mind when she asks, "Have you filed yet?"

After confirming Chloe is back outside with my dad, I slowly shake my head from side to side.

"Does that mean you're going to try to make it work?"

"We're starting counseling, week after next," I say, "but I'd rather the kids not know. I don't want to get their hopes up." *Or anyone's hopes*, I think, knowing full well my mother is the biggest cheerleader for our reconciliation.

Divorce might as well be a four-letter word to her. She wouldn't dare utter it, let alone condone the act by her own daughter. Even if I don't fully agree, I understand where she's coming from. It's a place founded by love and rooted in our shared faith. A place I can't fault her for and, in all honesty, weighs heavily on me as well.

Mom nods her approval, then reaches for the apple slices I've prepared for Chloe's snack. "She'll be happy with these. You're doing such a great job with her, honey. You know that, right?"

My eyes tear on cue, but I also smile and wrap her in a hug. "Thank you, Mom. I needed to hear that."

"Hey, hey, hey! No hugging allowed," my dad says, as he, Lucas, and Chloe charge into the house.

Laughing, I pull back from my mom. "Hey, hey, hey! Who let the hug police in here?"

As if part of a well-rehearsed skit, my dad busts into song, belting out the chorus of "Bad Boys" by Inner Circle. We all laugh and sing along with my dad, because… *why not?*

In the middle of our third repeat of the catchy lyrics, he cuts in with, "Jessica Marie, we need to have a serious conversation."

"Oh, yeah, Dad? What about?" I ask, still laughing.

Carlos Serrano straightens his back and walks into the kitchen, kissing my mother on the cheek as she exits with the snack for Chloe. The kids settle onto the floor in front of the TV while my dad looks down at me. He's not broad and towering like Brad at six feet, but he has about six inches over my five-foot-four stature. His tan skin, weathered by many years spent under the sun, is creased around his brown eyes. He earned his wrinkles—or badges of honor, as he calls them—running the successful landscape business he started after immigrating to this country, as well as playing countless rounds of golf and tennis once he semi-retired.

The stern expression on his face has me concerned he might be serious for a change. I stop laughing and hold my breath while waiting for what he might say. When he continues to wordlessly stare down at me, my gut clenches at the thought of him also bringing up the state of my marriage. My dad has never been Brad's biggest fan, especially not now, but he is also a man of strong faith who tends to side with my mom on most issues, if out of nothing but loyalty to her.

My parents celebrated their fortieth wedding anniversary last month, and my mom is always the first to remind me it didn't come easy. Marriage requires compromise and hard work from both partners. I know this, yet I can't help but feel that my situation differs from theirs on multiple fronts. Besides the infidelity, Brad has never shared my faith or even values. No one should have to compromise their values to make a marriage work. Right?

"I'm only going to say this once, Kissin' Bug," my dad says, using the nickname he'd given me as a small child. Apparently, I was constantly asking my parents for kisses.

"Stop rhyming. I mean it," he continues, completely straight-faced. All the air I had been holding leaves my lungs. My belly quakes with deep laughter while he completes the movie line himself in a high-pitched voice. "Anyone want a peanut?"

Giggles erupt from the kids in the family room, though I doubt they understand his reference to *The Princess Bride*. Tears return to my eyes, this time from laughing so hard I have to place a hand on my stomach to control it.

"Inconceivable!" I say once I catch my breath.

"That's it! You know what I'm gonna do?" My dad wags his finger near my face in warning. "I'm gonna tell him."

"Don't tell him, Carlos," I say.

"Don't be Cheeeeeeeeken!" my mom, kids, and I all shout in unison. Everyone in the room is familiar with Disneyland's *Pirates of the Caribbean* ride.

"Who's a chicken?" My dad spins around the room and then points at Chloe's half-finished snack. "Chloe, do those apples taste like chicken?"

When she shakes her head and squeals with laughter, my dad scoops her off the ground and mock bites at her stomach. "Just what I thought. You taste like chicken!"

After many hours, and much more silly banter, I prop my feet up on the ottoman next to the sofa where I'm seated. Kent is sitting in the oversized chair the ottoman technically belongs to, but his sockless feet are planted firmly on the floor.

"You threw a great party today," Kent says over the music blaring from the TV. His eyes are fixed on my sister dancing in front of it.

"Thanks. I'm glad you and Carole could make it."

"Woo-hoo! Five stars!" Noelle shouts as the music stops.

"Have you played this before, Auntie Elle?" Lucas asks, referring to the *Just Dance* video game they are playing on the extremely generous birthday gift from Natalie.

"Nope," my sister says.

"Then how are you so good already?"

"Do you want the modest answer or the truth?" she asks.

Lucas laughs. "The truth! Obviously!"

"Well, *obviously*," Noelle says, "the truth is, I'm naturally good at everything. Video games are no exception."

"Wow," I say, always amazed by my sister's confidence. "And what's the modest answer, Auntie Elle?"

Noelle turns and looks at me with wide eyes, as if she had forgotten she had an audience, then she shrugs. "That I got lucky with the video game, since I'm such a good dancer."

"So modest," Kent quips, earning him a brief glare from Noelle before she tosses her hair over her shoulder and turns back to Lucas.

"Ready to go again?"

"Yeah!" Lucas yells.

I nudge Natalie with my elbow and whisper, "Why don't you get in there and give Noelle some competition?"

Natalie stops scrolling on her phone and slowly lowers it to her lap. She then tilts her head, contemplating the idea.

"Come on. You know you want to," I prod.

Natalie turns to Derek on her left, who is seated at the other end of the three-person sofa. "I'll play if you play," she says to him, a teasing smile in her voice.

"You forget… I've got moves," he says.

"Oh, I haven't forgotten."

"Do I need to remind you two that children are present?" I bump Natalie with my shoulder before realizing it's my bad one. The immediate pain is a reminder that I need to do my stupid PT exercises if I ever hope to compete in games like this myself.

Natalie looks at me with a devilish grin. "No, Mom."

"We're in," Derek says, standing to grab the two extra controllers.

I try my best not to gawk at the biceps bulging from his fitted gray T-shirt, but… holy moly. *Well done, Nat.*

Natalie and I exchange knowing glances before she lifts off the sofa. "It's on!"

I smile, reveling in the fact that Natalie's competitive nature will give Noelle a run for her money. It might even knock Noelle down a peg, but Lord knows her ego could handle it. I'd kill for even an ounce of her self-confidence. Then again, I'd be confident too if I looked like Noelle. She got all the best genes in our family.

Despite being my little sister, she's two inches taller than me. And slimmer, too. Not model skinny like Natalie, but thin in the middle with curves where they count. Her hair is brown like mine—when it's not dyed blond, red, purple, or any other color she chooses on a whim—but her eyes are what stand out the most. Two emerald spheres that mesmerize anyone brave enough to look directly into them.

I once Googled the probability of green eyes, given both our parents have brown, and the answer was seven percent. A seven percent chance, and yet she got them. She also won five thousand dollars playing roulette in Vegas on her twenty-first birthday and was a contestant on *The Price Is Right*, twice. To say Noelle is lucky would be an understatement.

Fun fact: The popular game show's contestants are not drawn from the audience at random, as many might think. They are instead hand-selected through a brief interview process, which takes place while audience members are in line to enter the studio. Two questions are asked: What's your name, and what do you do for a living? From that alone, they gauge your stage worthiness. I know this because I was with Noelle both times she was selected, and I was not.

It would be easy to feel bitter, but I love my sister and want nothing but happiness for her. After my kids, Noelle is my favorite person on earth. We share a special bond I suspect only sisters can.

While Natalie is who I turn to for practical advice and gossip, Noelle is my go-to person for emotional support. My sister is gifted with the ability to remain neutral on matters of the heart, and she is also surprisingly good at keeping my secrets. Still, there are some things I could never share, even with my sister.

As my mind travels to such topics, it's interrupted by the sound of Kent clearing his throat. "Well, I better head out and get my mom back home. Thanks again for having us."

Glancing in his direction, I notice his face is unusually rosy. I then look over to see Noelle, Natalie, and yes, even Derek, engaged in what can only be described as sexy "Bollywood" dancing. They are gyrating their hips while making a triangle with their hands above their heads. Lucas—bless his heart—appears to be running in place rather than dancing, and the entire scene makes me bite back a laugh.

"Of course. I'll walk you both out," I say to Kent as I stand.

"No, please, sit and relax. I'll just grab my mom, and we'll be on our way."

My eyes travel to Carole on the backyard patio. She's been sitting out there in my old rocking chair for the last hour with her back to us, no doubt to escape all the noise. "How's she doing?" I ask.

Kent gazes in her direction as well. "Her doctors say the chemo is working, but she gets tired pretty easily. Today was a lot for her, even though she insisted on coming."

I wrap him in a hug. "Well, thank you again for coming and bringing her. I know it meant a lot to Lucas to have you both here." After letting go, I holler to Lucas, "Hey, bud, come say goodbye to Uncle Kent and Nana. They need to get going."

The game pauses, and groans come from all three adults, the loudest belonging to Noelle. My laugh is automatic as I shake my head. *My child is the mature one of the group.*

Lucas runs over and throws his arms around Kent's waist. "Bye, Uncle Kent! Thanks for coming to my party and for my RC car."

"You're very welcome, champ. Hopefully, we can race it together sometime soon. Let's go get your nana." Kent takes Lucas by the hand as they head outside.

Carole comes to life at the sight of her grandson. Her arms fold around him as he all but climbs into her lap.

"Take it easy with Nana, bud!" I yell from inside. Then I sigh, suddenly wishing Brad could be here too.

Noelle was right. It was weird having his brother and mom at the party without him. The extra-tight hug Lucas gave Kent seemed meant for his father, and as much as I don't want to, I feel sympathy for Brad.

Although Brad talked to Lucas on the phone today, he wasn't able to sing happy birthday or watch Lucas blow out his candles, and he'll have to wait until next weekend to watch his son play with the gifts he gave him. On top of that, Brad is also missing out on the opportunity to spend more time with his own ailing mother, who I know means the world to him.

Noelle slips her arm around my shoulders as if sensing my thoughts. "It's all going to be okay, Sissy."

Chapter 8

It was the eye contact that made everything better. It took away all the awkwardness I had been feeling. Those sweet brown eyes transported me out of the otherwise uncomfortable situation, muted Brad's grunts, and made me feel things I knew I shouldn't. All the while, a gentle hand generously explored my body the way one would travel a familiar path.

The exploration was one of reverence rather than discovery, like claiming land that had been adored from afar for way too long. Or at least that's how it felt when one finger and then another dipped inside me, stoking a combination of heat and moisture unknown to me before that night. *Seventeen years ago.*

An ache builds low in my belly as I mentally relive the most erotic experience of my life for the millionth time. I bite my lip and can almost feel myself being touched, stroked, loved. I also remember being aroused by the pleasure I was able to cause. It was easy to feel, easy to see. Her eye contact told me everything I needed to know.

"Earth to Jessica." My reverie is waved away by a slow-moving hand in front of my face, which immediately burns with embarrassment.

"Hey, Diego! Sorry. It's been slow tonight, so I guess I spaced out for a minute. How's your night going?"

"Slow, but the last lady I helped was a good tipper. Maybe she'll need restaurant recommendations, too," he says with a wink. "I'll try to send her your way, Smiles."

"Thanks," I say, admiring his smile as well.

"Oh, Baby Moses! No. It. Isn't!" Diego whisper-yells.

Following his gaze across the lobby, I see a tall man with golden skin and surfer-like blond hair walking toward reception. He's undeniably attractive, but I'm not sure it warrants the way Diego is freaking out and crouching down by my side. "Are you okay?"

"Do you seriously not know who that is?" The excitement in Diego's urgent whisper tells me it's someone important, but I shrug my shoulders and wait for him to continue. He lets out a breath like an audible eye roll. "It's Rome Jepsen!"

"Jepsen? As in related to the singer?" My question is sincere, but you'd think I'd murdered his pet by the glare I get in return.

"No. As in Rome Jepsen, the professional golfer… soon to be the best in the world! He's skyrocketing through the ranks." At my blank stare, he adds, "He'll be my generation's Tiger Woods."

His last comment strikes me in two different ways. One: It makes me feel unusually old—not only because I was already an adult when Tiger Woods was famous, but because he said "my" not "our" generation. Diego is ten years younger than me, but come on… a decade isn't a generation. Two: It amuses me that Diego is into professional golf. I shouldn't be surprised, though.

Diego isn't your stereotypical gay guy. He dresses and speaks like most other straight men I know, obsesses over muscle cars, and apparently likes sports as well. As dense as it may make me, I don't think I would have figured it out if he hadn't told me outright when we first met during new employee orientation.

We'd bonded over our Catholic faith that day, shared some laughs, and then he made a witty comment about his sexual orientation being the only orientation he needed. He later shared how difficult it had been to tell his parents, and even though he quickly laughed it off, there was pain in his dark eyes when he mentioned they hadn't spoken to him in over a year. In an obvious attempt to hide his pain, Diego joked it gave him a good reason to move from San Antonio to a city named after him.

"The PGA tour doesn't come to Torrey Pines until late January, but maybe he's here early to get familiar with the…" Diego's voice trails off as Rome Jepsen approaches the woman speaking with the front desk, then it comes back with a vengeance. "Holy guacamole! He's with the lady who tipped me a hundred bucks to unload their car. That means I touched Rome Jepsen's bags!" Diego caresses the luggage on the cart at his side with palpable giddiness. *Okay, maybe I would have figured it out on my own.*

"You're such a fanboy," I tease.

"I better go see if they need anything else!" Within seconds, Diego and his cart are across the hotel lobby and next to the attractive couple at the front desk, twenty feet or so from my concierge station.

My gaze stays fixed on all three of them as Diego gets the attention of Rome, who waves his hand in a gesture of modesty. Though I can't hear them over the annoying lobby music that's trying to lull me into a coma, it's obvious fanboy is shamelessly expressing his admiration of the hunky golfer. "Play it cool, Diego," I say under my breath as if he can telepathically hear me. Then, suddenly, it's me who needs to keep cool when the average-height woman with dark curly hair turns around.

Avery Emerald is here… at my place of work… with a handsome professional golfer, no less. After not seeing someone for seventeen years, what are the odds of running into that person *twice* within two weeks? The unfathomable math needed to calculate such a probability urges me to call Natalie. I pick up my desk phone and dial her number.

Two rings, then three. *Pick up, pick up, pick up.* I'm not sure why it feels like her answering will somehow save me, but the hope of not being alone in this situation is the only thing holding me together. On the fourth ring, I close my eyes and brace myself for voicemail when I hear, "Hello?"

But it's not Natalie's voice. I slowly open my eyes and see Avery Emerald's flawless face, looking as surprised as I feel, right as Natalie's outgoing message begins. "Hi, you've reached Natalie. If you're hearing this, it means I'm busy running a foundation, hanging out with my gorgeous boyfriend, or otherwise being awesome." I suppress a smile at my bestie's newfound confidence, hold up a finger to indicate I'll be with Avery after my call, and continue listening to buy myself some more time. *What the paper cut am I going to say?* "If this is a solicitor, don't bother leaving a message. I'm not interested. If this is a friend, send me a text. Seriously, who leaves voicemails anymore? Beep… Just kidding, the real beep is still coming. But don't wait for it!" Another brief pause is followed with, "You're waiting for it, aren't you?" Then there's an actual beep.

I clear my throat before speaking into the phone in a cheerful, professional tone. "Hello, Miss Roberts. This is Jessica with Bay Holiday Resort. I'm calling to confirm your poolside cabana rental for tomorrow. You should be all set when you arrive, but please feel free to call me back or stop by the concierge desk if you have any questions at all. Thank you!"

My failed attempt at a cry for help leaves my heart pounding as I place the phone back on the receiver and force a large smile in Avery's direction. "Thanks for waiting. How may I help you?"

"Um, the bellhop said I should talk to you to reserve a cabana." She fidgets with her hands as her large brown eyes bounce between me and the floor. Her obvious discomfort weirdly soothes mine.

"You've come to the right place! What day would you like the reservation?"

"Uh… Would it be possible to reserve one until August thirty-first?"

Since that's almost two months away, I ask, "You'd like to make a reservation now for August thirty-first?"

"No, I mean, we'd like one reserved every day from now until the end of August." She tucks a curl behind her ear and finally makes eye contact. "It's for Rome Jepsen."

"Oh, the golfer?" I ask, as if I don't already know and hadn't only heard of him tonight. Guiltily, my eyes dart around the lobby, but Diego and Rome have both vanished.

"Yeah, he'll be staying here for the next eight weeks while he trains."

"I see. Yes, I can reserve a cabana for each day of Mr. Jepsen's stay, and the charges will be added to his room at checkout. It shouldn't be a problem, but I can let you know if there are any issues. Are you his…?" *Wife? Girlfriend? Assistant?* My open-ended question lingers in the increasingly warm, thick air between us for a beat longer than comfortable before Avery fills in the blank.

"Traveling physical therapist. I'll be staying here as well… in a separate room," she says, looking flustered. "Rome appreciates convenience. Thanks for taking care of the cabana rental."

"It's my pleasure. That's what I'm here for." I hold my cheerful smile, hoping it doesn't falter, while my mind dissects her response.

Traveling physical therapist. It makes sense, given what I know of her travel adventures from social media, but it also stirs more unanswered questions. Worse, the fact that neither of us has yet to acknowledge we know each other creates a suffocating awkwardness. Forget the elephant in the room. It's a parade of elephants, and every other circus animal known to man, squeezing down a narrow hallway with walls that are closing in tighter by the second. It's unbearable.

Avery is turning to leave when I blurt out, "I'm sorry I didn't keep in touch… after high school."

She stops but leaves her back to me. "It's okay. You were with Brad."

Confusion over her standoffish behavior mixes with relief. *At least she's not pretending she doesn't know me.* "Yeah, I was. But we could have stayed friends."

She turns to face me with an expression that's equally soft as her voice. "We were never friends, Jess."

Her words alone would be cruel, if not for the vulnerability behind their delivery. I swallow down the lump of tears in my throat before they can fight their way north. "We could have been, Avery."

Her eyes, the color of light brown sugar, search mine as if trying to solve a riddle written in them. "Are you still with Brad?"

Does she have a problem with Brad? Is that why she ignored me at the adoption event? I want to ask her those questions and more, but all I can manage is a head shake.

Her lips curve into a closed-mouth smile before she says, "Maybe we can grab a drink sometime… when you're not working… to catch up."

"I'd love that! I work the day shift tomorrow and can meet up after, around seven, if you'll be free?"

Her smile grows by a fraction of an inch, or maybe only a fraction of a centimeter, but it's noticeable enough. She nods once and then turns on her heels—or rather, on her bright yellow flats, which are fashionably paired with a faded denim dress. As I watch her walk away, I can't help but beam. *I'm getting drinks tomorrow with Avery Emerald.*

Chapter 9

Nine years ago

"Can't we at least explore our options?" I ask, fighting back tears.

Brad runs his fingers through his sandy-blond hair and paces our small apartment. "This is why I didn't want to do those damn tests! We barely got the results yesterday, and you're already in crisis mode."

"We've been trying for four years, Brad. Four years! That's forty-eight months. Forty-eight cycles. Forty-eight times I've sobbed on the toilet after getting my period!" My cheeks are wet with tears, and my head wants to explode from the mounting pressure.

Brad stops pacing and sits next to me on the couch. He's close enough that our thighs are touching, but he doesn't hold me. Instead, he folds his hands in his lap and bows his head as if in prayer. I know he's not, though. Brad leaves all the praying to me.

"Look. I know how hard this has been on you, but the doctor said we can still get pregnant naturally. It may be more difficult for us, but it's not impossible."

"I know," I say, "but a blocked tube means I only ovulate every other month, and with your low sperm count, it could be years before it happens for us. If ever! What's the harm in learning more about artificial insemination? It would still be your sperm."

Brad springs off the couch. "Stop talking about my sperm! Jesus fucking Christ, Jess!"

My anger springs me upright as well. "Don't take the Lord's name in vain! And why can't we talk about this? I'm not even asking you to do anything. I just want to go down to the fertility clinic together to get more information, so we'll be educated when the time comes."

"When the time comes," he mocks. "And when will that be, Jess? If it were up to you, we would have gotten pregnant on our honeymoon. What's wrong with enjoying married life without kids?"

My heart sinks as hot tears fill my throat. "I thought you wanted a family as badly as I do."

"I do. I'm just saying, it'll happen when it happens. And in the meantime, we should enjoy the process and stop stressing about it."

"And if it doesn't happen on its own?" I ask, trembling with rage. "How long before you'll consider other options? It took me two years of nagging to get you into the clinic for testing. I don't want to wait another two years before we go back!"

"I'm done with this conversation," he says, grabbing his keys off the coffee table.

"What do you mean you're *done*? This is important, Brad."

"I mean, I don't want to talk about my sperm or fertility clinics ever again. Either we have kids naturally, or we don't have them at all. Aren't you the one always saying things only happen if it's God's will?"

I'm shell-shocked by that statement. *How dare he throw my faith in my face right now!* "I also believe God helps those who help themselves. He gives us all the tools we need, but it's on us to use them. Are you seriously saying you would be okay with never having children?"

"If it doesn't happen naturally, then yes."

His word-bullets pelt my chest. I've been shot, and it's hard to breathe. I look down, half expecting to see a puddle of blood at my feet. There's no blood, but I do see red.

"You keep saying *naturally* as if sex is enough. If you really wanted me to enjoy *the process*, you'd add in some foreplay and make it last longer than sixty seconds, Brad." I step forward so we're face to face. "I've also heard that a female orgasm can increase the chance of a *natural* pregnancy, and we both know you've never given me one of those."

Brad heads toward the front door. "Fuck you!"

"Fuck *you!*" I return as the door slams shut.

And then I cry harder than I ever have before. The tears burn my eyes like acid. They carry the combined weight of all forty-eight times I cried over not getting pregnant. But worse, there's a finality in my tears. We've fought plenty of times, but never like this. It feels like our marriage is over. Our hateful words have obliterated the hope of *maybe someday*, and left a bitter, barren woman in their wake.

An hour later, I park in front of the fertility center. I hadn't given it much thought before I hopped in my car and drove here. They'll be closed in forty-five minutes. Hopefully that's enough time to get my questions answered. I've been reading a lot online about artificial insemination, IVF, and ICSI, but I still don't understand how each option works, which is better, and, more importantly, how much each would cost.

We'll need to save up either way, as we can hardly pay rent most months, but Brad is about to get his general contractor license, which will help a lot. I've calmed down quite a bit in the last hour.

My marriage to Brad is not over. It was just a bad fight. *Okay, a horrible fight.* But we'll make up and get through it, like we always do. Divorce is not an option.

I place my hand on the handle to exit the car and then freeze. Going in there and getting a bunch of pamphlets will only incite Brad further. Maybe I should wait until he warms up to the idea, as I'm sure he eventually will, and then we can come back together like I wanted. But how long might that take? There's nothing wrong with getting information on my own, right?

If I can find out how much it costs, then we'll have a savings target. Brad doesn't even need to know what we're saving for until we've reached the goal. *If I'm not doing anything wrong, why do I feel guilty for even being here?* These thoughts and others swirl around my mind for the next thirty minutes while I sit in my car, unable to go inside.

Once I've had enough of my internal struggle, I start my engine and shift it into gear. *Screw it. I need a drink.*

Chapter 10

Now

"Thanks for meeting me here, instead of at the hotel bar," I say when Avery slides into the booth where I'm seated. "I didn't want us to get interrupted every five minutes by one of my co-workers stopping to chat."

Her smile reaches her eyes when she says, "You always were popular. And it was no trouble. I like the vibe of this rooftop bar, and it's nice to be downtown. I've missed San Diego."

Her comment about me being popular throws me a little, but my need to make conversation doesn't allow for time to overanalyze it. I was our ASB class president and played three different varsity sports. I suppose I was popular enough.

"That's right! You've been gone for a while. Didn't you move to LA after high school?" I ask, as if I don't already know.

"Yeah, I went to USC for undergrad and then stayed for my DPT degree. Seven years in total." Avery laughs. "It sounds like a prison sentence when I say it like that, but I enjoyed the years I spent there, working toward my goals."

"Wow. USC is impressive. Great football team, too. Go Trojans!" When her eyebrows lift, I explain, "My dad is a huge fan. He watches all of their games."

"Oh, did your dad go to USC?"

"No... he's just a sports fan," I say, feeling stupid for prompting the question. "What made you choose USC?"

"Well, they have an excellent program for physical therapy, and I figured Los Angeles was close enough to San Diego for family visits. I rarely made it down after the first two years, though." Sadness travels through her eyes before she shrugs. "Enough about me. Where did you go after high school?"

"Um, I stayed local and got my A.A. in Theatre at San Diego City College."

"That's great!" Avery says, with more enthusiasm than my two-year degree warrants. "Did you pursue an acting career?"

Another perfectly logical question I wish I hadn't set myself up to receive. *Because no... I didn't even try.* It was easier to assume I'd fail than to be rejected. Besides, my dream of being an actress in image-driven Hollywood was never realistic for someone overweight like me. If I'd made it at all, I would've been the sidekick cast for comic relief, not a leading lady.

I shake my head in response and push the plate of appetizers I'd ordered across the table. "Hot wings?"

"No, thank you. I'm vegan." She straightens in the booth and folds her hands in her lap. "I honestly always assumed you'd go on to be a big star. You were so talented and passionate in high school. Why didn't you go for it?"

A server walks up to our table, sparing me from responding. He's muscular and has a flirtatious smile. "Can I get you ladies anything to drink tonight?"

"I'll have the melon martini. With Grey Goose, please," Avery says.

She's looking down at her menu and therefore doesn't notice the buff server scrolling his eyes from her chest to her legs under the table. Avery's simple black dress is almost identical to mine, except she makes it look better. Her modest cleavage is on full display, and her shapely legs look long and lean in the nude-colored pumps I noticed when she first arrived. Our jacked server has clearly made the same observation.

As with most other hard-bodied guys in *Man Diego*, he looks like he spends a lot of time at the gym or surfing, or maybe both. A tight black T-shirt hugs his V-shaped upper body and appears to be cutting off circulation to his large biceps, where part of a tattoo is peeking out.

I'm trying to decipher what it says when he asks, "And for you, ma'am?"

Ma'am? Really? He's probably in his mid-to-late-twenties, but still. Ma'am is not sexy. Ma'am is not something you would call a woman you find even remotely attractive.

"The melon martini sounds good. I'll have the same."

"With Grey Goose as well?" he asks.

I'd rather not pay for the upgrade, but I say yes anyway. Buff guy lingers a few more seconds, with his eyes still glued to Avery, then finally disappears toward the bar.

Hoping to change the subject from my failure to pursue an acting career, I ask, "So, vegan, huh? You don't eat meat at all?" My question sounds even stupider out loud than it did in my head. *Good one, Jess.*

"No meat or animal by-products, like dairy or eggs," she replies.

"Not even cheese?" Another brilliant question. I'm on a roll. *But seriously, how does someone not eat cheese?*

"Not cheese made from dairy, but there are a lot of great vegan cheese alternatives these days. The options aren't as limited or bad tasting as they were years ago."

"Oh, how long have you been vegan?"

"I gave up red meat when I was eighteen, then went full vegan around age twenty. For me, it's about the treatment of the animals, but I don't like to talk about it. I feel like most people get weirded out or worried I'll judge them for eating meat when they learn I'm vegan. I see it as a personal choice. I'm upholding my own values, not looking to convert others to my cause."

That fills me with relief, given my love of meat, but also an insatiable curiosity. I have a zillion follow-up questions about what prompted her decision, but since she said she doesn't like to talk about it, perhaps it's a good time to change the topic… or to shift into a related one.

"Well, you obviously love animals. I thought I saw you volunteering at an adoption event a couple of weeks ago, but I wasn't sure if you recognized me." *There.* I put it out there. The hotel was not the first place we'd run into each other, and we both know it.

"Oh, yeah. Sorry about that." Avery's already rosy cheeks darken, and her eyes dart to the table. "I was surprised to see you there, is all."

Her sincere apology makes me feel guilty for bringing it up. It had been seventeen years since she last saw me. How should she have reacted?

"No worries. I was surprised too. My son Lucas turned eight last week and wanted a dog for his birthday. We adopted a poodle mix named Petey, who is settling in nicely and now goes by *Prince Petey of Bay Ho*. His name keeps getting longer and longer." I laugh and then gratefully reach for the martini our server hands me.

This time, I can read the tattoo on his bicep as it sneaks past the confines of his tight shirt. It says *Hayden*, but it should say *Pervert*, since he stares at Avery's cleavage again while handing her the second martini. She notices this time and crosses her free arm over her chest. Steam threatens to spill out of my nostrils as I glare at him, and then something even more concerning clicks.

Hayden. The "hot guy" who works at a bar and has his name tattooed on his bicep. The same Hayden who took my baby sister out to brunch last weekend. It has to be. Of course, Noelle is dating this jerk. She has notoriously bad taste in men, not that I can claim to have done much better in that department.

Hayden the Pervert is still standing in front of our table, so I clear my throat and sharpen my glare. "We're good now. Thanks."

He finally peels his eyes off Avery and looks in my direction. "I'll be back to check on you ladies in a bit."

Once he's out of sight, I mutter, "I bet you will, jerk."

Avery's blush deepens. "I'm sorry. That was my fault. I should have worn a cami under this dress, but I couldn't decide on a color and I was already running late."

"Don't apologize. Your clothing choices don't give him the right to objectify you, and that perv wasn't even trying to be discreet about it!" My blood is boiling when I let out a huff. It's not like me to express feminist outrage—that's much more Natalie's style—but this *toilet brush* dating my sister *and* ogling Avery has pushed me over the edge.

Avery brings her hand to her chest and gapes at me wide-eyed before blinking away her shocked expression.

Period cramps. I snapped at the wrong person. "I'm sorry. I didn't mean to…"

"No, you're right," she says. "As women, we apologize way too often—and for things that are not even remotely our fault. An impatient man bumped his shopping cart into mine the other day, and I said sorry to him. I've been trying to work on that, so thanks for the reminder."

Her kind smile makes me feel three inches taller as I straighten in the booth. "You're welcome. I apologize a lot, too, without even realizing."

Avery takes a sip of her drink, and a flash of black ink on the inside of her wrist catches my eye. I'm about to ask about it when she continues. "While we're on the topic of apologies, there's something else I need to get off my chest."

My lungs expand with a mind of their own, sucking in all the air around me as I brace for impact. *This is it.* We're finally going to talk about what happened all those years ago.

"The Petco adoption event wasn't the first time I was surprised to see you recently," she says. "I had bumped into you a few days prior at the rehab center. I was coming and you were going… we collided and you dropped your keys. I'm really sorry I ran off after that."

It takes all my strength to close my jaw. That was not what I was expecting at all. "I remember that day, but I didn't realize…" My train of thought is derailed as another one crashes head-on. "You're the new physical therapist there."

Avery's eyes once again meet mine as she gives a single nod. "I like to find a local facility to use when I travel with Rome. And when I'd called to inquire about renting space in their gym, they informed me they had a PT leaving and asked if I'd be willing to cover some of his patients, at least temporarily. I agreed, but I never expected to see you there… or at the adoption event… or at the hotel. I guess that's why I was so surprised. I mean, what are the odds?"

Her light laughter helps to break my shock-induced trance. *The odds, indeed.* I had wondered the same thing when I thought we'd had two chance run-ins. Turns out it was three. And more importantly… "My PT was the one who left. So, I'll be one of your patients?"

Another single nod from Avery. "I saw your name on my schedule for next week, but if it's too weird, I can…"

"It's not too weird," I cut in. "Why would it be weird?"

"Good," she says, not bothering to answer my rhetorical question. *We both know why it might be weird.*

With a smile that doesn't reach her eyes, Avery points her chin in my direction. "You have an eight-year-old son… with Brad? I saw on Facebook that you two had gotten married, so I'm assuming," she quickly explains.

My heart races at the seemingly innocent question. My skin flashes hot and then cold like a fever. I wipe away a few beads of sweat from my forehead, then nod. My mouth isn't quite ready to form words yet, though I know I'll have to talk about Brad at some point. To delay, I bring my drink to my lips and take the slowest possible sip.

"I believe I saw a young girl with you at the event as well. Is she your daughter?" Avery asks.

I lower my drink. "Yes, Chloe. She's five."

"She's cute. They both were."

"Thanks." I refrain from elaborating on Chloe's appearance by taking another drink.

"So, what else have you been up to since high school? Besides raising two cute kids, of course."

I should have anticipated the question, but it sinks my stomach like the Titanic. *What have I done with my life besides being a mom?*

"Oh, nothing interesting. I'd much rather hear how you got into physical therapy… and volunteering with a dog rescue. There has to be a good story there."

"I don't know about a good story," she laughs, "but we've already covered my love of animals. I try to volunteer with local rescue groups whenever I'm in a location long enough."

"And are you often in one place for very long?" I ask, grateful she allowed the focus to go back to her.

"Not often enough. Sometimes I check in and out of a hotel within eight hours. How long have you worked at the Bay Holiday Resort?"

And we're back to me. "I started part-time about six months ago. Before that, I was a stay-at-home mom and dabbled in direct sales—cosmetics, nutritional drinks, things like that."

"I'm sure being a full-time mother is a lot of work on its own," she says.

"Yeah, but it's my dream job." I realize no truer words have ever been spoken as soon as I say them. Being a mother—especially one fortunate enough to stay home with my children—was my greatest dream. *And I achieved that dream.* It's something I should be proud of, not embarrassed because I made it a priority above lesser goals. I sit up even taller. "My kids are everything to me. What about you? Do you want children?"

Avery's eyes dart down toward her drink, and I notice all the color drain from her face. *Oh no. What have I done?*

I, of all people, should understand what a sensitive topic children can be—especially when you want them but don't have them. How many times had I cried myself to sleep after being asked when Brad and I planned to start a family, as if the timing were entirely up to us? The worst was being reminded I wasn't getting any younger, even though I was only twenty-seven when Lucas finally arrived.

At almost thirty-five, Avery is undoubtedly aware of her biological clock if she wants children. And even if she doesn't, Natalie has told me numerous times how annoying it is when people constantly ask her about kids—or tell her all the reasons she should have them.

"I'm sorry. It was an insensitive question," I say when her eyes flit up to mine. "I still haven't learned how you became a traveling physical therapist. What's that story?"

Her eyes hold mine a few seconds longer. They're darker than usual under the dim lighting—milk chocolate rather than caramel—but they soften as color slowly returns to her cheeks. "You don't need to apologize. We talked about that, remember?"

"Ugh. That's right!" I smack my palm to my forehead, hoping to lighten the mood. "I'm sorry. I mean, I'm *not* sorry."

Her lips curve into a forced smile, but there is unmistakable pain behind it. Without thinking, I reach across the table and place my hand over hers. I feel a jolt; whether from her or me, I'm not sure. My breath hitches. I imagine Avery pulling her hand away, standing from the booth, and walking out of the bar. It's plausible since a love of drama runs through both our veins.

Avery doesn't pull away, though. Her body's only movement is the rise and fall of her chest with each breath. On the fourth or fifth rise, she says, "I can't have children. Not my own, at least."

I give her hand a small squeeze, biting my lip to avoid saying I'm sorry again.

"I think I would have liked being a mom," she continues, "but sometimes things don't work out the way you want them to and you have to adapt… figure out what God has in store for you instead."

"That's very true," I say, feeling her words in my bones. "I didn't realize you were religious."

She shrugs. "I went to a private Catholic school on the East Coast before moving to San Diego."

I'm not sure why that fact feels like a bigger deal than it is, but a surge of excitement flashes through me as I mentally catalogue our faith as another thing Avery and I have in common. "I can't believe I never knew that before. I'm Catholic too!"

She gives me a polite smile before saying, "I know… I mean, I knew you were back in high school. Your family was well known at the church by our school."

"You went to my church?"

"A couple of times," she says, "but then I stopped going."

"Why?" I ask, genuinely curious.

She shrugs again. "High school was a hard time for me. I guess you could say I lost my way for a while."

"Well, my family and I still go to the same church every Sunday morning, usually for the ten o'clock mass. You should join us… while you're here in town." When she seems to consider my offer, I add, "I always wished we could have been closer in high school."

Avery's eyes drop to my hand, which I now realize is still on top of hers.

"I mean, we should be friends. We have so much in common," I say, slowly retracting my hand from the gesture that was meant to be kind but lasted way too long not to be awkward.

Her silence is deafening. I break eye contact and take a long gulp of my melon martini. The drink that once had a strong kick is now sweet with a hint of mint on my tongue. *Why is she so resistant to being my friend?* I can think of at least one reason, but I push it back where it belongs—deep down.

"Yeah, that would be nice," she finally says.

I'm not sure if it's in response to attending church with me, being my friend, or both, but it makes my heart smile.

Chapter 11

"Here's a sheet with all the restaurants I recommend in the area. They are sorted first by cuisine type, then by budget. If you're heading downtown this evening, I also recommend checking out a sunset sail on the harbor. It's a gorgeous view and much cooler on the water if you want to beat the heat. A few tour companies are listed on the back of this sheet. They often run deals, so I recommend checking online before paying full price. Is there anything else I can help you with, Mr. and Mrs. Gunderson?"

"Wow, this is very thorough. Thank you!" Britney Gunderson says, waving her impressive one-and-a-half carat princess-cut diamond over the sheet I've handed her husband.

"Yes, thank you," the smiling John Legend look-alike says. He gazes lovingly at his wife before turning his attention back to me. "Our only other question is the best place to rent bikes. We'd like to take a ride around the bay tomorrow morning before it gets too hot."

"Our hotel has complimentary beach cruisers you can check out at the front desk. They are first come, first served, but I'll leave a note to hold two for you tomorrow morning," I say with a wink.

"Oh, thank you again!" young Britney says. "Come on, honey, let's go get settled in our room." She lifts her brows and puckers her lips at the tall drink of water by her side before they cross the lobby toward the elevators hand in hand.

I rest my elbows on my desk, balancing my chin on my fists, while I watch them hurry off. *Oh, to be young and in love*. Part of me doubts they'll even make it out of bed in the morning for that bike ride.

"Honeymooners," I say when Diego strolls up beside my desk. My eyes are still on the happy couple, watching them kiss as they wait for the elevator.

"Is that John Legend?" Diego asks.

"Right?!" I exclaim, a little too loud. "But no. He just looks like him, and I think his wife looks like a young Britney Spears."

"Pre-meltdown?"

"Obviously. Since *I'm old*," I say with an eye roll in Diego's direction, "most of the celebrities I can think of were famous decades ago."

"Who do you think I look like?" he asks. "And don't say young Mario Lopez."

I laugh so loud it comes out like a cackle before I throw my hand over my mouth. Diego is a cutie, but he's no Mario Lopez. He's missing the signature dimples and easy charm. It's adorable he would think that about himself, though.

I clear my throat once the laughter stops. "I actually think you look a bit like Tom Holland."

"Tom Holland?"

"From *Spiderman*," I explain.

"I know who he is, Smiles," Diego scoffs. "But he's a white, British guy."

"Yeah, well, you're Mexican Tom Holland."

It's Diego's turn to laugh so hard I see tears forming in his eyes. *"Mexican Tom Holland?* What would that even look like?"

"You!" I say, joining in on the laughter.

A minute later, we both compose ourselves, and Diego says, "Honeymooners are the best. They're too happy and distracted to complain about anything. Decent tippers, too, thanks to their honeymoon slush funds."

I pull my focus back to my computer and type a note about the bikes for the front desk, just in case. Tomorrow is my day off, and I'd hate for them to have any issues. "You're all about the tips, Diego."

"Damn straight. I don't haul around bougie people's heavy Louis Vs all day for the fun of it. Saturdays are how I pay rent. This is the first break I've gotten."

"I know what you mean. I've been swamped today, too." I eye Diego suspiciously. "If you're on a break, why are you here with me instead of spying on Rome Jepsen? I'm pretty sure he's at his cabana by the pool right now… shirtless."

Diego dismisses the idea with a flip of his wrist. "I'm over that."

"What? So fast? He only got here two days ago."

"I heard him sneeze," Diego says, as if that's explanation enough. When I stare at him in confusion, he adds, "It was a cartoon character sneeze. The loudest ahchoo I've ever heard in real life."

"Oh, well, that explains everything."

"Plus, he's a notorious womanizer anyway," he says, ignoring my sarcasm and laughter. "I wonder if he's banging that hot brunette he checked in with."

"She's his traveling physical therapist," I say, feeling the need to defend Avery's honor. And since when does Diego refer to women as *hot?*

"Yeah, I bet she helps with all his *physical* needs."

"She does not!" I yell and then immediately cover my mouth. People have halted their activity to look my way. *Well, stinky diapers.* I wave my hand in the air toward no one in particular to ward off their attention.

"Someone's defensive," Diego whispers once the lobby has resumed its normal buzz. "Spill it, Smiles."

"She's a friend of mine, is all. We went to high school together, and I know she's not the type of person to do that." Even as the words come out, I wonder if they're true. I hadn't asked Avery about Rome over drinks last night. For all I know, they could be mixing business with pleasure.

"That's so cool! Maybe she can introduce you to Rome, and then you can introduce your awesome friend Diego."

"I thought you were *over that?*" I curl two fingers on each side of my face in air quotes and laugh.

"I was playing it low-key. He may be a cartoon-worthy sneezing heterosexual, but he's still a golf god. Come on, Smiles… Pleeease! Promise me you'll try." The puppy dog expression on Diego's face makes it impossible to say no.

"Okay. I'll try."

"OMG! Maybe you'll date him, and then I could say I'm BFFs with Rome Jepsen's girlfriend!"

I laugh even harder at that. "Not likely, and I didn't realize we were BFFs."

"We will be… once you date Rome Jepsen."

At the mention of his name for the millionth time in the last five minutes, the bronzed golfer himself enters the lobby from the direction of the pool. He's wearing a pale-blue golf shirt and khaki shorts, not the swim trunks I saw him head to the pool in earlier. His stride is fast, like he's got somewhere important to be. Within seconds, he has crossed the lobby and is pushing his way through the revolving front door. Diego and I stare blankly at the exit even though he's already out of sight.

Across the lobby, the elevator dings, drawing my attention when a woman steps out. *Is that Avery?* The woman is the same size, but it's hard to tell. Her hair is pulled back under a baseball cap, and she's wearing dark sunglasses, a simple white T-shirt, and beige Bermuda shorts. It's the kind of nondescript outfit you would wear to blend with a crowd or evade the paparazzi as a celebrity.

With a large canvas bag thrown over her shoulder, she hurries toward the same revolving door Rome exited. Although her eyes are shielded, I swear she glances in my direction when she reaches the center of the lobby. I wave, like an idiot, and her pace increases—confirming she saw, yet chose to ignore me.

Three hours later, I'm nearing the end of my shift when Avery reemerges through the revolving door. She's wearing a floral print sundress now, with no ball cap or glasses, and her curly hair hangs loose over her shoulders. For a minute, I second-guess that the woman I saw earlier was Avery after all. But then I notice the same large canvas bag.

Not wanting to make a fool of myself like earlier, I look down at my desk and act busy in case she glances in my direction. I'm straightening the stack of handouts I print for guests who need recommendations when a throat clears. My eyes meet Avery's as soon as I look up.

The large canvas bag is now on the ground by her feet. Her head swivels side to side over both shoulders as she speaks. "Hi, Jess. About before, I was running late for… an appointment. I'm glad you're still here, though. I meant to come by and say hi earlier today."

"Thanks for stopping by," I say curtly before registering her face. The tight-lipped smile she offers doesn't reach her brown eyes, which are wide and full of unease. She keeps shifting her weight from one foot to the other, the way one might if waiting to use the ladies' room. "Is everything okay, Avery?"

"Um, yeah, everything's fine. Listen… I hate to ask for a favor, but do you mind if I stash my bag here and get it from you in a bit? It's heavy, and I'd rather not take it to my room right now."

"Oh, I could have one of our bellhops bring it up for you."

"No! I mean… I don't want to trouble anyone. Plus, it has valuable items, so I'd be more comfortable keeping it with you, if that's okay… since we're friends," she adds with another tight smile.

"Sure," I say, motioning for her to slide her bag under my desk.

No sooner than she does, I see Rome entering through the revolving door. He searches the lobby before landing on Avery and heading in our direction.

"Your boss is coming this way," I say, again wondering if there's more than that to their relationship.

Avery's back straightens. Her eyes widen even bigger than before, but only for a second. In the time it would take to peel off a mask, her expression morphs into one that's completely ordinary and relaxed. *She would have made a great actress.* Only I know the face she wears now *is* the mask.

"There you are," Rome says as he approaches.

She paints on a smile and spins around to face him, her back now to me. "Hey, Mr. Jepsen, I was about to get some restaurant recommendations, in case you're hungry. We could grab a bite to eat and discuss your PT schedule for the upcoming week."

"For the millionth time, please call me Rome. Mr. Jepsen was my father, and that rat bastard thankfully isn't here." He pushes a fallen strand of sun-kissed hair from his forehead and flashes a toothy Hollywood smile in my direction. "Good evening, ma'am. I don't believe we've met."

The hint of a southern drawl makes the "ma'am" sound less insulting for some reason, especially when paired with the flirtatious twinkle in his ocean-blue eyes. It helps that he's not some young kid, either. His ID on file with the hotel had confirmed he's thirty-seven. Heat rushes to my cheeks, my chest, even my toes.

"Rome Jepsen," he says, holding out his hand, which I lightly shake.

It's embarrassing that an attractive man introducing himself is all it takes to turn me to mush. Especially when said man is saying his own name like I'm supposed to be impressed. His loose blond curls, golden skin, and easy charm are appealing, but there's also an intensity I can't quite place. Maybe it's his athleticism or unwavering confidence.

I know a flirt when I see one. But darn it… I'm flattered that he's flirting *with me*. Then I remember Diego calling him a womanizer. *What's with me being attracted to blue-eyed playboys?*

My smile back to him is friendly and professional, but nothing more. "Nice to meet you, sir."

"Please, call me Rome. And what's your name?"

"Jessica. I'm a concierge here."

His smile widens. "I gathered that last part. When do you get off your shift, Jessica?"

Heat crawls up the back of my neck until it sets my earlobes on fire. Embarrassment, paired with I don't know what else, has my stomach in knots. I glance at the time before saying, "In about twenty minutes."

"Perfect! Why don't you join Avery and me for dinner? She mentioned you two went to school together, and a nice meal is the least I can do for all the help you've provided during my stay." He then turns to Avery. "I don't want to think about schedules or PT right now. Let's enjoy this lovely summer night, and we'll talk tomorrow. Sound good?"

"Sure, but Jessica probably has plans tonight already. We shouldn't…"

"I'm sorry. Where are my manners?" Rome interrupts. "Jessica, are you free tonight for dinner? I should have started with that question."

Painfully free, I think with an inner sigh. The kids are with Brad, and even Prince Petey is with them. Brad had caved on the allergy lie, saving face due to the poodle mix being hypoallergenic. Noelle, Natalie, and three other people I tried to make plans with are all busy tonight. If I don't accept Rome's offer, I'm destined to reheat a sad frozen dinner while watching a rom-com on my own. And frankly, I hate nothing more than being alone. I had thought to ask Avery if she wanted to come over, but now… here we are.

"I wouldn't want to impose," I say, searching Avery's face for any signs of opposition to me joining. There's something in her eyes, but I can't make it out. Her mask gives nothing away.

"Not at all!" Rome says. "Your company would be appreciated. Avery and I have been traveling together for months now. It's nice for us both to have someone else to talk to." He winks, then adds, "Plus, taking two beautiful women out to dinner would make my day. What do you say?"

His words make my mind travel places it shouldn't. Past places. Prohibited places. I resist the urge to fan myself. It's burning up in here. *Where's the blast of AC when you need it?*

Out of the corner of my eye, I see Diego cross the lobby with his cart full of suitcases. I'd loop him into this if I didn't already know he has a hot date tonight. At least, that's what he told me when I tried to rope him into my frozen dinner and rom-com plans. When Diego smiles in my direction and gives me a thumbs up, I remember his wild dreams for Rome and me. *I did say I'd try.*

"Sure. I'd love to join you both for dinner. I'll need to run home first to change, but it's close by." I hand Rome one of my handy printouts. "Here's a list of restaurants to choose from in the meantime. I'm happy to tell you anything else you may want to know about San Diego at dinner. I've lived here my entire life."

"That's great. This won't be a working dinner, though," Rome says with another wink. "I want you to relax and enjoy yourself. How about we meet you back here in an hour? Does that give you enough time?"

"Yeah, that works," I say.

"Perfect. See at seven-thirty then." Rome's blue eyes hold mine a moment longer. His picture-perfect smile sparkles white against his sun-tanned skin. He inches his fingers through his golden locks before slowly turning around and walking toward the elevator, glancing over his shoulder to wink one last time.

"So…" Avery says once Rome is out of sight.

Whatever trance I was in is broken. "Avery, I hope you don't mind that I'll be joining tonight."

"No, it's fine. But as a friend," she says through gritted teeth, "you should know Rome is not someone you want to get involved with."

"Because he's a womanizer?" I ask.

She shakes her head. "It's more complicated than that."

"Are you and he…?"

"Definitely not."

"Then, I don't understand. What's wrong with him?"

"Maybe nothing. I don't know." She sighs. "Let's just enjoy dinner, like he said. It'll be nice to have you there. I can take my bag back now, by the way. Thanks for stowing it while we chatted."

"Of course. Here you go." I pull the canvas bag out from under my desk. She wasn't lying when she said it was heavy. I feel like a little kid again, lifting my dad's bowling bag out of the car after league night.

Avery grabs it from me, and the black ink on the inside of her wrist again catches my eye. It appears to be words, but I don't recognize any of the letters. "Cool tattoo. What is it of?"

"Oh, it's just something I got in college," she says, angling her wrist out of my view. "Thanks again for holding my bag. I'll see you at seven-thirty, then. Here's my number in case anything comes up."

"Sounds good," I say, taking the business card she hands me. Once she's taken a couple of steps away, another question pops into my head. "Avery?"

She stops and turns to face me. "Yeah?"

"Has Rome ever hit on you?"

Avery's eyes scan the lobby, drop to the floor, then slowly move back up to meet mine. "Only once… when we first met. But I shut him down, fast, by telling him I'm a lesbian. See you soon, Jess."

Before I have time to process anything, I'm watching her hips sway and her dark curls bounce as she retreats toward the elevator with the large bag over her shoulder, never once looking back.

Chapter 12

Dinner with Rome and Avery had only been half as awkward as I'd expected it to be. Rome mostly carried the conversation, but not in the annoying way *Kevin the Jerk* had talked only about himself. Rome was charming and attentive. He asked surface-level questions about my life and experiences in San Diego and then used my answers to segue into interesting stories from his years on tour.

I didn't mind Rome's long-winded tales one bit. They limited my obligation to talk while still processing Avery's revelation. It had stirred feelings I don't quite understand and am definitely not ready to deal with yet. On top of that, the excitement threaded through those feelings seems premature. After all, Avery may have told Rome she's a lesbian just so he'd leave her alone.

But if that's the case, why isn't Avery interested in Rome? And why did Rome invite me to dinner? That last question occupied the lion's share of my headspace during our meal.

It's highly unlikely that Rome Jepsen would be interested in me, of all people. I've mulled over all the angles and keep coming back to one. True or not, Rome *thinks* Avery likes women. He was probably hoping to lure Avery into a threesome by using me as bait. *Wow, I sure have a type when it comes to men.*

Speaking of men, Brad stands from his chair when I push open the heavy wooden door to the office of Rebecca Wolverton, LMFT. He's taller than I remember, though still only six feet, and… *has he lost weight?* For someone who claims to have broken things off with the other woman, he is looking mighty fit.

"Sorry I'm a little late," I say, rushing inside but not closing the space between us. *Distance is good.* "There was traffic both ways when I dropped the kids off at my parents' house."

"No worries. Our appointment isn't until three forty-five anyway. You look really great, Jess." His baby-blue eyes bore into me while his compliment warms places I wish it wouldn't.

"Thanks. I thought it was at three thirty, but…" Realization sets in, and I cross my arms. "You knew I'd be late."

Brad shrugs. "I gave us a buffer so we'd have more time to talk. I've missed you so much."

I shift my eyes around the room, not knowing how to respond to that. We are alone in the large waiting area, which is decorated more like a living room. In one corner, a white leather sectional surrounds a glass-topped coffee table with a bowl full of seashells in the center and a small stack of magazines on the end. Coastal paintings in pastel watercolors cover the walls. The decor is likely meant to be relaxing, but it makes me wish I was at the beach—or anywhere but here.

On the side of the room where Brad was sitting, there are clusters of upholstered chairs with no apparent theme to their patterned fabrics. One is seafoam green with white polka dots, another pale blue with seahorses. There are two blue-and-white chairs, one checkered and the other in a chevron pattern. The chair Brad had risen from is sage green with palm trees.

Is this room some sort of test? Like where we each choose to sit says something about our personalities? To avoid finding out, I spot a beverage station and walk over to it. It's too hot outside for coffee or tea, but the ice water with cucumbers floating on top is calling my name.

"Yay for drinks. I'm so thirsty." I fill what appears to be a compostable cup and then spin around to find Brad two feet away, still staring at me.

"It's a good idea to hydrate," he says, reaching around my waist to grab a cup for himself. "This summer has been a scorcher."

The heat radiating off his body warms mine further. A quick "yep" is all I can manage. We're not touching, but my brain betrays me by remembering all the times we've stood like this with our bodies pressed together. Physical touch was a common love language for us. A simple hug in the kitchen before breakfast, or in front of the bathroom sink before bed, was how Brad said he loved me, wanted me, needed me.

But all that is broken now, I remind myself. It broke when he showed some other woman—Susan from the hardware store— how much he wanted *her*... in *my* kitchen. I break eye contact and pull myself away from the beverage table while he fills his cup with water.

"Thank you again for agreeing to meet me here," he says once he turns back to face me. "I'm sure this isn't easy for you. And I know you hate me..."

"I don't hate you, Brad." It's the truth, but saying the words aloud opens a floodgate behind my eyes. All the heat from earlier is channeled into burning tears. "It hurt that I wasn't enough for you, that *our family* wasn't enough for you. But as much as I want to hate you for that, I never could." I hold back all the reasons and wipe at my face.

"You're more than enough, Jess. You always have been. I screwed up... I screwed the *taxes* up, and I'm so sorry I hurt you. I don't deserve your forgiveness, but I'm willing to do whatever it takes to earn it, if you'll let me."

I laugh at his proper use of a T-bomb while sniffling snot back into my nose. I'm sure I look like a hot mess already, and our therapy session has yet to begin. An emotion that looks a lot like hope is reflected on Brad's face. For a moment, I worry about giving him false hope, but my thoughts are interrupted by the receptionist, who is now holding the door open.

"Mr. and Mrs. Clark? Becky is ready for you now."

Chapter 13

Thirteen years ago

"Jess, they're ready for you." After a quick knock, Natalie pokes her head inside my bedroom and then covers her mouth with her hands. "Oh! You look so beautiful!"

"I know!" I exclaim in my best Monica Geller impersonation. Then I turn back to the mirror I've been staring into for the last ten minutes and sigh. It's taken a year of dieting and practically living at the gym to fit in this gorgeous dress, but I did it. *Size eight and I feel great.*

"Your mom and sister are already outside by the willow tree you love. The photographer wants to take a bunch of pictures with the four of us ladies before we head to the church," Natalie says in a tone that's all business.

"Okay. Give me a minute." My breath is less steady than I need it to be, so I inhale as deeply as the corset-style bodice will allow.

In addition to admiring the intricate beadwork on the most expensive gown I'll ever own, I've also spent the last ten minutes questioning my decision to marry Brad. *Getting cold feet is normal,* I remind myself. But is it normal to have a sexual fantasy running through your head on the day of your wedding? One where your husband-to-be is *not* the main star?

It's been the same fantasy for the last four years, with Brad's role becoming less and less prominent in each version. But today, I will vow to be faithful to him and only him… until death do us part. Our impending marriage suddenly feels like a life sentence of unsatisfied needs. The church I love transforms into a courtroom, and our priest becomes the judge issuing my sentence.

"Are you okay?" Natalie crosses the room to stand by my side. "You look beautiful… but also a little pale."

"I can't breathe. Please, untie my dress!"

She does as I ask, and the relief of pressure allows me to double over. *I think I might get sick.*

"Hey. Hey. What's going on?" Natalie's concern comes through in her voice, even though I can no longer see her face. She places the back of her hand on my upside-down forehead and then on my cheek, checking my temperature in a motherly manner. Since Natalie is the least maternal person I know, the kind gesture is a hug for my heart.

"It's just nerves," I say, straightening to an upright position.

"Say the word, and I'll break you out of here. We don't need to go to the church today. We can hop in my car, drive to Vegas, and party the night away with free drinks at the craps table. No one will even bat an eye that you're in a wedding dress because… Vegas."

Natalie makes me laugh, but I know she's dead serious. She's never liked Brad, even though she hasn't told me directly. To be fair, I hated the jerk she dated all throughout college but never said anything. They broke up last month after she caught him cheating… again. I have to admit, the idea of being two single party girls together is appealing.

It's like she's reading my mind when she says, "Seriously, think how fun it would be. We're only twenty-two, Jess. The world is our oyster! And if you're deterred by the six-hour drive to Vegas, we could head south to Rosarito Beach instead. We'll fill up on cheap lobster and then dance the night away under the stars at Papas and Beer."

"Stop!" I laugh. "I'm not going to leave Brad at the altar."

"Rachel ran out on a wedding, and look how good her life turned out." Natalie smiles smugly, using our mutual love of *Friends* to try and win me over.

I shake my head, but I'm tempted. Brad and I started dating freshmen year, so I've never been a single adult. Worse, Natalie and I have both been so busy with boyfriends that we've never taken a girls-only trip together—unless you count camping with the Girl Scouts when we were ten.

Natalie's blue-gray eyes look at me expectantly. *She can see I'm caving.* I'm thinking of what to say when she tosses her golden-blond hair all to one side and twirls it with her finger. "You know you want to be like Rachel," she says in a teasing voice.

She's still trying to convince me, but her statement has the opposite effect. It hits me with all the reasons I *should* marry Brad. Natalie is blond and thin and gorgeous. She'll probably have a new boyfriend within the month. She's the Rachel of the two of us, and I'll always be more like Monica—before she unrealistically lost all that weight.

Brad was quarterback of the varsity football team and popular with all the girls in school, yet he chose me. He makes me feel beautiful, even on my worst days. It would be stupid not to want to spend my life with him. Plus, I've already given him my body more times than I can count. We should be married. *Getting married is the right thing to do.*

"I'm good now," I say, grabbing my veil off the dresser beside me. "Can you please lace me back up?"

Natalie's hands hesitantly cinch the satin ties on the back of my dress. "You know I'll support whatever you decide. I just want you to be one hundred percent certain before you sign up for a lifetime with someone. Are you sure you want to marry Brad?"

I place the veil atop my head and straighten its lace panels behind me. "Yes. Let's get moving. I'm getting married today."

Chapter 14

Now

Three rings proceed Natalie's voice projecting through my car speakers. "Hey, Jess. How did it go?"

"I don't know… It was emotional, for sure. That's part of why I called. I know we talked about me heading over to the women's center to unload on your therapy couch, but I started driving toward the beach instead. I think I need to put my toes in the sand and stare at the ocean. You know?"

"Sure. That's understandable. Are you okay, though?"

"I think so. Just confused. We didn't even talk about Brad's affair in this first session. It was more of a meet and greet with our therapist, who insists we call her Becky, by the way. Not Doctor Wolverton, not even Rebecca, but *Becky*. That's weird, right?"

"Totally weird. What did you guys talk about, then?"

"Well, *Becky* asked us a bunch of questions about how we first met; what qualities first attracted us to each other; the early parts of our relationship… It was a difficult trip down memory lane. I don't want to think about it anymore. How are things going for you at the center?"

"Mostly good. We had a *minor* security incident today, which I'm dreading telling Derek about, but everything is fine now."

"Oh no. What happened?" I ask.

"The soon-to-be-ex-husband of a woman staying in one of our protected housing units showed up in our lobby waving a knife. He was belligerent and threatening my staff, saying he'd kill everyone if someone didn't tell him where we were hiding his wife."

"Oh my goodness!" I'm not sure what's more shocking: a psycho with a knife making death threats, or Natalie's matter-of-fact tone when talking about it.

"It was quite dramatic for a Monday morning," Natalie continues, as if reporting on a sports event rather than a life-threatening situation. "I was in my office when he first arrived, but I came out when I heard the commotion. He seemed drunk and was slurring all kinds of profanities. Our security team is trained to deal with situations like that, though. They swooped in fast and tased the guy before he had a chance to do anything. The police showed up minutes later and took him away in handcuffs. End of story. He won't be bothering us or his poor wife again."

"Wow, Nat. Thank God no one was hurt! But you're right, Derek is going to freak when you tell him, if he hasn't heard already."

Natalie sighs. "I know. And I love that he's protective of me, but I hate worrying him over nothing. It really wasn't as bad as it sounds, and it was handled quickly. More than anything, I'm not going to let violent assholes deter the important work we're doing at Fresh Start. Men like him are the reason our women's center is needed in the first place. There's inherent risk in running the center—everyone knows that—but it's worth it to help women escape abuse and... well... get a fresh start."

"I'm so proud of you, Nat. What you're doing there is amazing."

"Thanks, but it takes a village. That reminds me... Our foundation is hosting another fundraiser next month. Can I count on you and your trusty bartending skills to help us out again?"

"More like *rusty* bartending skills, but of course! Send me the event details, and I'll make sure I take that night off from the hotel. Sweet! A parking spot." I hit the brakes and signal as a pickup truck pulls out onto Garnet Avenue, only a couple of blocks from the beach. "I should let you go now, but I'm in PB if you want to meet me before heading home."

"I'd love to, but I'll be here late. Today's incident set me back on some time-sensitive paperwork. Oh! One more thing I've been meaning to tell you, and then I'll let you go."

My natural curiosity stirs. "Ooh, what is it?"

"Derek and I want to buy a house together. We started looking last month."

"Dum-dum-da-dum. Dum-dum-da-dum," I sing.

"I don't know about that… maybe, though."

"Natalie Elizabeth! You've been holding out!"

"I haven't. I swear. My mother is the only reason we're even looking at houses. Honestly, I'm not sure how much longer I can take the three of us living in that apartment. It's bad enough we had to put a lock on our bedroom door to prevent Linda from *accidentally* walking in on Derek naked. But now, her latest boyfriend, if you can call him that, is *younger than us*."

Classic Linda, on both counts. I laugh. "Oh boy. Well… good for your mom, I guess."

"No, not good, Jess. A few nights ago, she let him stay overnight—which, trust me, my mom and I had words about—but the final straw was me waking up to this *random guy* wearing my mom's bathrobe and eating *my* cereal in our kitchen." Natalie lets out a defeated sigh. "Long story long, we need our own space."

"Which neighborhoods are you looking in? Please say Bay Ho."

"We've looked there—and also in Bay Park, Mission Hills, North Park, Bird Rock, Carmel Valley… anywhere in San Diego with homes for sale. In this market, we'll be lucky to find anything in our price range, but it's exciting to be looking. I can fill you in on more of the details later. Enjoy your time at the beach, and let's chat more soon. Love you!"

"Love you too!" I stuff my phone in my bag, kick off my sandals, and let out a long exhale.

The ocean breathes along with me, in and out with each crashing wave. The sand is still warm as I burrow my toes. I had walked here while Natalie shared her house-hunting news and salacious Linda gossip. Now, I'm sitting on the beach towel I always keep in the trunk of my car.

The spot I've chosen is a block south of Crystal Pier. Its wooden structure covered with white cottages is in my peripheral view, but I'm staring out at the deep blue sea. And I swear it's staring back. Like a star-filled sky, the vastness of the ocean has a calming effect on me. It puts the minor scale of my existence—and problems—into perspective.

I have no idea what to do about my marriage, but I trust the Lord will provide direction in some form. I close my eyes and say a quick prayer. When I open them, there's someone walking along the water's edge about six feet in front of me. *That can't be…*

Chapter 15

"Avery?" I call out in disbelief.

Her bare feet stop, and I notice the trail of impressions they've left in the wet sand. We exchange brief, awkward waves before she approaches.

"Hey, Jess, small world. I came here to get away from the resort and clear my head. I know Mission Beach is closer, but it's too touristy and crowded there." She pauses as we both scan the wide expanse of golden sand, which is covered with people, umbrellas, and chairs. "Not that it's much less crowded here, but…"

"I've always liked Pacific Beach better, too," I say.

Avery smiles, and I wonder if she's filled with all the same fond memories of this beach as I am. All the times we hung out here after high school flash through my memory like a fast-paced slideshow:

> Avery going into the ocean with me when no one
> else would; her freckles on full display as we took
> turns lathering each other's backs with sunscreen;
> Brad and his friends throwing a football back and
> forth while us girls sunbathed; Natalie getting a
> bloody nose when a bad toss came in her
> direction once; me asking the hot lifeguard for a
> Band-Aid; Brad getting jealous.

Once we got our driving permits, a bunch of us would pile into several cars—even though we weren't supposed to drive with passengers—and we'd take over a large section of the beach. Many people rotated in and out of our boisterous group, but Avery was a constant.

"I'm glad I ran into you, actually," she says, tucking curls behind her ears to no avail against the wind. "I've been wanting to clear the air between us… about what I said the other night before dinner."

Avery's shadow does little to block the glaring sun as I squint up at her. I scoot over on my towel and pat the spot next to me. "Do you want to sit down?"

"Sure. Thanks." She lowers herself onto the other half of my towel before angling her body toward me. "I should have clarified that my lack of interest in Rome isn't entirely about him. I'm not interested in being romantically involved with anyone right now."

"Okay," I say, unsure where she's going with this.

"It's just… I wouldn't want to have given you the wrong idea."

And there it is. The big fat elephant. She thought that *I thought* she was interested *in me*? As if Avery Emerald could ever be interested in me.

I shake my head. "I didn't think that, Avery."

Relief washes over her expression. "That's good to hear. The thing is, I've been focusing on self-love for the last few years." Avery's pink cheeks redden. "Not like that… that's important too… but I mean…"

I place my hand on her arm to comfort her nerves. "I know what you mean."

She smiles appreciatively. "Anyway, the first step was to stop blaming myself for things out of my control. The next was to learn how to be happy on my own."

"And did you learn how? Are you happy on your own?" *And can you teach me this superpower?* I want to ask.

"I think I'm getting there. It's a journey, not a destination, as they say. But I've learned one thing for sure: you can't cover your holes with someone else's love; you have to fill them yourself."

I know her comment was meant to be profound, but it takes everything in my power to push back the laughter rising from my belly. I bite my lip and hold my breath. Once my eyes meet Avery's, I'm a goner, because she's doing the same. Loud cackles erupt from both of us at the same time like a couple of schoolgirls.

"Okay. Okay," she says, wiping away tears after a solid minute of laughter. "As soon as I said it, I knew there was no way that didn't sound dirty."

"I'm sorry. I can't stop laughing. Maybe try replacing the word 'holes' next time."

"Cracks?" she offers, and we both laugh even harder. "Wow, we are *so* mature."

More laughter, more tears, and all my emotional stress from earlier has vanished. "I think we both needed a good laugh," I say. "In all seriousness, though, what you're doing sounds great. I wish I could be happy on my own."

"There's no reason you can't be."

"I've never been good at being alone. I can't explain why, but it makes me sad."

"You're a people person, Jess. You always have been. You shine in groups and you're extroverted, which means you get energized by being around others. There's nothing wrong with that. Being alone, though, means more time to think—and although I don't know you very well, my guess is it makes you sad because those thoughts are often self-critical."

"Wow. For someone who claims not to know me well, your guess explains it perfectly. How did you know that?"

"Because you're not alone," she says. "Most of us have an annoying, negative voice in our head. We let it pick us apart... unless we practice self-love."

"This is probably a stupid question, but what exactly is self-love?"

"Self-love is the healing kind," Avery says simply.

"Okay, but how do you practice it?" I ask, truly wanting to grasp the concept.

"You know the golden rule? Treat others as you would like to be treated?"

"Of course. It's technically from the Bible," I say. "Do unto others as you would have them do unto you."

"Right. Well... I don't think that always works. Too often, we treat ourselves *worse* than we would treat others. So, my golden rule for self-love is: Treat yourself as you would like *a loved one* to be treated."

At my blank stare, Avery continues, "The next time that negative voice in your head is being hurtful, do this: Pretend that voice belongs to a stranger, and the negative comment is being directed at someone you love—your best friend, a family member, maybe even one of your kids. Then think about what you would say to defend your loved one. Shut the negativity down on their behalf first, then practice defending yourself as fiercely. After all, you deserve to be on your own list of loved ones."

It makes total sense, and yet I would have never thought about it that way. I want to tell Avery as much and thank her for the advice, but I'm temporarily tongue-tied. It's like she's Yoda, and I'm Luke. Except she's female, and I never liked Luke Skywalker. He was too whiny. I'd rather be Leia.

Without further thought, I blurt out, "It's messed up that there wasn't a female Yoda for Princess Leia."

Avery blinks twice and then laughs as hard as we had earlier. I join in, soon folding over myself. Tears again escape the corners of my eyes, and my stomach muscles ache in a *hurts-so-good* way.

Once we both finally stop laughing, I straighten and say, "You have no idea how happy I am our paths crossed today. I needed this talk—and all the laughter—even more than I realized. Thank you."

"I've enjoyed our talk, too. I'm glad we're friends now."

Her words trigger some of my previous worries, and before I can stop myself, I ask, "Why couldn't we be friends before? Was it because of Brad?"

Avery shifts on the towel and stares out at the ocean. "Not exactly."

"That's not a no, though."

After a brief silence, Avery presses her hands into the ground as if to stand. "I should get going."

"Avery, wait." Feeling panicked, I grab her arm to stop her from leaving. "There's something I should tell you."

She settles back on the towel and turns to look at me. I feel the weight of her full attention, and it's both wonderful and frightening. My heart is thudding in my chest when I open my mouth to speak again.

"I found out, almost a year ago, that Brad had been having an affair. We're currently separated but still technically married. I saw him today for the first time since he moved out… at marriage counseling. I don't think I want to get back together with him, but I also hate the idea of filing for divorce. It's been stressful, to say the least." I move my gaze back to the ocean and finally release all the air I'd been holding in my lungs.

Even though I'm looking away, I still feel Avery's eyes on me. She inhales, exhales, and then asks, "Do you mind if I offer you some unsolicited advice?"

I half laugh while watching the waves crash in front of me. "Go ahead. You won't be the first person to tell me I should divorce him."

"I wasn't going to say that. And even if I did, you shouldn't listen to what anyone else thinks you should do about your marriage. Only you can make that decision." Her words pull my focus back to her as she continues, "My advice is to practice self-love before deciding either way. You can't truly love someone else until you first love yourself. And once you do, the answers you seek will become clear."

"Thanks for the advice," I say, genuinely grateful. "You really are a female Yoda. You're *Foda*."

She laughs. "Foda. I like that. If I were Foda, though, I would have said something like, 'Clear will become, the answers you seek.' My therapist is the real Foda. I'm just summarizing her sage advice from many sessions over the years."

I'm torn between wanting to joke about her spot-on Yoda impersonation, shrill voice and all, and wanting to ask why she's needed years of therapy, as invasive as that would be. They're such opposite directions that I'm unable to choose a conversational path. Avery is silently staring out at the ocean, so I allow myself to do the same.

Silence is a funny thing. It should be peaceful. It should give your brain a break from processing all the verbal information that's constantly thrown at it. Instead, it's when that annoying internal voice is at its loudest. My worry and self-doubt grow so loud that my mouth flies open, if only to stop the echo in my head.

"I'm afraid of failing as a mother." I feel Avery's gaze move to me, but I keep mine forward. My statement dangles in the deafening silence a moment longer before I continue. "Brad and I were good at parenting as a team, but on my own, I'm not sure I can handle everything required. And even if I can, it doesn't feel fair to our kids."

In my peripheral view, Avery's hand moves toward me, hesitates, and then falls onto her lap.

"I'm sorry for burdening you with my issues," I say, turning to face her while mentally kicking myself for sharing my parenting fears with someone who can't have children of her own. *Talk about insensitive.*

"No, I'm happy to listen," Avery says, and then, being the mind reader she often is, she adds, "I don't want you to tiptoe around the subject of kids with me just because I can't have any. I may not be able to offer practical advice, but it doesn't mean I can't provide emotional support. What specifically doesn't feel fair to your kids?"

"Mostly them having to split their time between Brad and me. They are home with me four nights a week, and then with Brad the other three when I'm working. Chloe, in particular, needs routine… and… I don't know."

"Have they not adjusted well to their new routine in the time you've been separated?"

"It was hard at first, but they do seem used to it now," I admit, unsure exactly how to put my lingering worries into words. *Avery needs all the information.* "Chloe had the most difficult time adjusting. She was born with a genetic disorder called Prader-Willi syndrome, which makes structure especially important."

"Oh, I didn't realize. I've heard of Prader-Willi in my studies, but I've never met anyone with the syndrome before. Do you mind me asking what her symptoms are?"

"No, I don't mind at all." Though the topic is depressing, talking about my precious baby girl breathes life into me. I feel energized as I continue. "Poor muscle tone is one of the early symptoms of PWS. But there's also delayed physical and intellectual development, sleep disorders, behavioral issues, infertility, vision problems, and so much more...

"Chloe sees a team of specialists at the Children's Hospital every three months. At six months old, she was started on daily injections of growth hormones to help build her muscle mass and achieve a normal height. We'll need to continue those until she's done growing."

"And the injections have helped?" Avery asks.

"They have, but even with treatment, Chloe didn't have the strength to take her first steps until she was almost two years old. Then, the worst symptom of PWS kicked in about a year ago, at age four." I take a deep breath to steady myself before continuing.

"It was lunchtime, and Chloe had just finished eating her sandwich. She turned to me and said, 'Mommy, I'm hungry. Can I have another one?' It's how I knew the insatiable food cravings had started. Constant hunger is a classic sign of Prader-Willi," I explain, wiping away tears. "My poor baby never feels full."

The hand Avery previously dropped in her lap lifts, and I feel the weight of it on my upper back, moving in small soothing circles. She has no idea how much her comfort means to me.

"Anyway, the constant hunger leads to other problems. Chloe is obsessed with food and prone to tantrums. She will also steal food if left unsupervised. We have to keep locks on the refrigerator, cupboards, and even the trash." I pause to wipe away more tears. "I'm sorry if this is too much information."

"No, not at all. I'm glad you're sharing this with me. I can't even imagine... I'm so sorry, Jess."

"Thanks," I say, forcing a light smile. "It honestly helps me to talk about it. A lot of people in my life try to avoid the topic or act like Chloe is a typical child, assuming they'll upset me otherwise. I know their hearts are in the right place, but it's easier to acknowledge the challenges than it is to pretend everything is fine."

"I can understand that. Have you ever considered talking with a therapist to help with the emotional toll?"

I shrug, not wanting to share that *yes, I've considered it, but my insurance doesn't cover mental health.*

Instead, I say, "There's an online support group where I sometimes connect with other parents. Most have children with autism, but there are a few dealing with PWS too. Prader-Willi children are often autistic as well," I explain, "but Chloe hasn't been tested for that yet. My primary concern is helping her stay at a healthy weight. People with PWS can eat themselves to death if their food intake isn't controlled for them, so she'll need lifetime support. One day at a time is what I tell myself."

"One day at a time is best," Avery agrees, giving my shoulder a gentle squeeze.

"Thanks again for letting me dump all that on you. I should get going now, though. I need to pick my kids up from my parents' house."

"Of course," Avery says, as we both press up to standing. "You have my number if you want to talk more. Please don't hesitate to use it."

I shoot her a grateful smile and wave goodbye as she turns to leave. After gathering my belongings, I'm halfway back to my car when my phone rings. The name flashing on the screen has my heart racing. *He never calls me.* My mind immediately goes to a list of worst-case scenarios.

Winded from the walk and my growing panic, my words come out in loud gasps when I answer the call. "Derek, is everything okay?"

"Hail Mary, full of grace, help me find a parking space." No sooner than the words escape my lips, a large SUV pulls out of a spot along Coast Boulevard. "Yes!"

I'd been circling for the last ten minutes. Parking is ridiculous in this area on the weekends, and what's worse, I'm not even sure I'm in the right spot. I should have asked more questions when Derek called earlier this week, but it's a little late for that now—as am I. *Ugh. Why am I never on time?*

Once the other SUV drives off, I pull forward past the spot, line my side-view mirror up with that of the car in front, shift into reverse, and parallel park this beast like a champ. My dad taught me well. As a teenager, I practiced parking one of his large work trucks between two orange cones, which he moved closer and closer together until the space practically matched the length of the truck. Thanks to my dad, I have no trouble maneuvering a large vehicle, driving a stick shift, or changing a tire—among other things.

My stress from running late melts away as soon as I step into the open air. A strong breeze off the ocean mixes with the sun's intense rays to moderate the summer heat, enveloping me in the perfect amount of warmth. Small puffs of white punctuate the otherwise azure sky, which will host a spectacular sunset within the hour.

The exact location I need to be at is only a guess at this point. I'm parked roughly at the midpoint of this one-mile stretch of treasured coastline. If I head north, I'll pass a beautiful park bordered by local art vendors and palm trees before reaching La Jolla Cove.

From experience, I know this area will be crowded with tourists picnicking in the park, walking along the golden bluffs, and taking selfies with sea lions against better judgment on the rocky beach. It's a gorgeous location—despite the cliffs being perpetually painted white by pelicans and seagulls—but I also imagine the stench will be especially offensive in today's heat. Therefore, I head south instead toward Cuvier Park.

Waves, far below, batter the base of the tall bluffs as I speed along the narrow sidewalk, squeezing past people from all over the world who are admiring the picturesque view. The sidewalk widens once it reaches a plaza overlooking the real gems of this area: the harbor seals.

There's a two-story lifeguard station here with public restrooms, and beyond it, a concrete breakwater curves several hundred feet into the ocean to form a horseshoe-shaped cove between it and the coastal bluff where I stand. Waves crash violently against the breakwater that doubles as an observation walkway, often splashing the people atop with sprays of water, but within its boundaries, all is calm. I pause briefly to admire the breathtaking view myself and immediately notice there are fewer seals than usual dotting the beach of the sheltered cove below.

It's not pupping season, so the rope that blocks off human access from mid-December to mid-May is absent. Most people are respectful enough to keep their distance without the physical barrier, but there's always at least one idiot. From atop the bluff, I spot a middle-aged couple—tourists, no doubt, with pasty white legs and a selfie stick in hand—trudging through the sand toward the few remaining seals at the water's edge. As expected, the alarmed "dogs of the sea" wiggle forward in a labored manner until they are in the ocean—safe from the human intruders, but no longer able to rest.

I wonder what Avery would think of that. Her love for animals is so strong she's given up eating anything that comes from them. The irritation creeping up my spine would be tenfold if I were her. It's probably what spurs me to yell, "Leave the seals alone!" before continuing on my way.

I scurry past street vendors—selling tamales, churros, ice cream, and tie-dye T-shirts with pictures of seals on them—until the sidewalk narrows again and the crowds thin. This stretch of coastline is my favorite. Its golden sandstone cliffs are bordered by white daisies with yellow centers, succulents with purple blooms, and tall sea lavender plants that overlook 180 degrees of sea and sky.

My gaze travels out to the thin blue line that separates the earth from the heavens. This gorgeous paradise is only a fifteen-minute drive from our house, yet it's the first time this summer I've visited. I shake my head as I walk. It's too easy to take God's gifts for granted… and to get so busy with life that you forget to enjoy it.

After logging a mental note to bring Lucas and Chloe to see the seals soon, I continue south past more people either walking, jogging, or sitting on benches—most likely all waiting for the sun's nightly color show. This reminds me of how late I am… hopefully not *too* late. I pick up my pace as I enter what I pray is the home stretch, opting to walk along the dirt path that crosses the bluffs rather than the arching sidewalk that climbs over them.

Once on the other side, I'm relieved by the sight of familiar faces gathered on the grassy enclave known as "The Wedding Bowl." Nestled lower on the bluff and encircled in flowering shrubs like sage and goldenbush, it's the perfect backdrop for any occasion.

My mom spots me first and waves as I make my way down the short staircase to the sunken lawn. Noelle is staring at her phone. *No surprise there.* My dad is making big gestures with his hands while talking with Derek and…

"Uncle Victor! Aunt Maggie!" I shout, surprised to see them down from Portland. I run to close the remaining ten feet between us and wrap my arms around them both.

"How's our favorite niece doing?" Uncle Victor asks, garnering Noelle's attention.

"Hey!" my sister shouts with a pout. "I know you tell us both that, but you could at least wait until I'm not standing right here."

I laugh and pull back from the hug. "It's so great to see you both!"

There are a couple of less familiar faces in the small crowd. One is a woman I believe used to be Derek's partner at the Portland Police Bureau, where my uncle is the Chief of Police. I can't recall her name, but I remember meeting the woman next to her and reach out my hand. "You're Natalie's friend, Leah, right? I'm Jessica."

The beautiful woman—tall, tan, and lean—shakes my hand firmly. "Right. You're Natalie's best friend. It's nice to meet you again under better circumstances. And I believe you've met my fiancée, Rhonda, as well."

"Yes! So good to see you again, Rhonda," I say, shaking her hand next.

I'm grateful Leah filled in the blank for my spotty memory. We'd first met when Natalie was fighting for her life in the hospital last fall—a time I'm sure we'd all like to forget. At that thought, I scan the area for Natalie and am relieved once more when she's nowhere in sight. *I'm not too late.*

The sun hangs low in the sky, casting golden light on what appears to be fifty bouquets of sunflowers arranged in the shape of a giant heart on the lawn. Inside it, Derek stands next to tall block letters outlined in white fairy lights that read, "MARRY ME." Even though I knew the plan for today, the beautiful sight causes my heart to throb and my eyes to water.

"Did Natalie get delayed?" I ask Derek, who is sharply dressed in a crisp white button-down. "I was worried I'd miss her reaction!"

"She should be arriving with Linda in about five minutes," Derek says, looking at his watch. "Linda texted me they were on track to be here at seven thirty when they left the house ten minutes ago."

"Oh, that's great! I thought they were supposed to be here at seven."

Noelle chimes in, "We told you to be here way earlier, because we knew you'd be late."

I place my fists on my hips but can't be mad. *They're not wrong.*

"I'm back! Sorry it took so long. Parking was a nightmare." The familiar voice belongs to Kent. I didn't realize Kent would be here, but I guess it makes sense. He and Derek talk a lot during our family gatherings, and Natalie has mentioned the boys go out for drinks sometimes. It's nice that they've become friends.

"No worries, buddy. You're a lifesaver!" Derek stuffs the small box Kent hands him into the pocket of his khaki dress pants and then bro hugs him with a quick shoulder bump and slap on the back. Wait. Did Derek forget the engagement ring? And Kent Clark saved the day?

Derek glances at his watch again while tapping his foot, then he folds his hands in front of him and taps his thumbs.

"Deep breaths," I say to him. "She's going to say yes, and she'll be ecstatic. You have nothing to worry about."

His hazel eyes remain fixed on the entrance. "Thanks. I'm sure you're right, but I'll feel better when I see her."

As soon as he finishes speaking, Natalie appears at the top of the staircase. Her hand is over her mouth in surprise, but a wide smile peeks around her fingers. A hushed silence falls over the group, then Noelle streams "Marry You" by Bruno Mars from the phone she's been cradling. *Well, paper cuts.* People had tasks, and I wasn't here on time to help.

Pushing down my guilt, I watch Natalie descend the stairs like an angel in blue. The silky sapphire gown has a high neckline and hugs all the curves on her thin frame as it drops straight down to her ankles. The ocean breeze blows her long blond hair back and out to the sides like she's posing for glamour shots, which prompts me to pull out my phone and start snapping pictures.

Natalie had been told her mother was giving her a ride to meet Derek at a charity gala, which they will technically attend after this sunset proposal. She hates surprises, or rather the torment of waiting to know something, but it's clear tonight has caught her off guard in the best possible way. She moves her hand from her mouth to her heart when she reaches the bottom of the stairs, and I capture every moment, switching to video as she approaches Derek.

He drops to one knee, and… *shoot, I'm crying again.* I watch through blurry eyes while trying to hold the camera steady. It's a dream proposal—unlike the one I received from Brad, but this isn't about me. My best friend is getting a second chance at marriage after losing her first husband in a tragic car crash, and the love she shares with Derek is absolute and unparalleled.

Derek pulls out a ring box and opens it. "Natalie, will you do me the honor of being my wife?"

"Yes!" she cries without hesitation.

Our entire group, plus a small crowd of strangers gathered on the sidewalk above us, all applaud and cheer as Natalie and Derek kiss. Noelle switches the music to play "Yeah!" by Usher, kicking off an impromptu dance party. My dad swings both Noelle and me under each of his arms, rolls us into his chest, and then spins us out before crossing the lawn and dramatically dipping our mother. Derek and Natalie deepen their kiss while dropping down low to the beat.

"Get a room!" Rhonda hollers, laughing as she shakes her hips near Leah.

The two women look so happy together, and I can't help but think of Avery. Has she ever had a girlfriend who made her as happy?

"Look alive." Noelle hip bumps me, then proceeds to mock smack my butt to the music.

I play along, dropping my hands to my knees and swaying my hips side to side.

"Ay, Dios mío," my dad mutters playfully, while moving his hand from his forehead to his chest, and then from left to right in the sign of the cross. He then spins and dips my mother again before resuming a waltz stance that only Carlos Serrano can pull off to hip hop.

Even Uncle Victor and Aunt Maggie are shaking their money makers, and, dare I say… grinding? Kent stands alone, nodding his head to the beat, so I hip check my sister in his direction when she's not paying attention. I might have put my full weight into it, because she flies three feet over and bumps into him.

It earns me one of Noelle's famous glares, but it was worth it to watch them feverishly part like the Red Sea. They love each other. They just don't *know* they love each other.

Once the song ends, Derek reaches into his pocket again. I fumble my camera app open and hold my breath, eager to know what's in the other box, which I now recognize as the one Kent had delivered.

"I have another surprise I hope you'll like," he says, before revealing a silver key. "It's to the house we were looking at last month."

Natalie's hands cover her mouth again. "The one I loved with the blue door and the granny flat over the garage?"

"That's the one," he says. "Escrow closed this afternoon, so I hope you still love it."

"I do! I do! And I love you… so, so much, Derek." Natalie bounces in place with happy tears glistening in her blue eyes.

Natalie's tears, of course, bring on fresh ones from me. I wipe them away just in time to see the last sliver of the sun dipping below the horizon. "Hey, everyone, the sun is setting!"

We all watch as the bright red-orange speck disappears behind the ocean, turning the scattered clouds in the distance into lovely puffs of cotton candy. It was the perfect proposal.

Chapter 17

Seventeen years ago

"We should have a threesome," Brad says while flipping through videos, like the topic is as casual as picking out a movie to watch tonight.

I laugh because, surely, he's not being serious. "As if! Like I'd ever let you cheat on me right in front of my face."

"It's not cheating if we're doing it together." His eyes widen, then he wiggles a DVD in my direction with the excitement of a young child. "Sweet! They have the *Fast and Furious* sequel!"

"Veto. Let's pick something we can both enjoy." I thumb through the romantic comedy shelf, looking for one with enough action to satisfy Brad. I've been wanting to see *Just Like Heaven* since it was in theaters, but I already know he won't go for it, so I keep browsing.

The last movie we rented together was *Troy*, which had something for us both. A love story for me. Graphic violence and nudity for Brad. Although Brad could rent it for us now that he's eighteen, we had to watch it at his house, since my parents would never allow me to watch a rated R movie like that one.

"Speaking of something we'd both enjoy…" Brad turns to me with a suggestive grin on his face. "You could pick the other girl, babe. Just no fuglies, okay?"

Is he serious right now?

"Brad, please, drop it already. It's never going to happen." There was a threesome in *Troy*. Maybe that's where all this nonsense is coming from.

Brad straightens his back, making himself look almost as tall and broad as he does when he's wearing all his football gear. His face is dead serious when he says, "Jess, we're going to get married someday, and we'll only have ever been with each other. Don't you want to be a little adventurous before we settle down?"

So many confusing feelings rush to me at once. We've never talked about marriage before. *Brad wants to marry me?* A tightness in my chest relaxes. I have felt guilty about our premarital sex ever since we stopped waiting last year.

After two years of making out practically every day, abstinence had been getting increasingly difficult. Brad had pointed out that most of our friends in shorter relationships were already doing it. I also know plenty of girls at our school who would be eager to sleep with Brad, so I suppose I didn't want to risk losing him, either. *But what's wrong with only being with each other?*

I swallow to settle my emotions before responding. "I like that we've only been with each other. It's special."

Brad wraps his arm around my shoulders and gives me a gentle squeeze. "Aw, babe, what we have will always be special. You're the only girl for me. All I'm talking about is spicing things up a bit. It'll be the one wild night we can look back on when we're old and gray, you know?"

"I guess that makes sense," I say without thinking. *Does it make sense?*

"That's my girl! I knew there was a reason I love you so much." Brad leans around and presses his lips against mine before sliding his arm down to take my hand. He angles his body to face me directly and looks into my eyes. "Jessica Marie Serrano, will you be my wife someday?"

There's no ring. He's not on one knee. *Is this a proposal?* I'm dumbfounded for a second. "You're asking me to marry you?"

"Yeah, someday," he says nonchalantly. "Like in three or four years. Let's get married when we're at least twenty-one so we can get legally drunk at the wedding." Laughter follows that statement.

Is this all a joke to him? Marriage is a holy union, a sacrament, not something to be taken lightly. "Would you convert to Catholicism for me?" I ask.

He stops laughing. "I would do anything for you, babe. You know that. I already go to church with you and your family most Sundays."

"Yeah, you do, but there's a lot more to conversion than going to mass. There's Confirmation and…"

"I'll do it," Brad interrupts. "You be adventurous with me this one time, and I'll jump through whatever hoops I need to. Whatever it takes."

"They're not hoops; they're sacraments," I correct. *And is he seriously bartering his soul for a threesome?* My mind cannot wrap itself around that, so it pushes it away. "I mean it, Brad. I want to get married by the Catholic Church, which requires you to be all in. And I'd want to raise our kids that way, too."

Brad loops his arms around my waist this time and pulls me in for a hug. His chin rests on top of my head. "I know, and I'm not kidding. I'm all in. Your faith is one of the things I love most about you."

"It is?" I ask, pulling back to look up into his baby blue eyes. It's always felt more like he loves me *despite* my faith.

"Yeah. You're so optimistic. You power through any obstacle. It's like nothing can ever get you down for too long, because you know God has your back. I wish I was more like that, but my brothers and I weren't raised that way." There's rare vulnerability on his face, and I think I love him even more.

"You can have that too, Brad. It's never too late to come to the Lord." I press my lips to his, and it's the sweetest kiss I think we've ever shared.

"Thanks, babe," he says after our lips part. "So, I'm thinking Richie Sampson's graduation party next weekend will be the perfect opportunity. He's got a huge house with lots of bedrooms, and his parents will be gone. What girl should we ask?"

And the tender moment is over. Talking about my faith and a threesome in the same conversation feels all kinds of wrong.

"Do we have to talk about this now… in public?" Looking around, I sigh when I see we're the only ones here, except for the bored employee at the other end of the video rental store. *I hope they don't go out of business.* "Fine. We can talk about it, but why does it have to be another girl? Couldn't we do it with another guy instead?"

"Ew! Gross, Jess! I'm not gay!" Brad sputters and throws his arms in the air.

"And I am?"

"No, it's different with girls. Girl on girl is sexy. Trust me."

I'm starting to trust him less and less. Nothing about that double standard makes any sense at all. But… I do have someone in mind. Butterflies form in my stomach. "Well, what if we ask another girl and she says no? That'll be embarrassing."

"Don't worry about that," Brad says. "Just tell me who, and I'll handle the rest."

"What does that mean?"

"It means I'll ask her, and I doubt I'll get a no. But if I do, I'll pretend I was joking or something." His confidence amazes me, and although he is often downright cocky, I must admit it's one of the things I find most attractive about him.

"Okay. I pick the girl, and I also pick the movie we watch tonight." My hand reaches for the DVD on the shelf behind us. "We're renting *Just Like Heaven.*"

"Ugh, a chick flick," Brad groans. "Okay, fine. Whatever you want."

I smile before the realization sinks in that I've agreed to compromise my morals in exchange for watching Reese Witherspoon and Mark Ruffalo fall in love tonight. Is that all it's worth? I should have called movie selection rights for life, at a minimum.

I'm mentally kicking myself when Brad asks, "So, who will it be?"

Her name is on the tip of my tongue, and the thought of saying it out loud sends a weird pulse of energy through my body. I take several steps toward the register, grab a box of Reese's Pieces, and then look back at Brad over my shoulder. "Ask Avery Emerald."

Part II: Avery

"You know, a heart can be broken, but it
keeps on beating, just the same."

–Fannie Flagg, *Fried Green Tomatoes at the
Whistle Stop Cafe*

Chapter 18

Now

I've seen Jess a handful of times in the week since the beach, including at our physical therapy session two days ago. Although her former PT had taken copious notes on the injuries from her recent car accident, it was clear he had done little to help her properly heal. Liquid fire had coursed through my veins upon the discovery of obscene amounts of scar tissue in her left shoulder.

Any PT worth their salt would have prevented that with a combination of massage and in-office exercises, rather than relying solely on patient compliance at home. I told Jess as much and recommended increasing the frequency of her sessions until we could improve her mobility. Gratitude had washed over her features, reaffirming the passion I have for my chosen career.

There is nothing more satisfying than aiding in someone's healing process. Before getting into PT, I had considered studying psychology. Being a therapist for the mind would be an equally rewarding profession, but the body doesn't lie. Physical trauma can't be hidden as easily as the emotional kind.

I kneel in the back pew while others file toward the altar, one row at a time, to receive Communion. It's been a while since I've attended a mass and even longer since my last confession. Partaking in the Holy Eucharist is not an option for me today, but I'm okay with that. Being here at all feels significant enough, and I'd much rather stay out of sight.

Jess returns to her pew, which is three in front of mine and to the right. She's accompanied by her two small children and an older couple that is unmistakably Carlos and Deedee Serrano. They've been pillars of this church and community since long before I moved to San Diego as a teen. I remember hearing all about how wonderful they were the day I first arrived.

A happy, loving family was the last thing I wanted to be around back then. It will be a testament to my personal growth if I'm able to manage it now, but the jury's still out. I want to be happy for Jess. I really do. But her perfect family is a reminder of everything I never had.

I look down at the Arabic script on my inner wrist, and in a rare moment of weakness, I think of my mother. I imagine her face and the pain she must have felt at the end; my father's grief; and my own suffering as a result. All of it intertwines in my mind's eye, unable to be separated from the concept of *family*. As if hiding my tattoo will erase the past, I tug down the sleeve of my cardigan.

Everyone stands for the final prayer, and my heart starts to race. Mass is concluding, which means I'll need to say hello to Jess… and likely exchange pleasantries with her parents. It's the right thing to do, since she encouraged me to come here today, but I can't help eyeing the door behind me. It wouldn't be difficult to slip out unnoticed during the closing hymn.

As I'm contemplating doing just that during the final verses of "On Eagle's Wings," I notice Jess turn and move her eyes over the crowd. It doesn't take long for them to land on me. Her mouth stretches wide into her usual megawatt smile and she waves excitedly. *Well, crap.* There's no escaping now.

I close the hymn book in my hands as the song ends and weakly wave back. People herd out the swinging double doors behind me, and I signal to Jess that I'll see her outside before doing the same.

Deep breaths, Avery. It's just her parents. I practically know them already anyway, given their presence at every school and community event—as well as all the aforementioned stories of their kindness and generosity.

Mr. Serrano's company had landscaped the front of our high school, in addition to his ongoing monthly maintenance of the church grounds—all without charge. Mrs. Serrano used to volunteer her time at our school library, and I hear she now runs a *Meals on Wheels* program within the parish that services the sick and elderly throughout San Diego County.

I'm a horrible person for wanting to avoid them. I know this, but the knot in my stomach doesn't seem to care. Doctor K would remind me to push through the discomfort. As with most advice, though, it's easier said than done.

Outside the church doors, I linger near the bake sale and stiffen when I see Jess walk out with her father's arm draped over her shoulder. She spots me immediately, but instead of approaching as expected, she points to the opposite side of the parking lot.

"Avery! I'm so glad you came today!" she says once I follow them over to where she pointed.

"Elizabeth! Nice to meet you!" her father says, sticking out his hand.

At my confused look, Jess laughs. "Dad! Her name is Avery. He's just being silly," she adds to me.

"More like being Carlos," Deedee Serrano says, approaching from behind with a child on either side. She has short silver hair and looks like a walking jewelry store—with large stone rings on every finger, bracelets up both arms, multiple sets of earrings, and *one, two, three* necklaces around her neck—and somehow, on her, it all looks great.

"My dad calls all of my friends Elizabeth," Jess explains. "It started with my best friend Natalie when we were four. Her middle name is Elizabeth… and now all friends are Elizabeths, apparently."

"You have a lot of friends, Kissin' Bug. It's easier to remember for an old guy like me." Carlos Serrano playfully nudges Jess with his elbow, then his mouth grows into the same megawatt smile his daughter wears effortlessly. His white teeth pop against his weathered tan skin, as do sparse amounts of white facial hair scattered among the gray and black of his neatly trimmed beard.

"Sixty-five is hardly old, Dad, and you started saying that thirty years ago," Jess teases back.

"God bless America!" Carlos randomly shouts before muttering something in Spanish.

"No one can understand you when you do that, dear," Deedee says.

"Ignore him, please," Jess says to me.

"Mommy, cake!" the small girl says, pointing across the parking lot toward the bake sale. *Chloe*, I recall, and my heart squeezes.

Jess' smile disappears as her whole body tenses. "No cake today, baby. We'll have a healthy snack when we get to your gigi and papa's house. You should join us," she says, turning to face me. Her smile returns but doesn't reach her eyes. "We barbecue at my parents' house every Sunday after church."

"Thank you, but I couldn't possibly…"

"Cake, cake, cake!" Chloe stomps her little foot with each word. Her chubby cheeks are red and wet with tears. Under thick glasses, her eyes are a bit crossed, and I'm immediately reminded of everything Jess told me about her daughter's struggle with Prader-Willi syndrome.

There's a look of defeat in Jess' eyes when she opens her mouth to speak. Before any words come out, Carlos scoops his granddaughter high into the air and buries his face into her stomach, making her squeal and giggle. "Tastes like chicken," he says with an exaggerated accent.

I watch Jess blow out a breath before she faces me again and places her hand on my arm. "I understand if you don't want to hang out with my crazy family, *trust me*, but I'd love your company. It would mean a lot to me if you'd join us."

The sincerity in her voice and pleading look in her eyes are more than I can bear. And just like that... my defenses drop, and all the feelings I've been suppressing for years come rushing back to the surface. There's a reason I've never been able to say no to Jessica Serrano.

"You're sure I won't be imposing on family time?" I ask.

Deedee cuts in to answer. "Family is everyone we choose to surround ourselves with, dear, related or not. You must join us! Plus, we always have way too much food. Carlos here thinks he's still a cook in the Army, feeding a whole platoon."

"It's true," Jess says. "There will be non-meat options, too. Corn-on-the-cob, beans, salad, pasta, bread... I'm not sure what else, but we can make whatever you like. So, what do you say? Will you come over?"

At my nod, Jess squeals like her daughter had. "Yay! It'll be fun. You'll see."

"Draw four and make it red," I say two hours later, unleashing a competitive side I didn't even know I had.

Jess wasn't wrong. This is fun.

"No fair," Lucas groans. He takes four more cards off the top of the pile before placing down a red "S" and yelling "Skip!" to his mom.

"I'll remember that, Lucas," Jess teases.

It's back to me, so I lay a red "D" on top of his red "S" before quickly shouting, "Uno! Sorry, bud… that's a draw two to you."

Lucas shakes his head and deadpans, "She's brutal, Mom."

"All's fair in love and card games," Jess says, laughing in my direction. She then surprises me by playing a yellow "D" on top of mine. "I can be brutal too. Draw two, Avery."

Lucas cheers as if avenged.

I mock glare at them. "A minor setback. You're both still going down."

"Intense game," Deedee says upon entering the dining room, and all the blood drains from my face. *Am I really trash talking an eight-year-old?*

I feel marginally better when Jess replies, "It is the way."

Her *Star Wars* reference, this time from *The Mandalorian* series, reminds me of our talk on the beach. Jess had called me Foda. I'd happily be her Foda.

Deedee nods what seems to be her approval before addressing her daughter. "Chloe was feeling tired, so she's napping in the back room."

Jessica's face goes serious as she presses to standing. "Is she doing okay? I'll go check on her."

Prince Petey of Bay Ho—the cutest dog ever—startles awake from his position at her feet.

"Sit, sit," Deedee says. "She's already asleep. And she's doing fine, just tired from all the excitement today."

Jess settles back into her chair, looking only half relaxed. "Thanks, Mom."

Deedee pats her daughter's shoulder and then takes a seat next to Lucas to watch the rest of our battle. "Who's next?" she asks.

"Right," I say, drawing two cards off the top of the pile before pointing my chin toward Lucas. "Your turn."

A devious grin spreads across his face when he lays down a yellow "R" card, reversing the direction of play back to me. It's in this moment I realize I'm no match for this kid. He knows what he's doing, and that "R" might as well stand for "Revenge." I bet he has a handful of *Draw Four* cards with my name on them.

But this also means Jess will feel my wrath now. I lay another *Draw Two* card, drawn as a result of her last play, and the war continues.

Ten minutes go by, and the number of cards in my hand grows substantially before Lucas shouts, "I win!"

In disbelief, I stare at his final card on the table—an innocuous green eight. *Beaten by an eight-year-old.* My battered ego snaps out of its trance when Jess laughs.

"Don't feel so bad. He's really good at this game. I still can't believe you never played Uno before."

"I didn't play any games growing up," I reply mindlessly.

At the sight of Jess' wide eyes, I immediately regret it. *Do all kids play games?* Hoping to divert focus, I add, "Congratulations, Lucas! You're the King of Uno."

He smiles at me before saying, "For what it's worth, you were a fierce competitor." *This kid is too cute.* "Mom, can I go play Mario Kart now?"

Jess gives Lucas a quick hug when he stands from the table. "Sure, but you'll have to ask your papa nicely. He might still be watching TV."

Deedee rises from her seat at the table. "No need. He's asleep in his recliner. I'll go help you get it started, honey."

"Are you sure, Mom?" Jess asks. "I can help him."

"No, no. You stay right there and keep your friend company. Gigi's got this." Deedee winks at us both and then follows Lucas out of the dining room.

Jess sighs. "My mom's the best. I'd honestly be lost without her, but her help also makes me feel guilty sometimes. She does too much for me."

"Your mom loves you and your kids. Sometimes taking care of people is the easiest way to show that." My eyes fall to the table, and I stack all the cards into a neat pile to busy my hands. "I know what you mean, though. My brother does way too much for me, too."

"Oh? I didn't realize you had a brother. I guess I should have thought to ask," Jess says, sounding apologetic.

"It's fine. Damien's four years older than us, so he'd already graduated from high school when we moved to San Diego. He left for college soon after to play soccer at UCSB. My brother was a proud Gaucho and their star forward… until an ACL injury during his second season."

"Ouch. He must have been devastated."

"He was. He couldn't play anymore that season and almost dropped out of school altogether. That probably sounds drastic, but Damien has been through a lot, and soccer was the one thing that brought him joy." I stuff the Uno cards into the box and do my best not to relive that horrible time. "Luckily, he was sent to physical therapy after his surgery, and a year later, he was able to return to the field. I saw the impact PT had on my brother's life, and I knew right then… I wanted to help others heal so they could get back to doing whatever they loved."

"What a great reason to become a physical therapist. I love that! I'm sure your brother is proud of you, too. What is he up to these days? Does he live here in San Diego?"

"He does. Damien moved back here after college, even though I left for USC that same year. He worked as a bartender while figuring out what he wanted to do, and now he's a lawyer."

"Nice! Natalie's boyfriend… excuse me, fiancé! They got engaged last night," Jess gushes. "Anyway, he's planning to go to Cal Western for his law degree next spring. You remember my best friend Natalie, right? She went by Natalya back in high school."

"Yes. Of course. And I heard what happened last year. It was all over the news. How is she doing?" As soon as I ask the question, I know it's a ridiculous one. *How would anyone be doing after almost being murdered by a serial killer?*

"That's sweet of you to ask," Jess says. "All things considered, she's doing amazingly well now, believe it or not. Her new fiancé, Derek, is the one who saved her. They're the cutest couple. And Natalie recently opened a non-profit women's center downtown to help victims of violence get back on their feet."

"Wow, I'm happy to hear it. That's incredible! And my brother can probably give her fiancé some tips regarding law school. If you want, I can text you his contact information to pass along."

"That would be *a-maz-ing!*" Jess says, emphasizing each syllable. "Damien sounds like a great brother, by the way."

"The greatest," I say.

"So, if you didn't play any games as a kid, what did you and Damien do for fun growing up?"

My body reflexively stiffens at the question, and Jess seems to notice. "I don't mean to pry. I was just wondering what your childhood was like on the East Coast, but we can talk about something else."

I hold up a hand and force my body to relax. I've answered this question hundreds of times before. "It's fine. Vermont is a lot colder in the winter than San Diego, and it's humid and buggy in the summer, so I stayed indoors a lot and focused on my schoolwork and chores. Nothing exciting."

Jess nods at my canned response, and I suddenly feel like a liar despite not saying anything dishonest. *Lying by omission*, as Doctor K would say. I owe Jess something more personal—a partial truth, at least.

I get my chance when she asks, "Were you happy to move to San Diego for high school, then?"

I would normally say yes, but that would be a lie. And I don't want to lie to Jess.

"Not at first. But looking back now, I know it was what was best for me. My childhood in Vermont… Well, it wasn't much of a childhood at all. Once Damien got home from boarding school, we came to live with my aunt in San Diego."

"Oh, Avery. I'm so sorry." Her hand immediately comes up to rest on my arm—a kind gesture I've come to crave from Jess. Rather than pity, her eyes reflect genuine compassion. Jess is as genuine as they come.

After a moment, her hand and gaze both slide down my arm to my wrist. Her thumb traces my tattoo. "What does this say?"

"No secrets," I answer honestly. "I got it as a reminder that no good ever comes from them."

Jess' body language morphs from relaxed to uneasy—tense shoulders, shallow breaths, a slow gulp—but the reaction disappears so quickly I might have imagined it. Her eyes move back up and seem to linger on my mouth a moment before meeting mine. They bore into me when she says, "I've always been glad that you moved here for high school… for selfish reasons… but now I'm happy for your sake, too."

My heart skips a beat under the focused attention of Jessica Serrano, the most popular girl in high school. Even though her world is full of familial love, and so different from mine, she's always had a special ability to make me feel like I'm the only person who matters. She probably makes everyone feel that way; hence, her popularity. But what did she mean by *selfish reasons*?

I clear my bone-dry throat, wanting to ask her, but the words elude me. *Time to change the subject.* "Is Chloe okay? You seemed worried about her earlier."

Jess shoots me a half smile I can tell is forced. "It's my job to worry. Chloe has sleep apnea—another common complication of PWS—so she gets tired a lot during the day. I'm working with insurance to get her a CPAP device, which should help her sleep better through the night, but in the meantime, frequent naps are a necessity."

As if summoned by the mention of her name, Chloe stands at the entrance of the dining room, rubbing tired eyes. "Mommy, I'm hungry."

"Sorry, I'll be right back." Jess stands and takes Chloe's tiny hand in hers. As the two walk off together toward the kitchen, I hear Jess ask, "How did you sleep, Princess?"

It makes my heart melt and break simultaneously. The emptiness inside me—usually the size of a pear—becomes the vast vacuum of outer space. I'm floating past Earth's orbit while watching life go on without me. My eyes water, but without gravity, the tears won't fall. *Foda wouldn't cry.*

Snapping out of it, I pull my phone out to text Jess that something unexpected has come up. And then I launch myself out the front door.

Chapter 19

At least I won't have to sneak past Jess this time, I think as I stroll across the hotel lobby in my flowy yet casual maxi dress. Stashing my giant bag of surveillance equipment under her desk before had been risky, and I'm certain she had noticed my outfit change. But that won't be a problem today.

It's Wednesday, and Jess only works here on Thursdays through Saturdays. She's told me as much, yet I still glance at the concierge desk on my way toward the exit. A young woman with sunny blond hair sits there, smiling at the hotel guests seated opposite her.

It's not the type of smile that lights up a room, though. *It's not Jessica Serrano's smile.* I'd always assumed her natural luminosity was the product of a perfect life. All sunshine and rainbows without a single storm. But when she opened up to me at the beach—about her fears and insecurities, her troubled marriage, and her daughter's challenges—what astounded me the most is how well her beautiful smile hides it all.

It goes to show that a well-executed smile is often our greatest disguise. It can cover our scars and mask our pain. Perhaps everyone is hiding something, keeping the ugliest parts of themselves concealed behind teeth and curved lips. Still, I never thought the sheer joy exuded by Jess could ever be faked—great actress or not.

Something tells me the worries she shared are only the tip of the iceberg when it comes to her emotional torment. If only I could help with more than the scar tissue in her shoulder…

I shake off the thought, adjust the wide-brimmed hat atop my head, and step out through the grand revolving door. Even with the oversized hat and my usual dark sunglasses, the brightness of another sunny, blue-skied day causes me to squint. The valet attendant is at my side within seconds, taking the ticket I hand him before disappearing to retrieve my rental car.

My mind returns to the task at hand while I wait. I may not be able to heal every wound—physical or otherwise—and I can't solve the world's problems or eradicate suffering, but I can be a voice for those who have none. I can help to end cruelty one innocent creature at a time. It's imperative I keep my head in the game and remember what's at stake.

The hat I'm wearing, more for discretion than sun protection, reminds me of those worn by women attending opening day at the racetrack—complicit in the overly romanticized "sport" of horse brutality. My heart aches at the thought.

Poor, innocent horses being whipped to go faster than nature intended. Captive "property" subjected to cocktails of drugs given to enhance performance and mask injuries. Beautiful colts, stallions, geldings, fillies, and mares forced to run until their lungs bleed and limbs break, and then—once rendered useless to their wealthy owners—sent to slaughter. Meanwhile, spectators flaunt fancy outfits and sip mint juleps.

My father used to love the races. The lack of an active track in our own state didn't stop him from betting on horses across the country. In our household, the Kentucky Derby was a bigger event than the Super Bowl each year. It was the only time we had guests in our ostentatious estate, which was far larger than necessary for our small family.

When I'd shown concern for the horses as a child, my father had insisted that they loved to run; they were born for it. And since racing allowed them to do what they loved, there was nothing wrong with it. It was logical enough for my adolescent brain. I suppose it's easy to believe almost anything before learning the terrifying truth. Too much of my childhood had been that way.

When a black sedan appears at the curb in front of me, I tip the valet, slide into the driver's seat, and open the "Find My Phone" app. The phone I had wedged between the seats in Rome's rental car is headed in the expected direction. I pull away from the hotel with a renewed sense of determination and mutter, "I know what you're up to, Rome, and I'm going to prove it."

The next day, repeated disappointment compounds into desperation during Rome's PT session. Not only was yesterday's covert expedition a bust, but it made me realize simple surveillance would never be enough. I've been following Rome for weeks—months if you count our time outside of San Diego—and all it has yielded are a few photos of his rental car parked outside a seemingly innocent residence.

But there is nothing *innocent* about it. I know it, and I'd be willing to bet my life that Rome knows it as well. Still, there's nothing I can do without evidence. I couldn't even get a shot of him with one of the puppies, let alone find proof that he's aware of their nefarious origin.

Using more force than necessary, I knead the knots under his shoulder blade. With his face down on the massage table and his arm pulled up overhead, I brazenly ask, "Where were you yesterday? I was hoping we could get lunch together, but you weren't at the pool or your room when I went looking."

"You went looking for me? I'm flattered," he drawls in that sickening flirtatious way he does with all women.

It doesn't matter that I've told him I'm only attracted to women. He seemed to take my declaration as a challenge to up his game, as if the right amount of charm could make me want his dick. Little does he realize, the real problem is the bigger dick it's attached to.

I suppose it would be easier to get the information I need if I could feign interest in him, but the one time I'd tried had been a disaster. Even now, the thought of his calloused hands on me stirs my simmering nausea. There isn't much I wouldn't do for a good cause, but I can't do that.

"Was your girlfriend not working yesterday?" he asks, conveniently evading my question.

"She's just a friend from high school. Is that where you were yesterday? Off with some mystery girlfriend?"

"Careful. You're starting to sound like a jealous lover." Rome laughs before shrugging his non-outstretched shoulder. "I was checking up on a business investment."

This could go somewhere. I already knew he had a financial stake in the business—based on bank records showing he wrote a fifty-thousand-dollar check to a Ms. Anabelle Rose of *Rose's Golden Doodles*—but he's never admitted to his "investment" before.

I steady my voice to sound as nonchalant as possible. "Oh? Here in San Diego? What type of business?"

"Okay. I'm done with that." Rome lowers his arm, uses it to push up to a seated position, and then draws a few circles in the air with his elbow. "My shoulder feels like it's been tenderized."

I take a step back but hold his gaze. *A little seduction couldn't hurt, right?* "We need to get you nice and loose before your next tee off."

He shoots me a crooked smile and doesn't need to voice his transparent thoughts. I already know he's now wondering how to get me *nice and loose*. Then he pauses as if considering something. "You'd be interested in this business, actually… given you're a vegan and all."

I suppress an eye roll at the label. Does the term "carnivore" define everything about a person who eats meat?

"I'm a silent investor for a local dog breeder," he continues. "She's all about the humane treatment of animals. She has a huge yard with only a handful of dogs to care for at a time, unlike those crowded puppy mills you read about."

Silent, my ass. You don't visit the business property three times in two weeks, traveling forty minutes each way, if you're only a *silent* investor. Eager to get this on record, I glance at my purse on the chair next to me before returning to Rome's steely blue eyes.

"That is interesting… and great for the dogs. But wouldn't it be difficult to make money operating a business that way?"

"It turns out you can," Rome says smugly. "There's a big market for people looking to responsibly source their new pet. They're willing to pay a premium for a humanely bred puppy, and if they're not happy, there's a cash-back guarantee. It's a win-win."

I cross my arms to demonstrate my skepticism, hopefully without showing too much of my hand. "How are the buyers ensured the puppies are bred humanely? I mean, couldn't the breeder lie to collect the premium price?"

"That's the cool part. Buyers can visit the property if they want and see the living conditions with their own eyes. And for those who can't make the trip, there's a twenty-four-hour live feed online, where you can watch the puppies play, eat, sleep, poop… you name it." There's a gleam in Rome's eyes I don't recognize—pride, maybe—before the blue spheres go dark and scroll down my body in an all-too-familiar mental undressing.

My body instinctively stiffens, but I force my hand up to my chest and fiddle with the top button of my V-neck blouse to draw his attention there. "That *is* cool," I say, lowering my voice and acting as impressed as I know he wants me to be. "What about when the dogs are… you know… making the puppies? Filming them doggy-style without their permission would be bad form," I say with a suggestive wink that makes my stomach crawl up into my throat.

Rome laughs and stands. He's less than a foot in front of me, and his hot breath is against my ear when he whispers, "I bet you'd like that. But no. The dogs get their business on off-camera."

"Like… at a separate location?" I ask, desperately needing him to admit what I already know.

My prying causes Rome to lean back and tilt his head. That crooked smile reemerges. "Why are you so interested in dog sex, Avery? It's been a while for you, hasn't it?"

I clear my throat and attempt to take a step back before realizing the wall is mere inches behind me. The heel of my shoe hits it with an echoing thud.

Rome laughs again and takes a step back. "Relax. I'm not trying to hit on you. I know you've got it bad for that hottie in concierge, even if you won't admit it."

I open my mouth to protest, but no sound comes out. How did we get on the topic of Jess?

Dammit. I can't bring the conversation back to dog breeding without him getting overly suspicious. This is the closest I've ever gotten to him implicating himself. It's the closest I'll probably ever get, and now the opportunity has passed.

"I can't blame you, though. Those jugs," he says, motioning with his hands a good foot in front of his chest. "It's a shame you won't let me join you two."

"She's straight," I blurt, immediately regretting my truthful words when the corners of Rome's lips curl.

"Is that so?" he drawls. "Maybe I should ask her out, then."

Bile rises from my stomach. Everything inside me wants to scream at him to leave Jess alone. I could tell him she's married—another terrifying truth—but something stops me. Perhaps it's my desperation to expose Rome. Or perhaps it's my need to prove I'm not into Jess.

Either way, I instead say, "Go ahead."

Chapter 20

The sun, low in the sky, scatters its golden beams across the still surface of the bay as I pull up to the hotel. Sparkling light refracts off the murky water like a prism, casting diamonds across a blanket of blue. The oversized revolving door into the hotel couldn't possibly move any slower. *It's not a big deal. I'll just talk to Jess before Rome asks her out, and everything will be okay. It's not a big deal.*

When I finally push my way inside, I'm relieved to see Jess sitting alone at her desk with Rome nowhere in sight. He must have gone somewhere else after our PT session. Before I can let myself question his whereabouts, I cross the lobby and stop in front of the concierge desk right as Jess stands.

"Hey, I was hoping to catch you," I say.

"Well, you're in luck," Jess returns. "I was about to go clock out for the day, but I can help you first if there's something you need."

"Oh, this isn't hotel related. Um… What are you up to tonight?"

"I've got a hot date…" Jess smiles at me with a devious glint in her eyes, and my heart drops.

I'm too late. How am I too late? Did Rome beat me back to the hotel, ask her out already, and then disappear? My nausea from earlier returns with a vengeance, and the room slowly spins in one complete rotation.

"With myself!" Jess finishes with a laugh. "I was going to try a night of self-love, like you recommended. I'm getting my favorite takeout on the way home, and I'll probably eat it in front of a movie. Maybe take a long bubble bath after." She shrugs before taking in my face, which must be ghostly pale from the feeling of it.

"Avery? Are you okay?"

Her warm hand on my shoulder breaks me out of my stupor enough to nod, but I'm not capable of much else yet. My initial panic over the thought of her going out with Rome fades into an image of her in the bathtub. The blood that had drained from my face rushes to other parts of my body—long neglected parts now warmed with sizzling intensity.

I wouldn't be feeling this way if I hadn't sworn off sex entirely three years ago, I remind myself. It's a perfectly natural reaction. It doesn't mean I'm still pining over Jess.

I force my lips into a smile. "Yes, yes. I'm fine. I was hoping we could talk, but I don't want to interrupt your…"

"You should come over tonight!" Jess interjects.

"But you already have plans."

"Trust me, I'd much rather have company. I was only trying to make a 'date' with myself sound fun. Plus, I thought you'd be proud of me for listening to your advice, but I can do that another time."

"Are you sure?"

"Yes, definitely! I need to go clock out now, but you can come over whenever you want. I'll text you my address. We can talk, eat, drink, watch a movie… It'll be great!" Jess says, squealing with excitement.

I gulp down my own. "Okay, see you soon."

Several hours and glasses of wine later, my worries from earlier become a distant memory. Warmth spreads ubiquitously through my body. I should have probably stopped after one glass, but *carpe momentum*.

It's been far too long since I've felt this good. My belly is pleasantly full. My tongue is laden with the delicious taste of veggie tempura, mixed with the velvety richness and subtle tannins of this exquisite cabernet.

"Dark chocolate?" Jess offers. "It's vegan."

"You're speaking my language." I reach for the small bag in her hand and accidentally graze her knuckles with my fingertips.

It gives me enough of a jolt that my hand freezes over hers. Though it lingers for mere seconds, an eternity of desire surges from the contact. Everything tightens and aches as I remember the feeling of that soft hand from years ago. Her warm skin awakens all of my senses to the memory as if it were yesterday. My breasts swell and pebble, and maybe it's the wine or my imagination, but I swear hers do as well.

I grip the bag of chocolates and force my hand away. "Thanks," I say in an attempt to clear my dry throat.

Jess shifts next to me on the couch as if reading my thoughts. We're close enough to touch when she pulls her legs up and tucks them under her, moving into a slanted seated position. She's wearing jean shorts and a boatneck top that completely covers her large chest.

Most women would wear a plunging neckline to flaunt such assets, but not Jess. *Never Jess.* She's a gift one has to earn the right to unwrap. I've always admired that about her.

Her breath sounds labored when she says, "I was thinking we could watch *Fried Green Tomatoes.* Have you seen it before?"

"Of course. I love that movie," I say, leaning in closer to breathe in the floral scent of her perfume.

"Great. I figured it was appropriate for tonight. You know… Towanda!" she says dramatically and then laughs.

Appropriate isn't a word I would use to describe any of the emotions currently surging through me. The concealed sexual tension between Idgie and Ruth feels all too familiar; their unexpressed love, a perfect parallel. And Jess wants to watch that movie… with me.

My eyes slide down from her plump lips to the tender spot where her neck meets her collarbone. My mouth, previously dry, waters at the sight of her delicate skin. I imagine pressing my lips against it, hearing her moan. My mind goes blank. I'm pulled forward as if snared by a tractor beam until…

"Down, boy," Jess says firmly.

I shake my head, immediately sobering, and then look at the fluffy white dog pawing and whining at Jess.

"Do you need to go out?" she asks the dog in a loving tone before looking at me. "I'll be right back. I'm going to let Prince Petey into the backyard, in case he needs to go potty."

Alone with my thoughts, I want to slap myself. *What the hell was I thinking?* If not for the interruption, I would have kissed the neck of Jessica Serrano-Clark. The same Jessica Serrano-Clark who is still married—to Brad—and very much not interested in me. At least not *in that way*. We've finally gotten to a place where we can be friends, and I was about to throw that away like an idiot. Thank goodness I was saved by the dog.

The dog. The despicable breeder. Rome. How could I have forgotten why I came here tonight in the first place? I need to warn Jess about Rome.

"Sorry about that," Jess says, reentering the room. "Having a dog is like having a third child. And this one is particularly clingy."

"That's sweet, and no worries about the interruption."

Prince Petey trots over to the couch, and I reach down to pet him, running my fingers through his soft curls. Gratitude radiates through my energy—a language I know he can read. "You're a good boy, aren't you? Yes, you are, Sweet Prince Petey of Bay Ho who loves his mommy."

"Oh no. Let's not add to his already too long title," she says with a laugh. "Should we get the movie started?"

"Actually, we need to talk first."

Her face straightens at my serious tone. "You felt it too?"

"Yeah, but that's not what… Wait. Felt what?"

Jessica turns away from me and paces the floor with Prince Petey at her heels. "Umm… an earthquake, I think… or more like a tremor… when I was in the backyard with the dog. But if you didn't feel anything, it was probably nothing."

Her nervous energy is reflected in the dog now pawing at her feet. If I didn't know better, I would assume she's truly rattled by thinking there had been an earthquake, rather than being unnerved by the lie she just told. Her performance would be solid, but for the bizarre timing of her behavior. She had been laughing and talking about her dog's clinginess when she first came back inside.

"Anyway, what did you want to talk about?" she asks, reclaiming her seat next to me on the couch.

"It's about Rome," I say.

"Oh? Did something happen between you two?"

"No, it's nothing like that. But he's planning to ask you out."

"Me?"

"Yes, you. But you have to say no."

Jess' eyebrows knit together before she asks, "Why?"

"Because he's trouble."

"Okay… but how is he trouble? He seemed nice the other night at dinner. Is it the womanizing?"

I sigh, wondering how much more I should share. "Womanizing isn't the half of it."

Jess looks at me expectantly, and it isn't long before her silent gaze breaks me. *I need to tell her everything.* The sudden onset of this resolve has me up and pacing the floor.

"What I'm about to tell you can't leave this room."

"Of course. What is it?" Jess curls her legs up and snuggles Prince Petey, who happily occupies my vacant spot on the couch.

"Rome is involved in something despicable… and most likely illegal. I've been following him since he arrived in San Diego, which was a couple of weeks before we checked into the Bay Holiday Resort. If anyone found out, though, especially Rome, I'd be in a lot of trouble."

"I won't say anything. I swear. What is he involved in?"

I stop pacing and look into her inquisitive eyes. "How familiar are you with puppy mills?"

"That's where they breed a bunch of puppies to be sold for profit, right?"

"Basically. The conditions are horrendous, though. Imagine rows and rows of stacked wire cages, some so short the dogs can't even sit up, let alone stand. When the dogs in the upper cages go to the bathroom, it covers the ones below them. But that's the least of their problems. They're often malnourished, exposed to extreme weather, and not given proper veterinary care. Then, when the dogs can no longer breed due to sickness or age, they're either abandoned or killed."

Jess' hand flies to her chest. "That's awful!"

"I know. The worst part is that many puppy mills are legally licensed by the USDA and local state authorities, and the few regulations that exist are rarely enforced." I run my fingers through my hair to rein in my temper. "Anyway, the point of my soapbox is that most people buying puppies don't realize this. They assume a breeder having a license must mean everything is okay."

Prince Petey nudges closer to Jess on the couch and rests his head in her lap, as if affected by the conversation. Sweet soul that she is, Jess soothingly strokes his floppy ears. "I don't understand why anyone would get a dog from a puppy mill, though. I'm not very educated on the topic, but even I know not to buy from one of those places."

"The sad fact is that most puppies sold in pet stores and online are from puppy mills. Buyers are usually unaware of the source… or don't care as long as it's the breed they want." An overwhelming desire to sit leads me back to the couch.

"I guess that's why you hear: *Adopt. Don't shop*," Jess says as I settle next to Prince Petey.

"Definitely. But some people will always prefer to use a breeder. And that brings me to what Rome is involved in… which takes evil to the next level."

"Next level, how?"

"A responsible breeder will happily show you where the puppy was born and raised and even let you play with the mother. Rome claims to be a silent investor for such a breeder of golden doodle puppies here in San Diego, but I have reason to believe the operation is a scam. They're able to charge a premium price to socially conscious buyers by putting on a show—a pretense of happy puppies playing in a quaint backyard setting—when they are actually trucked in from an atrocious puppy mill based in Mexico. Only God knows the conditions those poor animals are living in, but we've been trying to get insight for years."

"We?" Jess asks with a tilt of her head.

"I'm part of an animal advocacy group that monitors puppy mills here in the U.S., mostly in the Midwest. But we were tipped off about the puppy trafficking into San Diego by our sister organization across the border."

"Sorry for all my questions, but how did you learn about Rome's involvement? And how long has this been going on?"

"I can't answer your second question definitively, but I learned about Rome's financial involvement when his personal assistant, Cameron, reached out to me two years ago. Cam told me Rome needed a new traveling PT, and he also informed me of some large checks Rome had written to the breeder. It's why I took the job with Rome… so we could figure out what was going on and expose the truth."

At Jess' confused look, I add, "Cam and I met through the animal advocacy group five years ago during a protest against animal testing. We became instant friends and have stayed in touch ever since."

"I see."

I shift on the couch to better face Jess, careful not to disturb the now sleeping dog. "Anyway, we already knew *Rose's Golden Doodles* wasn't a respectable breeder, based on reports of buyers receiving sick puppies—some of which died only days after being purchased. And while it's typical for puppies from puppy mills to suffer from a variety of health issues, Annabelle Rose claims that's not the kind of business she runs. It got her on our watchlist fast."

Jess takes a large gulp of wine before setting her glass down. "Let me see if I've got this straight. You know this lady is selling sick puppies—most likely bred in horrible conditions in Mexico and then smuggled over the border—but she's claiming to be a responsible breeder here in San Diego to charge more money for the pups. And you also know Rome invested in her business at least two years ago."

"Correct, but I've only recently been able to prove that he's more than a *silent* investor. He's visited the breeder's home several times already since arriving here. Plus, he canceled his PGA tour this summer to train in San Diego, which I know can't be a coincidence."

"So, why not go to the authorities? Isn't there something they could do?"

"Not to sound cynical, but the authorities aren't helpful. Like I mentioned, the USDA regulates puppy mills, but even if we could get them to come out for an inspection, they wouldn't find any violations on-site. And the puppy trafficking falls under the U.S. Border Patrol's jurisdiction. I called them and was told they'd look into it... right after they solve other problems like drugs, guns, and human trafficking. Dogs aren't high on their priority list." I cross my arms, holding back the anger I'd felt after making that call.

Jess mirrors my pose, her bottom lip protruding into a rare yet adorable pout. "There must be some way to stop it."

"The best way is to end the demand by informing the public, but that's unfortunately a lot harder than it sounds. Most people don't bother to educate themselves before purchasing a puppy, and those that do are getting duped by scammers like Anabelle Rose. That's what makes her operation so monstrous. But Rome's involvement gives us hope."

"How so?"

"Once we have enough evidence, we can alert the press. A story like this wouldn't go very far on its own, but with a celebrity athlete involved, it could make national headlines. That will get us the platform we need to raise awareness."

"And ruin Rome's career in the process," Jess says in understanding.

"Yes. That's why I have to be absolutely sure he knows what's going on, rather than being scammed himself. I've been following him around, but it's difficult to get anything concrete so far."

"I see." Jess gets a far-off look in her eyes. "Then I should date him."

"What? That's crazy."

"No, it's perfect! I can get close to him to learn his secrets. Since he's an investor in the business, he'll probably want to brag about it on a date. Guys always try to impress women with how much money they make."

"No, Jess. Things could get messy. I don't want you to get involved in this."

"I'm already involved. How could I know this is happening to sweet, innocent dogs and not be?" Jess squeezes Prince Petey by her side, which might as well be my heart. "Please, let me help. I want to do this."

Her words bore into me. There are people who get under your skin; there are others who reside in your bones. Jess is the latter. The feelings I didn't think could run any deeper solidify in my marrow. No amount of time, distance, or prayers could ever eradicate my unrequited love for her. While I've always known that, I hadn't realized it could grow.

"Okay," I agree, "but you'll need to be careful. Rome may come across as simple-minded, but he's not stupid. He'll get suspicious if you ask too many questions."

"Got it. I can do this, Avery. We're going to take them down and save the pups!"

Despite being moved by her enthusiasm, I smile tightly and nod. It's all I can manage. I pray this works… for her sake and the dogs'.

With a bounce, Jess lifts onto her knees, causing her furry companion to hop off the couch and resettle on the floor. She leans forward, a touch off-balance, to retrieve her wine. After downing and refilling her own wineglass, she reaches toward mine with the bottle. "Let's cheers to our new mission!"

Already feeling the effects of the two large pours I've had, I reflexively pull my glass into my chest and cover the opening with my palm. Before I can open my mouth to decline, cool liquid is hitting my shirt, my bra, my skin.

"Shoot!" Jess exclaims. "I'm so sorry!"

What happens next is so quick and surreal I must be imagining it. That's the only explanation for the warmth of Jess' hand on my left breast, vigorously rubbing my wine-soaked T-shirt with her palm as if it were a towel.

"We need to get this off before it stains," she says a bit frantically before her soft brown eyes lock with mine.

Still on her knees, she's looking down at me from her elevated position. Her hand slows to a massage, and she bites her bottom lip before giving my small breast a gentle squeeze. Her eyes glaze over but never break their stare. *Is this really happening?* She can't possibly know what she's doing right now. It must be the wine.

I'm torn between stopping her and seeing where this goes when my hand makes the decision for me. It hovers briefly above hers without touching—ready to interrupt the most glorious sensation I've felt in years—and then moves up to her face instead. I stroke her previously pouty lip with my thumb, eliciting a breathy moan so quiet I'm not sure if it comes from her or me.

"Touch me," she whispers.

She has no idea how badly I want to—how badly I've wanted to all these years—but I'm frozen. I'm reminded of that night seventeen years ago. The night that was both the best and worst of my life. It was the night I realized I enjoyed the touch of a female infinitely more than that of men. It was also the night I knew I was in love with Jess… and that she'd never be mine.

As if sensing my hesitation, Jess halts her caress and stumbles back from the couch. "I'm so sorry. I don't know what happened. Let me go get another shirt from my room for you." Her words come out in a slur, even though I'm positive her previous ones were clear as day.

"It's okay. Don't bother. I should probably get going anyway." I stand and grab my purse from the oversized chair next to the couch. "Raincheck on the movie?"

"Are you sure? We both had *a lot* to drink," she says with emphasis. "You shouldn't drive yet."

Her pointing out our alcohol consumption only confirms my decision. "I'll take an Uber. My rental car should be fine parked on the street here overnight, as long as that's okay with you?"

"Of course. But I feel awful about spilling on you! Your white T-shirt is covered in wine. I guess I'm more drunk than I realized."

I open the rideshare app on my phone and busy myself to avoid looking at her. It was foolish to believe she might actually want me. *Of course, it was the wine.* Jess insisting as much only adds insult to injury. Feeling vulnerable, I suck in a breath and steel myself to get through the next *eight long minutes* before my ride will arrive.

"Are you sure you don't want to borrow a clean shirt? I'm a little bigger than you, but I'm sure I can find something that fits."

Changing my shirt will help burn some time, so I nod. "That would be great. Thanks."

Jess exits the room, and my whole body sighs. She'd made it perfectly clear all those years before. *She is a straight woman of strong faith—a faith that doesn't "believe" in homosexuality. Her involvement in the threesome was strictly an expression of her love for Brad. Her touch was meaningless. She planned to marry Brad, and she did.* I shouldn't need to be reminded of these facts, but I recite them in my head anyway. I'll repeat them for the next eight minutes if I have to.

"Try this," Jess says, returning with a V-neck top I wouldn't have assumed she owned. "I'd need butter for my rolls if I wore this, but it'll look perfect on you."

Although she's laughing, there's pain in her eyes. My previous desire to curl up into a ball and disappear is overwhelmed by an even stronger need to defend her. I ball my fists on my hips. "Jessica Serrano, what did I tell you about self-critical thoughts?"

She blinks at me several times before responding, "To practice self-love?"

"Exactly. And how do you do that?" After what feels like a lifetime of silence passes, I answer for her. "You defend yourself as you would a loved one. So, what would you say to your mother if she implied she wasn't happy with her body?"

Jess shifts weight onto her right leg, then her left, then right again. "Umm… I would say she still looks great after having two kids, and that she should stop comparing herself to others. She's the most beautiful woman I know, inside and out."

"That's perfect." I close the distance between us and take the blouse from her hand. "And it *one hundred percent* applies to you as well. Where should I change?"

"Uh, you can use my bedroom. It's down the hall, first door on the right."

I attempt to head in the direction of her pointed finger, but it's suddenly wrapped around me; both of her arms are. My still wet chest mashes against her well-endowed one as I realize I'm being held in a tight embrace. Jess is known as a hugger, but it dawns on me that I've never been a recipient of one of her hugs before. I allow myself to breathe in her intoxicating scent once more. Cinnamon, sunflowers, and honey. *Maybe she's a bee charmer like Idgie.*

"Thank you," she says, still squeezing me against her.

I intuitively know she's thanking me for more than the self-love exercise. The same way a dog can read a person's energy, positive or negative, my receptors pick up on a deeper gratitude. She's grateful I'm letting her sweep the groping experience under the rug—the same way neither of us talk about our night at Richie Sampson's graduation party. People tend to leave unsaid the things they wish never happened.

"You're welcome," I say, stepping back once Jess loosens her grip.

Walking down the hall toward her bedroom, I glance at my phone to check on my ride. *Five more minutes.* I'll change my shirt, say goodbye, and go on pretending I'm not hopelessly in love with someone who will never be mine—the same way I always have.

Chapter 21

Three years ago

"Do we have to go out tonight, Char? Wouldn't it be nicer to stay here with some wine and a movie… maybe share a bath in that huge tub of yours?"

I'm hoping the promise of sex will spare me the torture of making small talk with endless strangers while pretending to enjoy it. There is literally nothing worse. Okay… there's animal abuse, murder, world hunger, war, climate change, humanity's impending doom… but attending a party where you only know the person you came with is high up on that list.

My girlfriend pokes her head out of the bathroom. Half of her auburn hair is held messily up with a claw clip, while a strand at the bottom is wrapped several times around the barrel of a curling iron. She's upside down, as my head hangs backward off the foot of the bed, but I can still make out her frown when she says, "It's Charlize. You know I hate when you call me Char."

Technically, her given name is Charlotte, but she legally changed it after she saw *The Italian Job* and became obsessed with Charlize Theron. It's hard to blame her for idolizing the tall, blond, South African bombshell. Char's passionate nature is what drew me to her in the first place. Still, I have a hard time calling my short, ginger, American girlfriend Charlize.

I clear my throat and do it anyway. "Sorry, Charlize. Can we please stay in tonight?"

"No way, babe! Tonight's party is at a legit mansion up in the hills. This super rich guy—I think he's a movie producer or something—invited my friend Lacey, and she got us on the guest list. This is not the type of event you pass up. Trust me, it'll be insane!"

"You say that like it's a good thing."

"It is! Now stop being a party pooper and come get ready with me."

Defeated, I lift my head and roll over onto my elbows, allowing all the blood pooled in my brain to return to my body before slowly peeling myself off the bed. I would hate Char right now if she weren't so damn sexy in that tight red dress. It leaves nothing to the imagination, and yet there are a few things I can imagine doing to her later.

It's been a while since we've been intimate, come to think of it. When we first started dating, after volunteering at the animal shelter a year ago, we couldn't keep our hands off each other. When did that change? After the first month? After two months? Six months?

I suppose it's difficult to assign an end date to a honeymoon phase. It's more of a gradual decline that begins the moment yearning morphs into having—a cruel joke upon the human condition. We long for what we do not have, and if we get it, we're not satisfied.

As I dig through my overnight bag, hoping I brought something appropriate for tonight's gathering of *who's who* in Hollywood, I'm flooded with unsolicited thoughts of Jess. Though many years have passed, the torch I carry still burns as brightly as when first ignited. I briefly wonder if that would change if, in some alternate universe, we were ever together. But in my heart, I know it would not. She was the apple in my Garden of Eden, and one bite will never be enough.

I'm jarred from my thoughts by Char's reappearance in the doorframe. "I love you, Avs, but we both know there's nothing in that bag suitable for a mansion soiree. Squeeze your hot ass into something from my closet, and let's go get our drink on!"

And there they are, the three words that breathe life into me. Her generous 'I love you' keeps me going, even if I know she's not the one for me. Not everyone finds *the one*, I remind myself. Others find and lose it. And then there are the people like me, who yearn for the one from afar while settling for what's right in front of them.

Char is a far cry from a second-place trophy, though. She is wild and fun; kind-hearted and passionate; beautiful and brilliant. And she loves me. That is more than enough. Of all I've ever yearned for, being loved takes first place.

The party is as insane as Char promised. All twenty thousand square feet of the three-story palace of glass and stone are filled with scantily clad bodies. I know the home's size because I'd been compelled to look it up online when we first arrived. After we'd driven through the massive security gate, we were greeted by a large circular drive straight out of the movies, complete with a large fountain in the center and a valet to park our car.

Inside, wall-to-wall windows provide an amazing bird's-eye view of downtown Los Angeles, shining brightly against a blanket of black, but no one else seems to notice. They are all too inebriated, and I don't mean from alcohol, although there's plenty of that flowing as well. Beyond the coat check in the first-floor foyer, there was a marble pedestal table with a bowl full of Molly, offered as casually as dinner mints by a nearby attendant.

Char seemed to consider it a moment before following my lead and politely declining. I like to think I can be as fun as anyone, but drugs are not my scene. I didn't succumb to temptation in my teens and twenties, so I'm certainly not going to now at a far wiser thirty-two. In my youth, it would have been easy to latch on to something that could numb my constant pain. But that's precisely why I never tried drugs. I knew I wouldn't be able to stop if I did.

Sober and anxious, I'm a minority among the gyrating throngs of euphoric socialites. The indoor lap pool in the west wing I've ventured into is the scene of what can only be described as a Molly-induced orgy audition—with all of its inhabitants, either topless or completely nude, groping each other in small clusters.

"I'll take two of those," I say to my personal savior walking by with a tray of champagne flutes.

This party may be a literal clusterfuck, but it's also marked by wealth. Servers in black-and-white attire have been circling with passed hors d'oeuvres and Dom Pérignon all night. When I'd earlier asked a young woman offering caviar if there were any vegan options, she mentioned some cucumber and cream cheese sandwiches also being served. She said it so kindly I didn't have the heart to tell her that cream cheese is not vegan. *Liquid diet it is.*

If one is driven to double fist, it might as well be with expensive champagne. I take two glasses off the tray in front of me and scan the crowd, looking for Char. She disappeared about ten minutes ago, leaving me to wander this labyrinth of a house alone. I'm more than a little relieved not to see her among the sea of flesh in the pool. Ignoring the knowledge that this is *absolutely her scene*, I down the first glass and then the second, not even bothering to savor the crisp, opulent taste.

I turn on my heels to leave the area and smack into something hard and wet. *No, not something… someone.*

"Whoa there, beautiful. Let me help you with those." Masculine hands swiftly grab the empty glasses from me right as my fingers release them in shock.

The tan, muscular form in front of me is *sans* clothes and dripping with water. My tongue-tied brain processes this while concurrently realizing that the solid chest I bumped into is not the only thing hard on him. I will my eyes to look away but can't erase the image.

"I'm Rome. Rome Jepsen," the naked man says, shifting both glasses into one hand to offer the other.

I hesitantly shake it, still dumbfounded.

"You might recognize my name from TV. I'm a professional golfer," he continues, clearly not modest in any sense of the word. "Care to join me in the pool?"

My ability to converse returns. The deejay is blasting EDM at ear-piercing decibels, so I yell, "No, thank you! I'm here with my girlfriend."

"That's no problem. She can come, too." There's a slipperiness to his drawl—and a calculated meaning behind his phrasing—both of which send shivers up my spine.

I need to get away from this man, and his erection, stat. I'm not afraid of penises, per se, but his has the characteristics of a heat-seeking missile: indiscriminate and set to conquer. Remembering that women often refer to their platonic female friends as "girlfriends," I decide it best to clarify and again yell to be heard over the music.

"I'm a lesbian!"

Of course, this is the exact moment the deejay winds down the track, fading the current trance song to near silence before slowly increasing the volume into the opening notes of "Sandstorm" by Darude. For a hot second, I forget what decade I'm in, and then I'm drawn back to the present when I notice multiple sets of eyes pointed in my direction. *Well, crap.*

Spotting a nearby staircase, I flee the scene of my mortification without a second's hesitation.

Chapter 22

Now

Mission accomplished. It required getting up with the metaphorical chickens and staying away from the hotel until nightfall, but I've successfully avoided running into Jess for the last two days. After our uncomfortable parting at her place Thursday night, I figured some distance would be best… until Monday, when I'll have no choice but to face her at our next physical therapy session.

The balmy night air caresses my skin as I exit my car, hand the key fob to the waiting valet, and head toward the revolving door. Jess would have long gotten off her shift by now, and she doesn't work tomorrow, so I'm in the clear… until Monday. I push the thought away, reminding myself what Doctor K always says about dwelling on past pain or future worries: *Why put yourself through it more than once?*

It's best to live in the present. At the mental cue, I stop walking and take in my surroundings. The welcoming scent of the fragrant plumeria shrubs planted outside the hotel is reminiscent of a Hawaiian vacation—sweet, citrusy, and tropical. Similar to jasmine, this varietal's blooms are white and pop against the dark-green contrast of its glossy leaves.

After inhaling the floral air, I pause at the top of my breath. A symphony of chirping crickets can be heard nearby, while the crashing of distant waves travels to me by zephyr, as does a tang of salt in the air. It is not enough to "stop and smell the roses," I remind myself. True mindfulness comes when all senses are fully immersed in the moment.

Like snowflakes, moments are unique snapshots in time that can never be repeated, yet so many pass us by unnoticed. I stand outside a few more minutes, mindfully taking in the sights, scents, sounds, tastes, and feelings as if they are the only things that matter. In the grand scheme of things, I suppose they are. That is, until my past crashes into my present.

"Avs?" a familiar voice asks.

The short redhead—swiftly approaching from about ten feet away—is smiling… at me. The tight blue cocktail dress she's wearing matches her stiletto heels. She looks wicked good, as always… and happy, I think. *God, I hope she's happy.*

"Char… I mean, Charlize. Sorry. What a surprise seeing you here," I say, trying to sound as friendly as possible.

She laughs and waves her hand in the air like she's wiping away an invisible smudge. "Please. I went back to Charlotte. We both know I could never pull off Charlize. Anyway, I came down from LA this weekend with some friends for Comic-Con. Well, for the afterparties. What about you? Are you living here now?"

"No. I'm a traveling PT these days, here in San Diego with a client. I've been bouncing around the last couple of years since leaving Los Angeles." As soon as I say it, the obvious hits me. *I don't have a home.* I'm not sure I ever did, but LA had come close after seven years of school followed by another eight getting my career off the ground.

"That's fun," Char says. "And you're staying at this hotel too? We should totally get a drink to catch up!"

Her enthusiasm throws me. *Does she not remember the brutal details of our breakup?* She should be sticking pins in a voodoo doll of me right now, not wanting to chat over drinks. But I've never been one to take a blessing for granted, so I nod my agreement and follow closely behind as Char makes her way into the hotel and across the lobby.

We've cleared the elevators and are about to turn the corner toward the hotel bar when a loud, intoxicating laugh fills my ears. I'd recognize that laugh anywhere. It both warms my heart and freezes it. *Oh no. This can't be happening.*

Char continues forward, unaware of the looming disaster, and I follow. It doesn't take long for my eyes to confirm what I already heard. Jess is sitting at the bar, laughing and playfully touching a man's arm. Not any man's… Rome's. Jess is having drinks with Rome.

My heart beats like it's trying to escape my chest. This might all be easier if it could. *Run away, my tender heart. Run and hide.* But it's too late. Char is already pulling out the high-backed barstool immediately next to Jess.

"Are these seats taken?" Char asks, referring to the only two open stools at the crowded bar.

For a second, I wonder what I did wrong to deserve this. Then I remember. *Karma is a far greater bitch than she gets credit for.*

"They're all yours," Jess says cheerfully to Char, before angling her head to see me standing behind them. "Avery! What a surprise to see you here. Rome and I were just getting better acquainted."

I could be hallucinating, since it feels like my spirit is hovering a safe distance above my body to watch this train wreck, but I swear Jess winks at me. It makes sense now, though. She is on a date with Rome to get information about his involvement in *Rose's Golden Doodles.* Involving Jess in my war against animal cruelty is yet another mistake for which I'm sure I'll pay… probably right now.

"You two know each other?" Char asks.

Her question is directed at me, but I'm still deciding how to best answer when Rome chimes in with, "Oh, yeah! Avery and Jessica go way back."

Where the hell is this guy's karma? I wonder, while watching Char for any signs of recognition.

"I'm Rome Jepsen. Nice to meet you." He reaches his hand out to Char, and I briefly imagine turning it around with my mind to choke him with it. *Too bad I'm not really a Jedi. Foda could easily end this torture.*

Char shakes his hand. "Rome Jepsen, the golfer?"

"The one and only," Rome says.

"I think we've met before, actually… Were you at a mansion party in Hollywood Hills a few years ago?"

Just when I think this couldn't get any worse, a devilish grin spreads across Rome's face.

He looks at me and then back to Char. "That's right! I met Avery for the first time at that party, and now I remember you, too. You were the girlfriend she was in such a rush to get out the door."

"Yeah, I suppose our meeting was cut a little short." Char cuts me a glance, and my mind travels back to that horrible night.

After I had embarrassingly bumped into "the one and only" shamelessly naked Rome Jepsen, I had frantically searched the second and third floors for Char so we could leave the party. Only, I didn't find her upstairs and eventually made my way back down to where I started. There Char was, stripping off her clothes and heading toward the pool, about to engage in a non-golf-related foursome with Rome and two other women.

She'd been out of her mind on drugs, which I'd chosen not to be mad about at the time. I just needed to get her out of there. It took some convincing, but I got her to leave with the promise that

I'd make it up to her when she got home. I didn't realize then how wrong my promise would turn out to be.

"I'm Charlotte, by the way. And I'm sorry, but I didn't catch your name." Char has released Rome's hand and is now focused on Jess, who looks slack-jawed.

"Oh, I'm Jessica. Nice to meet you, Charlotte."

The two women shake hands, and it's like watching my worst nightmare unfold. I hold my breath, waiting for the name to click. Her reaction is delayed, but I immediately notice when it happens. Char's hand drops to her side, her back stiffens, and she pivots on her heels toward me in slow motion.

"This is Jess?" Char's hazel eyes are wet and pleading when they lock with mine, but she doesn't need me to answer. Her heartbroken expression tells me she already knows.

"I'm so sorry." My words come out empty, even though I mean them more than I'm able to express. I never wanted to hurt her, and here I am doing it all over again.

Char storms away from the bar, and I'm flooded with emotions. Shame, sorrow, gratitude… she could have easily made a bigger scene but left instead.

"Um, sorry to interrupt your evening," I say. "I better go check on her, but please enjoy your drinks."

I then chase after Char without waiting for a response.

Chapter 23

I know it was cowardly, but I called out sick from the rehab center today. Another PT will assist my Monday patients, including Jess. I'm not ready to face her. Not yet.

"Why don't we start with what's clearly bothering you today?"

"Nice to see you too, Doctor K." My voice drips with sarcasm, even though I know it's unwarranted.

Doctor K is short for Doctor Angela Katai. Even though I'm one of the few who know how to pronounce her last name, *Kuh-Tay*, Doctor K is a nickname I've used for as long as I can remember. It oddly makes me feel closer to her.

My fifty-something therapist merely tilts her head and waits for me to begin. She doesn't waste any time in getting straight to the terrifying truth of any matter. She's also become quite skilled at disarming my evasive tactics, but it doesn't stop me from trying.

"What makes you think something is bothering me?"

Her face is immovable under her dark-framed glasses and platinum-blond bob. "For starters, you requested an emergency session today, and you're here in person."

"Well, as previously mentioned, I'm currently in San Diego for work. It was a short drive to LA, and your comfy couch was worth the trip."

The one-hundred-and-twenty-mile journey ended up taking almost four hours, thanks to multiple accidents and insufferably common congestion on I-5, but she doesn't need to know that. Besides, her couch really is comfortable. There's something cathartic about lying here with my feet propped up and my nose toward the ceiling. The world is a scary place, but during this hour, here on this couch, I know I'm safe.

"A video call isn't the same," I say with a horizontal shrug.

At Doctor K's continued silence, I decide to take down my outer shield. "I ran into someone from my past on Saturday night. An ex-girlfriend."

I'm not sure why I'm being cryptic with my therapist. She knows all about my former relationship with Char, including my shameful mistake that ended things. She also knows—from our last video session two weeks ago—that I ran into Jess while in San Diego, but a lot has happened since then.

"I'm not sure where to start," I admit.

She taps the end of her pencil against her lips, like she always does when she's thinking. I've told her she may want to consider taking notes with a laptop or tablet, but she stubbornly refuses. She's old-school, yet it's weird to think of her as *old*.

When we first met, Doctor K was about the age I am currently, and her two children were both in diapers. Now, her oldest has recently started college, same as I had when I started coming here. Though we've all grown older together, the gaps between us remain the same, and in an odd way, it feels like none of us have aged at all.

I still assume the role of resistant, smart-mouthed teenager, and Doctor K plays the stern mother-figure who practices tough love. I like that about our relationship.

"How did you feel when you first saw your ex-girlfriend?" Doctor K finally asks.

"Confused," I say. "She was being nice to me, even though I broke her heart."

"And that upset you, because you don't believe you deserve her kindness?"

"Yes, but no. That's not why I'm here today." Frustrated, I sit up on the couch and pout.

Doctor K sits back in her chair, waiting for me to continue. She strategically uses her silence against me, and it works every time.

"The ex I ran into was Char, who incidentally goes by Charlotte now again."

Doctor K nods knowingly. Of course, she knew it was Char all along. It's not like I'm in the habit of breaking people's hearts, and Char was my most recent girlfriend. My sexual moratorium started the day after we broke up, so I wouldn't hurt anyone else the way I had hurt her.

I clear my throat and then reveal my terrifying truth. "We went into the hotel bar to get a drink and ran into Jess instead. They introduced themselves."

The whites around Doctor K's blue eyes widen and then shrink almost as quickly, but I catch it. She broke her usual stoic stare, which means, of all the horrible things I've shared with her over the years, this is the one that took her by surprise. I imagine she's dying to know where the rest of this story goes, so I lie back down and use silence to my advantage this time.

After what feels like several minutes, Doctor K's curiosity gets the better of her. "Did Charlotte tell Jessica what had happened between you two?"

I take a deep breath for suspense, then say, "No. She easily could have, though. The hurt in her eyes before she stormed off was unbearable."

I'm still staring at the ceiling, but I hear all the air exit Doctor K's lungs as if she had been holding her breath. Odd as it may be, it gives me mild relief to know there's someone else in this world who knows exactly how high the stakes were in that situation. And more importantly, there's someone else who cares. That's all it takes for the rest of my defenses to come down.

I turn on my side and hold the gaze of the woman I've often wished was my mother. "I'm here today because I feel horrible for breaking Char's heart... again."

She straightens in her chair. "It sounds like you blame yourself for Charlotte's reaction to meeting Jessica. Am I interpreting that correctly?"

I know what she's doing. It's textbook cognitive behavioral therapy, whereby she exposes my underlying thought pattern as irrational to invalidate my feelings. But my feelings are valid, so I ignore her question.

"The worst part was, after I caught up to Char in the lobby, she asked me to at least tell her I was happy now with Jess. She said her heartbreak would be worth it if she knew I had finally fought for my happily ever after. She was a romantic like that." I sniff back snot as hot tears run over the bridge of my nose and pool on the sofa cushion beneath my cheek. "I couldn't even give her that."

Doctor K leans forward with a tissue box, which I take, and then she crosses her arms. "Avery, I've known you for a long time, and I've never known you to feel sorry for yourself. Please don't start now."

Her words have me springing up on the couch. She's always practiced tough love, but this is new. "Are you seriously scolding me for crying?"

"For crying? No. Sometimes a good cry can be the best therapy. But do you even know *why* you are crying?" Her steely gaze does not waver.

I use a tissue to blow my nose and then defiantly throw it on the floor. Okay, I may have regressed from resistant teenager to pissed-off toddler, but *what the F, Doctor K?*

"Have you been listening to me at all? I'm crying because I hurt Char, not because 'I feel sorry for myself.' Geez, Mom."

She blinks several times but remains silent. One minute elapses, then another. It takes me that long to realize my slip up.

"I meant that you're acting like a mom, not that I think you *are* my mom."

She nods slowly and writes something in her notes. I hate it when she does that. It's like talking behind someone's back.

"What are you writing?" I ask.

"Just a note to circle back to why you never talk about your mother."

"I don't have a mother. You know that already."

"Yes, but we never talk about her death, or how you felt growing up without her. Let's put a pin in that for now, though. I'd like to better understand how you hurt Charlotte Saturday night… since that's why you say you're crying." She removes her eyeglasses, places them and her notebook on the side table, and then folds her hands in her lap. "Please, humor me, Avery. Did you orchestrate the meeting between Charlotte and Jessica?"

"No, of course not. I was horrified that it happened."

She gives her usual knowing nod. I'm starting to think she gets a twisted amount of pleasure out of asking questions she already knows the answers to.

"So, you didn't know Jessica would be at the hotel bar before you walked in with Charlotte?"

"No. I mean, I heard Jess laughing when we walked in, but Char was ahead of me and it was too late to stop her. It all happened so fast."

"Okay. What was the first step of self-love I taught you?" she asks.

I sigh, finally seeing where this is all going. "To stop blaming myself for things outside of my control."

"Great. Let's recap," she says. "You came here upset today, allegedly because Charlotte was heartbroken after running into Jessica, but their meeting was outside of your control. So, you are either blaming yourself for things outside of your control, which you know better than to do, or you are upset about something other than Saturday night's encounter. Which is it, Avery?"

"You really do act like a mom, you know."

She smiles for the first time this session. "I know. And you know I care about you as if you were one of my own children, professionalism be damned. But I wish you'd take down your walls, Avery. Other patients have shared more with me in seventeen minutes than you have in seventeen years."

It's the first time she's ever said this so bluntly to me, and I'm at a loss for words. Therapy with Doctor K has been such a huge part of my life. I honestly feel like I let down all my defenses when I'm in this room… eventually, at least. I'm more open with her than I've ever been with anyone else, and now I learn I've been feeding her breadcrumbs. *What does that say for the rest of my relationships?*

"I guess I'm still upset with myself for what happened three years ago," I admit, "and more than that, I'm upset that the pain I caused was all for nothing. I'm upset that Jess will never love me the way I love her."

Doctor K smiles at me again, and it's obvious she already knew the real reason, even before I did. She also already knows exactly what happened three years ago.

After I'd gotten Char home from the nightmare mansion party and her Molly-induced buzz had calmed down, she was still feeling frisky. Since I promised to show her a good time, I rallied despite being far from *in the mood*. I wanted to want her. But after a night full of anxiety, I was exhausted.

It didn't help that Char had disappointed me by partaking in drugs and then almost cheated on me with three other people. I wasn't holding that against her, though. Or I don't think I was.

I started caressing her body, thinking it would be easy to get her off in her heightened state, but she soon made it very much about me. Char's mouth was ravenous, traveling every square inch of flesh. I tried to relax, tried to enjoy it, but my body was nonresponsive. Char could tell, because she asked me what was wrong.

A smart, emotionally balanced woman would have been honest with her. I should have explained that I was tired and stressed from the party, but my overwhelming fear stopped me. I was afraid Char would withdraw her love if I could not be what she needed in that moment. So, I said everything was fine and then conjured memories of my one passionate night with Jess to force myself to relax.

Char's bedroom was dark. Char's hands became Jess' hands. Char's mouth became Jess' mouth. Soon, my body melted under her touch.

I knew the mental fantasy was wrong while I was doing it, but it was working. Char moaned into my slickness, clearly pleased that I was aroused. It was a little white lie, intended to spare her feelings, I told myself.

Once I pushed my guilt aside, I could fully embrace the fantasy. It was Jess moaning I love you—again and again—into the sensitive flesh between my thighs. It was Jess stroking my breasts while burying her tongue deep inside me.

I weaved my fingers through her soft hair as my hips began to buck. My sweet edge had been reached, and I was free falling on the ride down. I remember seeing stars against a black sky before bursts of pleasure rippled through my body and curled my toes. Everything went dark as I screamed out in ecstasy, "Oh Jess! I love you, Jess!"

Chapter 24

Now

"Avery," a voice calls from behind.

Come on, come on. The elevator is only one floor away. The ding of its arrival is music to my ears. Finally, the gold-plated doors part to welcome me in.

"Hey, Avery, wait up!"

The second attempt to get my attention is louder, but I step into the elevator anyway. I'll think of an excuse later. *I'm so close.* Without looking up, I push the button for the fifth floor.

The elevator doors are about to kiss shut when a delicate hand slides between them and they part once more.

"Hey, I was trying to catch you so we could talk," Jess says, sounding like she'd sprinted across the lobby.

In a panic, I hold up my index finger in the universal sign for "one moment, please." Then I pretend to remove wireless earbuds—grateful my shoulder-length curls are hiding my ears— and I fake toss them into my purse. "Sorry, I was listening to music. What were you saying?"

"I was hoping we could talk..." Jess scans the hotel lobby behind her, then adds, "privately."

The elevator buzzes angrily due to being held open. I briefly debate stepping out when Jess says, "Can I come up to your room with you? I'm off my shift."

The incessant buzzing makes it impossible to think, so I nod, and before I know it, Jess and I are riding up the four quick floors toward my hotel room. My heart is racing by the time we're standing outside my door.

"This is me," I say, trying to act casual when nothing about this feels casual at all.

Logically, I know she's only here to talk. *About what* is an entirely separate question, which I won't allow myself to ponder right now. But the human body ignores logic. It only knows how to react, and right now, an unprecedented event is unfolding before my eyes. *Jess is entering my hotel room.*

There's something uniquely intimate about a hotel room. Perhaps it's because they're so often associated with clandestine affairs and romantic holidays. Or perhaps it's due to the giant bed in the middle of the room, which steals your focus the second you walk through the door, as is happening now.

My room is not a suite like Rome's. There isn't a kitchenette, a sofa, or even a desk. A king-sized bed occupies most of the relatively small, square-shaped space, while the bathroom is tucked away behind the door near the entrance.

"Sorry, it's not very big," I say, feeling my heat level rise at the sight of the crisp white linens on the freshly made bed. Something primal in me wants to rip off the comforter and roll around until the sheets are thoroughly rumpled and…

"No worries," Jess says. "You're staying here a long time, though. I bet we could get you a free upgrade. I'll talk to the front desk before I leave tonight."

"That would be amazing. But please don't go through any trouble. This room works for me."

Or it works when I'm alone. It's twice as small right now, and ten times as hot. Did housekeeping jack up the temperature?

"It's no trouble," Jess says, as I walk over and fiddle with the thermostat.

It reads a cool sixty-eight, and I hear the steady stream of forced air coming from the vent above, but that can't be right. My skin is radiating its own heat, like that of a bad sunburn. My chest, in particular, is on fire, and my forehead is damp with sweat. I double-check that the thermostat is set to "cool" not "heat." It is.

"Is everything okay, Avery? You look a little flushed."

"Yeah, I'm just…" My brain stalls trying to finish the sentence. *Sexually frustrated because you're in my hotel room. Panicking because I don't know how to act. Or… having a hot flash, because I forgot to take my estrogen pill. Dammit.*

Jess is still looking at me with her brows pinched in an expression of concern. Her kind-hearted nature reminds me why, once again, I'm a lovesick fool. Turning off long-rooted feelings is akin to willing yourself to cease breathing. It's impossible. No matter how long you hold your breath, your body eventually hijacks the process.

"Make yourself comfortable. I'll be right back."

Shutting the bathroom door behind me, I rest my palms on the cool marble countertop and stare at my reflection in the mirror. Flushed was an understatement. My face, neck, and chest are as red as my dress and aglow with perspiration. I first splash cold water on my face, welcoming its cooling touch, and then I dampen a washcloth to press to the exposed skin of my neck and chest.

A simple, open-heart pendant rests on my décolletage. It was a gift from Doctor K, given years ago as a reminder to keep my heart open to love. *What a joke.* If only I could close it. My heart is not some locked door, where only Jess holds the key. That would be easier.

No, my heart is wide open and brimming with love. I'd happily offer it often and freely. The problem is, it has become a graveyard for unreturned, unwanted love. All the plots are full, and my cemetery of a heart cannot accept any more corpses.

At the thought, I remove the gold necklace and reach for the pill pack in my toiletry bag. After enduring a hysterectomy at such a young age, my doctors had warned me that my production of estrogen would stop earlier than usual. But I'm only thirty-five. And this is hell.

Opening the pack, I realize I've skipped a few doses this week, including Monday's pill. That might have contributed to the irritation I'd felt in Doctor K's office. I should apologize to her—and I will—but first, I use water from the bathroom sink to gulp down the pill from the Thursday slot.

After checking myself in the mirror once more and fluffing my hair, I emerge from the bathroom as ready as I'll ever be. When I turn the corner, nothing could have prepared me for what I see. I told Jess to get comfortable, but this…

"Feeling better?" Jess asks from her reclined position on my bed. Her tan, muscular legs are stretched long in front of her, while her head is propped up by a triangle formed between her shoulder, elbow, and fist.

Unable to speak, I slowly nod.

"I hope it's okay that I'm on your bed. There wasn't anywhere else to sit."

I nod again, or maybe I never stopped nodding, because I'm feeling lightheaded. She's not wrong. There's nowhere else to sit in this room, but I wouldn't exactly call what she's doing *sitting*. She's lying on my bed… in my hotel room. The black cocktail dress she's wearing has crept ever so slightly up her smooth thighs.

"Water," I croak. "Would you like some water?"

"No, thanks. I'm fine."

I walk the two steps to the mini fridge anyway and take out two bottles of Evian. "In case you change your mind," I say, before opening and chugging my bottle.

When I finish, I take a deep breath and ask, "What did you want to talk about?"

"A couple of things, actually." She shifts to a somewhat more seated position with her back resting against the surplus of pillows on the bed. "Why don't you get comfortable, too?"

Because I might burst into flames, I want to say, but I smile and move toward the spot on the bed she's patting. As I lower myself onto the plush mattress with the care of someone defusing a bomb, Jess laughs and says, "I don't bite."

A million rejoinders flood my brain, none of which are appropriate to say aloud. Thank God she keeps talking.

"First, I wanted to update you on what I learned from Rome during drinks Saturday night and dinner tonight. It's not a lot..." She raises her hand as if stopping me from getting my hopes up. "But I wanted to share what I found out right away."

"Okay," I say, trying to ignore that she saw Rome again tonight. Two dates within a week? That's more excessive than these decorative pillows.

"Your dress is pretty, by the way. Did you have a hot date tonight? With your girlfriend... Charlotte, right?"

"Ex-girlfriend. And no. I just like to get dressed up." Even though it's true, everything coming out of my mouth sounds like a lie. My tone, too defensive, implies I'm hiding something. But how do I explain that putting on a nice dress, even when I have nowhere important to go, makes me feel better about myself?

I use my hand as a fan, still feeling the effects of the ongoing hot flash. "Is it warm in here?"

"I don't think so," Jess says, before casually placing her hand on my thigh. "Oh, you're sizzling hot!"

Her relatively cold hand on my superheated skin feels like heaven… and then hell when I remember it means nothing. Jess is a tactile person. She's a hugger, and she touches people when she talks to them. That's her norm, and that's all this is.

"So, what did you learn… on your dates with Rome?"

"Right," she says with a small sigh. "Well, for starters, it was easy to get him to talk about the dog breeder. All I had to do was mention that I recently adopted a rescue dog, and he jumped right in with how 'rescue dogs are nice and all,' but if I want a purebred dog, I should go to *Rose's Golden Doodles*. He also referred to himself as a business partner, not an investor."

It's hard for me to concentrate with her hand still on my thigh, but I force myself to say, "That's interesting. But Rome could be trying to impress you by making himself sound more important to the business than he is."

"That's what I figured, too, at first. But then…" Jess pauses, no doubt for dramatic effect. Her eyes light up and her features become even more animated as she continues. "I asked him how he knew this *Rose lady*, acting like I was jealous or something, and he claims their relationship is strictly professional. He said he met Annabelle Rose through a mutual friend, who is their third business partner. They each have a one-third share of the company."

"Wow, that's great intel!"

"I know!" Jess exclaims, imitating a character from her favorite show. "But wait… there's more."

Her enthusiasm is utterly adorable, even when she's delivering a cheesy infomercial line. I would buy anything if I turned on my TV at three a.m. and saw her smiling face selling it.

I'm completely captivated by her when she says, "The third partner is also a professional golfer, and guess where he lives?"

I opt for the obvious. "San Diego?"

Jess shakes her head. "Guess again."

"I don't know." I shrug. "Where?"

"Rosarito Beach… Mexico!" Jess gives my thigh a firm squeeze on the last word, and my mind is split in two.

Half of my mind has a million follow-up questions and can't believe she's uncovered the connection to Mexico that's been missing this whole time. If we can learn who this third business partner is, we might finally be able to locate the Mexican breeding facility and get proof of the cross-border puppy smuggling.

The other half can't stop thinking about the hand still touching my bare thigh.

"That can't be a coincidence, right?" Jess asks.

"No, it cannot. You're amazing, Jess." It's something both halves of my being agree on without a doubt.

Her puppy brown eyes widen as if surprised I would say such a thing. Then they lock with mine. "You're amazing, Avery… for everything you do to help both people and animals. I'm grateful to contribute."

"You sell yourself short." I stop myself from adding that she always has, as it might come off as unintended criticism.

More than anything, I wish she would see herself the way I do—as a strong, beautiful woman with many talents and unlimited potential. One incredible talent is her ability to make anyone feel safe and welcome with a single smile. I'll never forget walking into our first class together as a new student freshman year.

I'd felt like a scared animal. One being introduced into a new environment after a lifetime of captivity and abuse, unsure of whom to trust. Then Jess smiled at me. She didn't say anything, and I had no idea who she was, but her smile was enough to put me at ease. I chose an empty desk in the aisle next to hers, one seat back, and finally felt safe. I didn't realize it at the time, but I think that was the day I first fell in love.

Jess shifts beside me on the bed. Her hand moves off my thigh as she straightens herself upright. I feel the loss but know it's for the best. There's a good reason for my three-year-long sexual moratorium. My declaration of love for Jess during the heat of passion with Char caused irreparable damage. I can't let that happen again with anyone else, Jess included. No good would come from it.

"I unfortunately didn't get the name of the third business partner in Mexico," Jess says. "But I'm hopeful I can find out this Saturday night when Rome takes me to the driving range. It'll be easy to bring up the other professional golfer in conversation there without it being suspicious."

"A third date?" There's shock, disgust, and a tinge of jealousy in my voice, but I can't help it. "Jess, you don't have to do that. You've already gotten more than enough information to help, and I'm worried…"

"It'll be fine," Jess interrupts. "I'm being careful, like you said. I promise."

I was going to say *I'm worried Rome will try to get physical after a third date*. But maybe she *wants* to get physical with Rome. He's outwardly attractive to most women who like men; never mind his darkened, puppy-slinging soul. Or maybe something has already happened between them… No, I can't let myself believe that.

"Are you okay?" Jess asks, prompting me to wonder how long I was lost in my own head.

"Hmm? Oh, yeah, I'm fine." Unable to lie to her face any longer, I turn my attention to the clock on the nightstand. "Wow, I didn't realize it was getting so late. It's almost ten o'clock."

"Yeah, sorry to keep you up. I could go, or…" Jess stops herself.

"Or what?" I ask, hope blooming in my chest.

"Well, there was one other thing I wanted to talk to you about," she says, bringing me back to reality.

"That's right. You mentioned there were a couple of topics. What's the other thing?"

Jess looks down and picks at her fingernails, which I now realize are bare and bitten short. "It's not important. We could talk about it later if you'd rather I leave."

"I don't want you to leave."

My words dangle in the air like fireflies in the night. Jess' eyes once again meet mine, and I swear they twinkle.

"Do you ever think about that night?" she asks.

Her words don't require any clarification. We've never talked about that night before, but it seems we're about to. I can't believe this is happening. *Is this really happening?*

I'm in too deep of a dream state to pinch myself—or even speak, it seems—and my stalled reply dims the light in her eyes. Perhaps it's why my traitorous mouth blurts, "All the time."

And just like that, I've shared my terrifying truth. I hold my breath, waiting for the world to end. Instead, I see instant relief spread across her beautiful, heart-shaped face.

"Me too," she whispers.

"You do?" I ask in disbelief.

She nods, still holding my gaze. "It's the only time I've ever…" She stops herself again and breaks eye contact.

"Ever what?" I ask, desperately needing to know the rest of that sentence.

The rosy makeup on her cheeks deepens to crimson. "It's embarrassing to say out loud, but… no one else has ever given me… I mean… besides that night, I've never had an…"

"Oh," I say. Then the voice in my head screams even louder. *Oh! Oh! Oh!*

I'm equal parts shocked, thrilled, and tongue-tied. Jess is back to picking at her bare fingernails as silence settles in around us. Watching her discomfort feels like an invasion of privacy, so I let my eyes shift down her curvy body until they land on her hot pink toenails.

"I was with Brad for twenty years," she finally says, "and I enjoyed feeling wanted, but I never enjoyed sex with him. It just felt like something I should do, you know, to make him happy. It was never about what I wanted."

"And what do you want?" I ask, bringing my eyes back up to hers.

Her eyes darken and drop to my mouth. "I think you know."

We're both still on the bed, mere inches apart, and I only know one thing for certain: my sexual moratorium is over.

Chapter 25

The next day is spring blossoms, summer vacations, autumn leaves, and winter holidays all combined. It's like waking up from the best dream imaginable and realizing it was all true. Jess is asleep next to me, her hand gripped in mine. After our mind-blowing night, she had fallen asleep right as the sun had risen. I'd lain awake a while longer, studying her face in the early morning glow before dozing off myself.

It turns out Jess snores as loudly as a hibernating bear, but that's okay. She's an adorable bear, like a koala or panda—neither of which hibernate, incidentally, and okay, koalas aren't even technically bears—but my point is, she's perfect. No amount of snoring could change that.

Awake once more, I again admire the sleeping beauty beside me. Her cute snub nose, supermodel beauty mark, and deep smile lines on either side of her plump lips all define *perfection*. If one were to look up the word in the dictionary, they'd find a picture of Jessica Serrano.

Not to brag, but it makes sense that she's exhausted. After climaxing *seventeen times*—once for each year we've been apart—anyone would be dead to the world. Truth be told, I didn't think it was physically possible. But her body had been primed like a finely tuned instrument, humming all the right notes with the simplest strokes.

She'd moaned her first release as we made out like sex-crazed teenagers. The second had erupted only minutes after I'd brushed aside the soaked fabric of her thong. After that, our bodies became a symphony composed of sound, touch, and love—with Jess giving as well as she received.

She stirs beside me but doesn't open her eyes before mumbling, "What time is it?"

I glance at the clock and reply, "Almost noon."

"What day is it?" she asks, springing to a seated position.

"Friday," I say with a laugh, although the sight of her nude has me thinking it would be easy to stay in this bed for days.

Her large breasts—previously splayed across either side when she was on her back—are now perked to life as she sits upright. I'm reaching out to massage one, as I had so many times last night, when she exclaims, "I was supposed to start work an hour ago!"

"Sorry, Sunshine. If I'd realized, I would have woken you up sooner. Maybe you should call in sick… and stay in bed all day with me," I say, still in a dream state.

Jess is already out of the bed, picking articles of clothing up off the ground, but she pauses as if considering my brilliant idea. "I wish I could, but I don't have any paid time off."

Despite knowing it would come off wrong, I want to offer to reimburse her missed wages so she can stay with me today. I'd give her my credit card and take her shopping on Rodeo Drive, too, if it would make her happy. Money has never mattered to me, but, realizing it's a sensitive topic for most people, I bite my tongue.

"Thankfully, my work clothes are in my locker, since I changed here before dinner," Jess says while pulling on her black cocktail dress. "But now, I have to do the walk of shame in last night's dress while running super late for work and coming from…" Trailing off, she stops frantically tugging at her clothes long enough to look at me.

"Avery, last night was… special. But can we please keep what happened between us?" When I stare at her, unsure how to respond, she quickly adds, "We wouldn't want Rome finding out I'm not really interested in him, right?"

"Right," I say, because there's nothing else I can.

"I have to get going, but I'll call you later. Okay?" Without waiting for a response, she's out the door, and I'm slapped with a new terrifying truth: *Jess is ashamed to be with me.*

I spent the rest of the day wallowing, though I'd told myself I was merely savoring the remaining traces of Jess by staying in bed. The sheets still smelled of her perfume. Their rumples faintly resembled the outline of her body. Even the air in the room was deliciously tainted with the memory of her soft kisses and low moans. I couldn't leave that—especially not when leaving my room also meant seeing Jess in the hotel lobby.

With the help of room service and several long naps, I've made it to eight o'clock at night without stepping foot outside. While drifting off earlier, I remember flecks of light dancing inside my eyelids, similar to dawn's first rays bouncing off water. The glimmer then faded into a sunset over the ocean, glowing magnificently on its way to darkness.

That sums up Jess for me perfectly. She is my first light, and my last, and everything in between. *My sunshine.* I'd envied the sunflowers she adored back in high school, but perhaps I've been one all along—a lone sunflower in a field, tracking her shine across the sky to survive.

If I am a sunflower, Jess is most definitely the sun. But what am I to her? After all, a star burns brightly regardless of the existence of flowers.

The buzz of my phone on the nightstand jolts me from my thoughts. The steady thud in my chest triples in speed as I reach for it. Jess had said she would call me. It has to be her. I don't bother looking before answering.

"Hello. Jess?"

"No. Who's Jess?" a much deeper than expected voice replies.

I close my eyes and suck in a breath, both disappointed and relieved at the same time. At least it's my favorite guy in the world. "Raldy! How are you?"

"I'm doing well, but I still want to know who this Jess person is," he says teasingly.

"She's… someone I was expecting a call from. I can catch you up later. First, I want to hear all about your trip. Please tell me you're finally back in San Diego."

"I am. My plane landed about an hour ago."

"Thank goodness. I've been here for over a month now and have only seen you once. This is what happens when you're a hotshot lawyer, you know. No time for the little people," I tease.

"Sadly, that's true. Little sisters are the exception, though. Can you meet me for dinner tomorrow night?"

"Sure! Do you mind if I invite Jess too? I'd love for you to meet her, and vice versa." I'm not sure if Jess will want to come, but that's an entirely different problem I won't allow myself to brood over yet.

There's a long pause on the other end of the line. Too long.

"Damien, is something wrong?"

More silence ensues before he says, "I was hoping we could talk privately at dinner. There's something I need to share with you."

His tone is serious. And familiar. I'll never forget Damien's fateful call my sophomore year in college. No one had wanted to tell me that Aunt Robin's cancer had returned and spread six months prior. So instead, I got slapped with the terrifying truth after it was too late to say goodbye.

I couldn't stay mad at Damien, though. Aunt Robin had made him swear on our mother's grave not to tell me until she passed. She was a true angel, who had taken us in when we had nowhere else to go. Although I hardly let myself think about them, I like to believe both sisters are happily reunited now.

"What is it?" I ask, matching his somber tone.

"I think it's best if we talk in person."

"Tell me, Damien. *Now.*" My fist is on my hip as I pace the floor of my hotel room. He's crazy if he thinks I'm letting him off this phone without telling me his news.

He sighs his resignation. "It's Henry. He's sick. After my business meeting in Boston, I drove up to Vermont to visit a friend. That's how I found out."

"How sick?" I ask.

"Less sick than he deserves. The bastard should still be rotting in prison," Damien growls. "But he seems to be experiencing the early stages of Parkinson's."

"How do you know that?" I ask, ignoring the nausea brought on by the memory of our father's early release from prison years ago.

"Let's just say I know someone who works at his doctor's office. Sharing the information with me was a HIPAA violation, so this needs to stay between us, but I didn't want to keep it from you."

He doesn't need to say *like I did with Aunt Robin*. We both know he still feels guilty for keeping me in the dark. We'd made a pact back then: No more secrets ever again.

As I often do when thinking about family, I look down at the tattoo on my wrist. Though the language is not one I speak, my finger traces the Arabic letters that have become a part of me: لا اسرار. I silently recite their hallowed meaning, my new life mantra: *No secrets.*

"Thank you for telling me," I say.

"Ems, are you okay?"

I nod, but since he can't hear that, he repeats the question. The use of my nickname—short for Emerald, our mother's maiden name—has me tearing up. We've been calling each other Ems and Raldy ever since that awful day when I was thirteen.

After finding the words, I finally say, "Yes, I will be. Thanks again for letting me know, but let's not talk about it anymore. I want to have a nice conversation with my charming big brother at dinner tomorrow. And hopefully you can meet Jess too, if she's able to come."

"Sounds good. I'll ask my assistant to make a reservation for three somewhere nice, and I'll text you the deets."

"*My assistant.* Someone's gotten fancy."

"Despite the paltry salary, being ADA isn't without its perks."

"You mean DDA, right?"

"Um… I guess I failed to mention it, but I was promoted from my deputy position to ADA a few weeks ago."

"Shut the front door! Assistant District Attorney Damien Emerald. That's huge, Raldy! I can't believe I'm barely hearing about this now, but congratulations! We'll have to celebrate. Dinner is on me tomorrow."

"My student loans and I never say no to a free dinner, but you don't have to, Ems."

"I want to. It's the least I can do. You're the best brother a girl could ever have." My voice cracks on the last sentence, and like the amazing brother he is, Damien knows best to change the subject.

"So, tell me more about this Jess person, who may or may not join us for dinner tomorrow."

Damien doesn't know anything about Jess. Not about my burgeoning crush on her in high school, nor about its culmination into an undying love.

My brother and I generally avoid the topic of our physical relationships. Damien is a handsome man, and I've met a number of his girlfriends over the years, but the "deets" of his conquests are best left undiscussed. Similarly, I've been elusive when it comes to my love life. Though I'm fairly certain he knows I favor women, I've never explicitly told him.

Our pact comes to mind: *No more secrets ever again.*

Damien already knows my darkest secret, but not because I'd confided in him as I should have. He'd come home from boarding school unexpectedly, shortly after my procedure, and found out the terrifying truth all on his own. He'd helped me back then. I need to trust he'll support me now.

And just like that… I tell my brother everything.

Chapter 26

Seventeen years ago

My thumping heart is in perfect time with the rapid beats of the bass downstairs. The distant party music grows quieter as I make my way toward the closed bedroom door at the end of the long hallway. That's where Brad said they'd be. With each step closer, my breaths get shallower until I'm panting for oxygen. I still can't believe I agreed to this.

A blond guy from our graduating class stumbles out of the bathroom, smelling strongly of alcohol as he passes me in the dimly lit corridor. He gives me a suggestive look, like he knows where I'm headed, and it makes me feel self-conscious. Why did Brad ask me in the first place? Was it because he assumed I'd say yes?

Contrary to popular belief, I am not promiscuous. A few guys on the football team, who I had the displeasure of tutoring, claimed to have slept with me, but they were total liars. I had shot down each of their advances, and their battered egos apparently couldn't handle it. The false rumors started sophomore year and only grew, but I didn't mind. It was better to let everyone think I was a *jock whore*, as some called me, than to have them learn about my secret crush.

Jessica Serrano—a jock in her own right, and an overall amazing human being and actress—is the only person I've had eyes for throughout high school. It's sad to think that I'll be leaving for college in a few short months, but at least Los Angeles isn't far from here.

Tonight could change everything—for better or for worse.

Fearing I might hyperventilate, I stop outside the door and force myself to take deeper breaths. Jess is in there… waiting to have a threesome with me. All doors and windows to my heart are wide open, ready to welcome her in. The idea of being kissed and touched by Brad makes my skin crawl, but knowing she'll be there too somehow makes it all better. I can pretend it's just the two of us, a fantasy come true.

To avoid walking in on anything, I knock before creeping the door ajar, and I'm relieved when Jess tells me to come in. Her luminous smile brightens the whole room as I close the door behind me. Once our eyes lock, I immediately know everything will be okay.

"All right. Let's get this party started," Brad says.

It sounds like he's rubbing his hands together, but I don't look at him. I don't plan to break eye contact with Jess the entire night.

"Before we get started," Jess says, still holding my gaze, "you should know that Brad and I plan to get married. This is only a one-night thing."

"Buzzkill," Brad directs at Jess.

"I just want her to have all the facts, in case it affects her decision. She deserves that." Though she's responding to Brad, her eyes never leave mine.

"I understand. Thank you," I say, trying not to sound as deflated as I feel.

"Do you still want to do this?" she asks.

My gaze slides to the plump bottom lip she's biting, and I nod.

"I think we should go first," she says.

I'm not sure if the *we* she refers to is her and me, or her and Brad, but then she takes several steps forward, closing the distance between us. My heart gallops even faster. She means *her and me*.

"Sweet! Kiss her, babe!" Brad cheers from his seat on the bed.

I do my best to ignore him, but... *damn, he's annoying.*

Jess takes my hands. "Is this okay?"

Again, I nod.

"Do you want to kiss?" she asks, sounding more timid than usual.

"Do you?" I ask in return.

She nods while nibbling on her lower lip. I take that as my cue and lean in. Meeting me in the middle, her warm lips press against mine. There are hoots and hollers coming from Brad, but my brain successfully blocks him out as soon as our mouths begin to move. All I can hear is the sound of our combined breath, our smacking lips, and a low moan when I find her tongue with mine.

Her hands slide up my bare arms before they cup my face, lighting a fire inside me. Having done nothing like this before, I follow her lead and place my hands on either side of her pretty face while we continue to make out. *OMG, I'm making out with Jessica Serrano!*

When she deepens the kiss, my fingers instinctively weave through her silky hair and tug her closer. Our chests, already touching, smash together as our hips make contact. We're about the same height, so it's easy to imagine our body parts melding into each other. The Spice Girls song "2 Become 1" plays in my head.

Breaking our kiss, Jess asks, "Should we move to the bed?"

Brad says something again—I have no idea what—and my next thought is that there's a reason they say three is a crowd. It's not *3 Become 1, Brad.* I wish he would go away and leave Jess and me alone, but that wasn't the arrangement. I knew what I was getting myself into when I agreed to this. Pushing back my disgust, I remind myself: Jess is worth it.

"Sure," I say, focusing on our precious eye contact.

She takes my hands again and leads me to the bed.

This time, I hear Brad when he says, "My turn."

"Not yet," Jess snaps. "Move over."

He groans but does what he's told. Jess and I settle onto the edge of the bed, and the rest happens both quickly and in slow motion. We resume kissing, as if we had never stopped, but this time, our hands travel up and down each other, exploring reverently while greedily seeking pleasure. Jess lifts her shirt off, I think at Brad's prompting, but I can't be sure. I've blocked him out again.

We continue kissing, intimately removing clothes, and touching for what might be five minutes or hours. Time no longer exists. My hands explore every mountain and valley on her perfect landscape, lingering in all the places I appreciate her touch in return. Before long, a river runs through us both, connecting us in ecstasy. Our bodies are trembling, like once still ponds shaken by the force of a waterfall.

It's the best moment of my eighteen-year-old life. Until we are rudely interrupted by Brad.

"Okay, my turn now," he says.

Jess sends me an apology with her eyes before replying to him. "Fine, but you have to be with me first."

He grumbles something but doesn't seem to object.

Pain shoots through my chest when I watch him roll on top of her. On top of *my Jess*. As if sensing my discomfort, she reaches out and laces her fingers through mine. Brad is all over her, but her loving brown eyes once again lock with mine. It's as if we're having a silent conversation, and she's telling me everything will be all right.

As I hold her gaze, we're the only two in the room. I give her hand a squeeze, and the smile I get in return is enough to stop the earth from spinning. My body relaxes, and I push the dread of what's to come aside, focusing only on her.

Suddenly, there's a loud rap on our locked door. "The cops are here! The cops are here!"

"Shit," mutters Brad, who thankfully rolls off Jess.

We all rush to redress, then run down the stairs and out the back door of Richie Sampson's house. Once outside, the panicked throngs of drunken grads scatter like dandelion petals in the wind.

Completely sober, I head toward my car and catch a glimpse of Jess climbing into Brad's pickup truck. A smile is still plastered on her heart-shaped face, which turns in my direction. The corners of my lips curve upward as well when I realize our "threesome" never went much past an incredible twosome. *Saved by the police and underaged drinking.*

Part III: Jessica

"And now these three remain: faith, hope, and love. But the greatest of these is love."

—The Bible (NIV), 1 Cor. 13:13

Chapter 27

Now

"That's good. Now, relax your grip a little, and then pull your arms back like so." Rome's front side is pressed against my backside as he swings the golf club in my hands. "Following through after you make contact with the ball is key," Rome continues, motioning with his arms stretched in front of me.

Follow-through *is* key, and I'd left Avery hanging after the most incredible night of my life, again. Coming on this date was a major mistake. I knew it before I even got here, but now all I want to do is throw this stupid club and go see Avery. She'd seemed hurt after I told her I couldn't meet her and her brother for dinner tonight.

"Thanks for your help," I say, trying to sound engaged. "It's nice getting tips from a professional golfer. Are most of your friends professional golfers, too?"

Rome straightens after we complete my swing, thankfully taking a step back. "Not really. It's hard being friends with someone you may one day have to compete against. I've got my eye on the prize."

The bright lights of the driving range suddenly feel like they're all pointed at me. I watch his eyes scroll over my body, but I don't feel flattered by his attention. Quite the opposite. His gaze is that of someone craving a steak while staring at a prized cow. The loud thwacks all around us become the sound of meat cleavers hitting butcher blocks.

Refocusing on the mission, I ask, "What about your business partner who's also a golfer? What was his name again?"

Rome's steel-blue eyes stop scrolling and lock with mine. "I don't believe I ever mentioned his name. Either way, we're not friends. Business is business."

The playful charm usually present in his voice is gone, and the way he's looking at me makes my stomach clench. I break eye contact first by stepping aside and pointing toward the tee. "It's your turn now. Let's see what you've got."

He doesn't budge at first, but when he finally reaches for his special driver and steps up to the tee, I release my breath and discreetly grab my purse. I'm not sure exactly how to get out of this, but I'm certain I need to leave, right now. Phone in hand, I put my acting skills to the test.

"Oh no! I just got a text that one of my kids is sick. I need to pick them up A.S.A.P." I feel guilty for using my kids as an excuse, and fear my lie could come true, but desperate times call for desperate measures. When Rome looks skeptical, I double down with, "It's Lucas. He's throwing up all over the place. It must be from the Happy Meal that *my husband* let him have earlier."

After letting that last part sink in for a second, I make a break for the parking lot while hollering over my shoulder. "You stay and work on your golf swing. I'll see you later!"

An hour later, I pull up in front of what had once been my dream home—complete with pink stucco and a white picket fence. I had raced all the way from the golf center in Del Mar to the Mexican restaurant in Old Town only to find Avery and her brother already gone. My three calls to Avery's cell also went unanswered. It was stupid to think I could catch them. I've blown my chance.

As I push open the heavy wooden front door, I'm greeted by an excited Prince Petey, whining and pawing at my legs. From his reaction, you'd think I'd been gone for two days rather than the two hours since I left for my date.

"Hi there, good boy! Aww, thank you," I say, kneeling down to pet him after locking the door behind me. "I missed you, too! Yes, I did."

My mood instantly elevates. It's nice coming home to someone so happy to see me. It's nice coming home to anyone, really. I look around my otherwise empty house and frown.

The formal living and dining rooms within view have hardly been used lately. Two floral sofas, handed down from my parents, sit neatly decorated with various pillows and a knit throw over the back of each. One pillow reads, "FAMILY IS EVERYTHING." Another is embroidered with, "LOVE NEVER FAILS." Both mantras taunt me, even though I know they're true.

With my loving dog at my heels, I head toward the kitchen via the dining room and try to remember the last time we used the "fancy china" I'd insisted on adding to our wedding registry. My grandmother had passed down a nice set of gold-rimmed dinnerware that is also stored in our curio cabinet, but at the time, I'd felt it was crucial for Brad and I to pick out our own china pattern as "man and wife."

Twenty-two-year-old me had held a lot of unyielding convictions. A woman was supposed to find a strong man to take care of her. She was supposed to get married and have babies. End of story. I love my children more than anything and wouldn't trade them for all the happiness in the world, but I had never considered another path even possible.

Until two days ago, I'd convinced myself that the night of Richie Sampson's graduation party was just a wild experience with my future husband. The longing that persisted years after was chalked up to youthful nostalgia. It had felt less wrong that way.

Last Thursday night with Avery had felt both wrong and so very right. With the memory of her sweet kisses still lingering on my lips, I wonder what that makes me. *A lesbian? Bi-sexual? An adulterer? A hypocrite?*

I shamefully recall how I once viewed homosexuality as a sin. It's what I'd been taught my whole life—thanks to several ongoing misinterpretations of the Holy Bible. I've since come to realize that *all love is love*—and since God is love—it can never be immoral.

But is that what this is? Are the feelings I have toward Avery love? Or only lust? The latter is one of the seven deadly sins, and I can't help but worry my faith is being tested. Is Avery the love of my life? Or is she forbidden fruit tempting my soul? I am still married to Brad, after all.

After letting Prince Petey relieve himself in the backyard, I plop down on the couch in the family room with a long sigh. Adultery is a sin any way I slice it. Although Brad cheated on me, two wrongs don't make a right. My mind unwillingly travels back to that awful morning nine years ago, and my sigh deepens into a groan. Three wrongs don't make a right, either.

I check my phone for the millionth time. *No return calls or texts from Avery.* My heart aches at the very real possibility that I've lost her before she was ever mine. I should have called her sooner. Instead, I waited two days, declined her dinner invitation, and went out with Rome again. I wouldn't call me back, either.

The storm of grief pouring down has me again wondering: Am I in love with Avery?

Needing a distraction, I pick up the remote that hopefully controls our smart TV and hit the home button. The screen turns on, and much to my delight, it goes straight to the movie I plan to watch: *Fried Green Tomatoes*.

Chapter 28

Toward the end of the movie, a knock at my front door has me springing up before I can register the late hour. I wipe my tear-soaked cheeks with my palms while making my way to the door. *Avery. It has to be Avery.* I'm both disappointed and alarmed when I look through the peephole.

"Brad?" I swing the door open and panic when I see my two babies in tears. "What happened? Is everyone okay?"

"They're okay. Just shaken up," Brad says, as Lucas and Chloe rush forward and grip onto my legs.

I wrap my arms around them and look sternly at Brad. "What is going on?"

"There was a fire… at my apartment building. The unit beneath mine, it…" Brad sucks in a breath, steadying his voice. "The kids were already in bed, and I'd fallen asleep in front of the TV. By the time the smoke detectors went off, the floor was burning hot already. I ran into the kids' bedroom, scooped them up, and ran us out of there."

"It was scary," Lucas says with a snot-nosed sniff.

Prince Petey, also near my legs, licks Lucas' hand. My eyes instinctively drop, and that's when I notice the bandages around Brad's feet, poking out from under his Adidas slides.

"Your feet got burned!" I whisper-yell.

"Only first or second-degree, according to the paramedics." Brad shrugs. "It doesn't feel too great to stand on 'em, though."

"Come in. Come in," I say, ushering Lucas and Chloe inside the house and directing Brad to follow. "Please, have a seat. Can I get you anything?"

Brad lowers onto the previously unused sofa in the formal living room. "No, thank you. I'm sorry to show up so late like this. I tried calling first, but your phone kept going straight to voicemail, and the kids wanted you."

"Big fire, Mommy," Chloe says through sobs.

"It's okay, baby. Mommy's here now." I squeeze her even tighter before turning to Brad. "Thank you so much for bringing them home."

"There was so much smoke, and it was really hot, Mom," Lucas says, calmer than earlier, "like when you open the oven door and I'm standing too close. Once we got outside, we saw orange flames everywhere! The whole building was on fire."

I lock onto Brad's weary blue eyes, silently begging him to tell me it's not true, but he nods. "Everything is gone."

I want more details, but not in front of the kids. "How about I tuck you two into my bed for the night?"

Lucas and Chloe, both clad in dinosaur-print pajamas, nod their sweet, sleepy heads. Once my babies are snug on what used to be Brad's side of the bed, I kiss their foreheads and tell them I love them more times than I can count. "Mommy will be right back. Try to get some sleep, my loves."

After I lower the lights and exit my bedroom, the magnitude of the situation hits me. *My children… and their father… could have died tonight.* Thankfully, the Lord was looking out for them, but still. *They could have died.*

I navigate the short hall back to the formal living room where Brad sits motionless. As I join him on the sofa, pure emotion has me burying my face in his chest. He smells of smoke, with hints of sweat and cologne, and he feels one hundred percent like Brad. Never before have I felt this grateful for the mountain of a man beside me. The strong man who carried our children to safety tonight.

"I'm so glad everyone is okay!" I pull back to look into his eyes as another thought surfaces. "*Is* everyone okay?"

Brad's gaze drops to the floor. "There are still some people unaccounted for, but they won't know for sure until they've either contacted everyone who might have been away, or…" He stops, understandably unable to finish the horrendous sentence.

"We'll pray for them," I say, lacing my fingers through his.

Brad's eyes return to mine, and in them, I see gratitude and something else I can't quite name. He also looks tired, rattled, and disheveled. He opens his mouth to speak but then closes it.

"How?" I ask.

"They think it was a grease fire that originated in the kitchen of the unit below mine. It spread hot and fast. The woman who lives there made it out with only minor burns, luckily, and then she called nine-one-one. You just never think…" Brad shakes his head. "You don't think these types of things will happen to you… until they do."

We both sit in silence for a few minutes, holding hands, before Brad says, "I should probably figure out where I'm gonna go. My mom's house is nearby, but I don't want to wake her so late. Do you think I could get a discount at that hotel you work at?"

"You'll stay here… for as long as you need," I say without a second thought. The idea of him leaving to check into a hotel right now is absurd. "Both of the kids' beds are empty tonight, or we could pull out the sleeper from the sofa in the family room."

"Thanks, Jess." His blue eyes soften, causing an involuntarily flutter in my chest. "The couch is plenty comfortable as is."

It's hard to believe an inanimate object can carry so many memories, but they're unleashed on me all at once. We'd gone to every furniture store in town for six consecutive Saturdays before settling on the tan, microfiber, king-size sleeper sofa for our family room. I wanted to be able to have guests, and I'd had faith that the extra bedroom now belonging to Chloe would someday be occupied.

Like a set prop in a film production, our couch has played a role in many life scenes. It's where family and friends have gathered and relaxed on numerous occasions. Lucas lost his first tooth while hanging upside down off it. Chloe said her first word—*dada*, much to my disappointment—when I'd been holding her on that couch. Brad had slept there the nights we'd fought, and we'd sometimes made up on it the next morning.

Dropping his hand, I stand and motion for him to follow me into the family room. Once there, I open the ottoman footrest and pull out the extra blanket and pillow stored there.

"Here you go. Is there anything else I can get you? A drink, maybe?"

Brad limps over to the couch and stops so close I can feel his breath on the top of my head. "I'm fine for now. Thanks. If I need something later, I'll help myself… if that's okay?"

"Of course," I say, looking up to meet his eyes again. The nameless emotion in them from earlier is clear now. It's hope. My breath hitches as I feel its pull. The inscriptions from the throw pillows flash in the forefront of my memory: *FAMILY IS EVERYTHING*, and *LOVE NEVER FAILS*.

I wrap my arms around Brad's solid body once more, tears forming in my eyes. "I'm glad you're okay."

His hands run up and down my back. "I've missed you so much. You have no idea."

The cracks in his husky voice force the tears down my face and into Brad's shirt. I have no idea what I'm doing right now, but I know this feels right. It feels familiar. *It feels safe.* My arms hang on a moment longer before I finally step back.

"Well, good night. I should get back to the kids."

I grab my phone off the arm of the couch and stride toward my bedroom, needing to put space between us. In the hallway, I pause, Brad's earlier words finally striking a chord. *I tried calling first, but your phone kept going straight to voicemail.* I hit my phone's screen, but nothing happens. The battery must have died while I was watching the movie.

I think of Avery for the first time since Brad and the kids arrived. My first thought is: *She might have tried to call.* My second thought is much more frightening. *What am I going to do now?*

The next morning, my nostrils are lured awake by the aroma of coffee and bacon, also known as *Heaven.* Not fully conscious yet, I move Lucas' arm out of my face, rub my sleep-filled eyes, and look around. Chloe is near the foot of the bed, curled around Prince Petey. The clock on my nightstand reads 7:14, and both kids are miraculously still asleep—no doubt because of their ordeal last night. They can use some extra sleep.

I roll out of bed as carefully as possible, finger-comb my hair, then pad my way toward the kitchen. The sight of Brad at the stove, shirtless, has me stopping short. His back muscles flex as he flips a strip of bacon. *Has he been working out?*

I clear my throat to announce myself. Brad turns, and only then do I realize how scarcely supported I am by the thin weight of my snug cami. I stretch an arm over my chest, but not before Brad's eyes widen. And yes, he *has* been working out. His chest and abs have definition I haven't seen on him since high school. Over the years, we'd both gone soft in the middle, but now…

"I thought I'd make breakfast as a thank you for letting me stay over. I hope that's okay."

I close my jaw and hope it wasn't too obvious I was gawking. "Yeah, of course. But… you don't cook."

"Bachelor Brad had to learn a few things." He says this with a chuckle as he returns his attention to the bacon, but there's sadness in his tone. With his muscular back to me, he says, "If it's okay with you, I was hoping to attend mass with you and the kids today."

Unexpected excitement surges through me. Brad is asking if he can go to church with us. What alternate universe am I living on right now?

"Of course!" I say. "The kids and I would love to have you there."

Chapter 29

"Lucas, I'm not going to ask you again, bud. Please turn off the video game and get your shoes on. The dog needs a walk, and you said you were going to help, remember?"

"Yes, I remember," Lucas groans.

"That's the spirit!" I say, while lacing up my own shoes. I've already helped Chloe into hers, put the harness on the dog, and filled several water bottles for our Wednesday morning walk.

If nothing else, having a dog has been great for getting regular exercise. In the month since we brought home *Prince Petey the Personal Trainer*, I've lost ten pounds and my clothes are finally fitting looser. Moreover, the results have motivated me to stay on a path of health and fitness. As of this week, I've decided to eliminate red meat and most dairy from my diet—except cheese. *I still need cheese.*

We're halfway out the door when I say, "Oh, wait. We need a tennis ball for when we get to the dog park. Can you go grab one, bud?"

Lucas runs back in as asked, and a minute later we're on our way. Though barely nine o'clock, it's already hot and dry outside. *Like an oven*, I think, remembering Lucas' description of the apartment fire. I gently squeeze my son's shoulder, which is being pulled forward by the leash—*Prince Petey the Personal Trainer* likes to work our upper bodies as well—and then I lean down to kiss the top of Chloe's head as we walk hand in hand through our neighborhood.

Set on one of the many hills overlooking our fine city, Bay Ho is full of quaint charm, friendly faces, and picturesque views. Most of the homes here were built in the 1950s, but they are well-maintained and artfully landscaped. Small green lawns are surrounded by pops of color: reds, pinks, purples, and an occasional splattering of yellow and orange.

I wave to Mrs. Anderson, watering her rose bushes, as we continue down the tree-lined sidewalk. A few of our other neighbors have opted for more draught-resistant landscaping, as we did with the help of my dad. Their yards are dotted with of a variety of succulents surrounded by neutral-colored stones set in geometric patterns.

After looking both ways, we cross the street to the side with the most shade, as there will easily be a ten-degree temperature drop once we get there. The air here is always cool, even when the sun is intense and unforgiving. The thought makes me think of Avery. It's been three days since she saw Brad with me at church, and I fear she may never speak to me again.

Though much has happened since, my mind travels back to the first time she met me at church over two weeks ago. We'd had a great time at my parents' house, playing Uno and sharing stories. There had been a connection between us that day, even if I wasn't able to see it then.

The realization hits me like a ton of bricks. *I miss her*, and not just for the physical aspects of our complicated relationship. I yearn for the opportunity to get to know her better and to simply be around her. My heart aches with the knowledge that I've ruined any chance of that now.

It's not like I could have told Brad *not* to come to church, though. The man had saved our children, burned his feet, and lost all his belongings in a single night. Allowing him to stay at the house also felt like the right thing to do. He hasn't stopped paying the mortgage—so it's technically his house too—and then there's the fact that we're still married…

"Is Dad going to live with us again?" Lucas asks as we make our way down the sidewalk.

I'm jarred from my thoughts by his question. "I don't think so, bud. He's just staying with us until he finds another apartment."

"But Dad said you guys are trying to fix your marriage. How can you do that if you don't even live together?" Lucas persists.

"Daddy loves you, Mommy," Chloe says.

I'm going to kill Brad. We had agreed to keep the kids out of this and not tell them about marriage counseling, which, coincidentally, we have again this evening. It will be our third session, and based on the way I'm feeling right now, it will also be our last.

Our second counseling session occurred a few days after Avery had come over to my parents' Sunday barbecue. *Becky*, as she still insists on being called, had finally broached the subject of Brad's infidelity. We'd discussed the general consequences of unfaithfulness in a marriage—such as its impact on trust, self-confidence, and intimacy—but the session had only left me with more questions. Did Brad and I truly have any of those things to begin with? And assuming we did, were they broken long before Brad ever slept with Susan?

I wrap an arm around each of my babies as we continue walking slowly downhill toward the community park. "Sometimes, there are things grownups can't fix, even when we try. But it doesn't mean we don't love each other—and both of you, very, very much."

Lucas shrugs me off, pulling faster ahead. "No, you don't! If you did, you'd try harder."

I stop short in my tracks. Chloe continues forward, following her brother. The park is within sight now, and I watch as they both head into it with Prince Petey leading the charge. I want to join them, but I'm frozen in place.

My gaze moves beyond the park, scrolls over the sea of rooftops, and lands on the palette of blues painting the background. The deep azure of Mission Bay catches my eye first. The lake-shaped splash of dark blue is surrounded by green trees, and above it, a sprawling expanse of baby blue sky attempts to steal the show. Nestled between the two, a denim-blue strip of distant ocean demands my attention. I need it to remind me how small and insignificant my problems are, as it so often does.

I stare and stare but nothing changes. The pain of Lucas' words, and the knowledge that he's right, feels anything but insignificant. I *would* try harder if I was in love with Brad.

Chapter 30

The afternoon sun is bright and blazing as I wade knee-deep into the ocean. Staring at it from a distance hadn't been enough to shrink my problems, so I dropped the kids off with my parents after the dog park and drove straight to the beach.

The salt stings my freshly shaved legs, but I don't care. I need to clear my head before facing Brad at our third, and possibly final, counseling session. I still can't believe he involved the kids by telling Lucas we were trying to "fix our marriage." *Whatever that's supposed to mean.*

I close my eyes and say a silent prayer. The waves beat at my legs, but I stand strong, focusing on the decision I need to make. I imagine its weight lifting off my shoulders, forming into a droplet, and falling into the vast sea of God's master plan. For a brief moment, I feel at peace. But then I remember, someone will get hurt either way.

If I stay with Brad, it will make him and the kids happy, but I'll certainly never hear from Avery again. And if I choose Avery, assuming she'll even have me, there could be more collateral damage than I'm able to fathom right now. It seems the odds are stacked in Brad's favor, three-to-one, so why isn't this an easier decision?

A seagull cries overhead, and I open my eyes to the sight of a large wave coming right at me. I quickly turn and then brace myself as the charging water crashes against my back, drenching my previously dry clothes. I wish I'd had the foresight to wear a bathing suit, but such is life. The water rushing back to sea causes my knees to wobble. Rather than fight it, I'm all in.

I yell an unbridled "woo" before diving into the next set of waves. The water is cold and refreshing as I swim farther out and stop at the point where I'm barely touching the ground. And then I laugh. I laugh like a maniac. I laugh harder than I've laughed in days, possibly weeks. And I again think of Avery.

An earlier version of myself would have considered it selfish to be splashing around in the ocean without my children. Blowing off marriage counseling and staying here all afternoon to have fun alone might also be selfish. But now, it's exactly what I plan to do… because it's what I *want* to do, and because it's what I'd want for a loved one in my situation. Avery's voice echoes in my head: *You deserve to be on your own list of loved ones.*

This is self-love, and I finally get it. It's not about sitting at home by myself to prove I can be alone. It's about doing something that makes me happy for one simple reason: *it makes me happy*. Self-love is not selfish. It's liberating!

I dive under the next set of waves with joy in my heart. When I surface, my decision is crystal clear. Wanting Avery might be selfish—maybe it is, maybe it isn't—but I know choosing her will make me happy.

My kids will be disappointed when Brad moves out again, and that will be tough, but they'll have a happy mother. If my mom would be happier with someone other than my dad, despite how much he means to me, I would want that for her. Because I love her. And now… I love me, too.

As Foda once said: *Once you love yourself, clear will become the answers you seek.* And she was absolutely right. The answer has never been more obvious, and I need to tell her. I use the next wave to propel me toward shore, praying the phone and keys I'd wrapped in my beach towel are still there unperturbed.

I'm shaking off water like a wet dog when I hear, "Jess?"

I freeze and then turn in the direction of the voice. "Avery!"

She drops the sandals in her hand. "What are you…"

I don't let her finish the sentence. In two quick strides, I'm directly in front of her. My hands fly up to her face, and I capture her lips with mine. My heart flutters when she leans in rather than pulling away. Then… *fizzle, pop, boom, pow.* She's kissing me back. Her lips and tongue are moving in unison with mine—parting, swiping, and nipping hungrily.

"You're here," I whisper breathlessly, feeling as if I somehow prayed her into existence.

"I'm here," she whispers in return.

Her fingers weave into my wet hair, gently pulling me closer. I moan into the kiss, and in this moment, we're not standing on a crowded public beach. We're at the water's edge on a deserted island, drenched from a torrential tropical storm, and kissing as if our lives depend upon it. It's a mashup of movie scenes in my head—the passionate kiss in the rain from *The Notebook,* the sexy pool kiss in *Wild Things,* the emotional kiss at the end of *Castaway,* the romance of *Gone with the Wind, Casablanca,* and, of course, *The Princess Bride,* all rolled into one—only a million times better. It's the most romantic kiss of my life.

I almost whimper when she pulls back. My hands instinctively grasp onto hers to preserve our connection. We stand there, eye to eye, holding hands. So many questions stare back at me.

"I owe you an explanation," I say.

"As to why you were swimming in your clothes?" she asks with a smirk.

"That… and about Brad." When her eyes drop to the sand, I release one of her hands so I can tilt her chin up. "It's not what you think."

"And what do I think?"

"That I'm getting back with him. But I'm not!" I lean to get her attention when her gaze darts to the side. "Please, look at me, Avery. I need you to hear this. There was a fire at Brad's apartment Saturday night while the kids were there."

Avery's brown eyes widen. "Oh, Jess, that's awful!"

"It was, but the kids are okay. *Thank God.* Brad carried them out. He burned his feet and lost all his belongings in the fire, but he's otherwise okay, too." I let out a breath to stop myself from reliving all the emotions. "Anyway, he showed up with the kids late that night, and I'm letting him stay on the couch until he finds a new place. It felt like the right thing to do."

"It *is* the right thing," Avery says.

Grateful for her understanding, I continue. "Then he asked if he could join us at church on Sunday, and I got excited because I thought it would be good for him. So, I said yes, but I didn't think about the impact it would have on you, and I'm so sorry for that."

"You don't need to apologize, Jess."

"Yes, I do. You were clearly upset after you saw us there together, and you had every right to be." I rest my hand on Avery's shoulder, needing to feel the warmth of her skin. "While I'm apologizing, there's something else I need to get off my chest. Until today, I wasn't sure what I was going to do about Brad, and I'm so sorry for leaving you in limbo. That wasn't fair of me. I'm actually supposed to be on my way to marriage counseling right now, but I'm not going, because I've realized I don't want to be with Brad. I want to be with *you.*"

Avery's shoulders go slack under my touch. Tears form in her eyes before she closes them. She shakes her head side to side, and then, an eternity of silence.

"Please, say something," I plead. "Am I too late? Do you not want to be with me?"

Her eyelids slowly open. Small teardrops cling to her bottom lashes before rolling down her cheeks. She sniffs and then wipes at them.

"Believe it or not, I'm not a big crier. I rarely feel sorry for myself, but with you…" She shakes her head again. "With you, I'm a different person."

"I don't understand," I say.

Avery pulls her hand from mine and takes a step back. My other hand drops from her shoulder like a fallen solider and hangs limp at my side. I try my best to ignore the strong feeling of loss.

"That's right. You don't understand," she says. "I wasn't upset for the reason you thought when I saw you and Brad at church. I didn't think it meant you were getting back together. Not necessarily, at least. I was upset because… you looked right together."

"What? No…"

Avery holds up a hand to stop me. "I need you to hear me. You and Brad, with your family, looked *right* together. Your kids looked *right* with both of their parents. You looked *right*—and happy— with both of yours. It's when I realized that what I'm doing *isn't* right. I'm selfishly putting myself between you and your happy family. I can't be the reason your kids don't get to live with both of their parents. I won't. I'm sorry."

"Wait!" I grab Avery's arm when she takes another step back. I'm not going to let her go, not again. "It's my turn to be heard. *Please.* Can we go sit on my beach towel?"

Avery hesitantly follows me over. After texting Brad that I won't be meeting him, I spread my towel on the hot sand, sit, and pat the spot next to me. She looks at it with apprehension.

"Jess, I already told you. This is wrong. I shouldn't have let last Thursday night happen, and I shouldn't have kissed you back today."

Her words cut me, but I force a smile. "And I already told you, it's my turn now. Please, sit with me. You're not doing anything wrong."

Once she lowers herself onto my towel, I angle my body to face her. *This is it.* This is my one shot to convince her we belong together, and I need to not blow it. *No pressure.* I open my mouth to speak, but suddenly the words are not there. It's like I've forgotten my lines on opening night.

"Jess, are you okay?"

Her question snaps me out of my trance. "Uh, yeah. Sorry."

How long had I been staring wordlessly? And more importantly, what do I say next? I've never had stage fright before, but I'm certain this is what it feels like. Performing had always come easy to me in high school. And then… *I've got this.*

"It all started in our freshman drama class," I begin. "I don't know if you remember, but on the first day of auditions for *Romeo and Juliet*, we both read monologues from *The Diary of Anne Frank*."

"I remember," she says.

"Good. Well, I remember being on stage, reciting my lines, and thinking of you. I couldn't see anyone in the audience because of the lighting, but I visualized you, watching me perform. It was the best feeling in the world, and when I got off the stage, your opinion was the only one that mattered to me. I didn't understand the feelings I had toward you then, but I do now."

Avery sucks in an audible breath and then sighs. "I wish I'd known that then, but that still doesn't change…"

"I'm not done," I interrupt. "This is going to be what I call a *long story long*. Good thing we're both comfortable."

She lets out a small laugh when I motion to our seats on the towel, and I consider it a win. I'd do anything to make her smile.

"Anyway, you didn't seem to like my monologue," I continue. "You weren't smiling or applauding, and—in true drama queen fashion—I felt devastated. Then when you went on stage, I was terrified you were going to recite the exact same lines, because I knew your delivery would obviously be better."

"Are you serious? There's no way my delivery would be better than yours!" Avery laughs, tucking her hair behind her ears before meeting my eyes. "Actually, I *had* planned on reciting the same monologue that day. But once I heard yours, I knew I could never do it justice the way you had, so I had to quickly pick something else. The look you saw on my face was panic. It didn't mean you weren't great. I always loved watching you perform. It's like you were born for the stage."

My mouth drops open in utter disbelief. "This whole time… I can't believe… Well, I wish I'd known that then, but unfortunately, that's not how the rest of this story goes. While you were on stage, Brad threw notes at me, asking me out."

"Yeah, I knew that," she says, looking down at the sand.

I gently tip her chin up. "But you don't know why I said yes. One of the notes he threw had said, 'Yours was better,' and it was the confidence boost I'd needed that day. Back then, I craved external validation—and still do sometimes, if I'm being honest— but I've been working on that." My heart smiles as our eyes lock. "Anyway, I thought you didn't like my performance *or me*. But Brad did. That's why I said yes to him."

Avery reaches for my hand, as if finally understanding, but waits for me to finish. She must sense my *long story long* isn't over, and she's right.

"Earlier today, I found out that Brad told Lucas we were trying to 'fix our marriage.' It made me furious, because we'd promised not to give the kids false hope, but it also got me thinking. I found myself asking the same question over and over: How do you fix something that was broken from the start?"

My cheeks and neck are soaked before I realize I've been crying. Avery wraps her arm around me, and I lean into her warmth, hyperaware of my cold, wet clothes. After a few more sobs, I pull away from Avery's shoulder so I can look into her eyes. She needs to hear this.

"I shouldn't have married Brad. He was never the one for me. I think about that night seventeen years ago all the time, not only because it was amazing, but because it's when I should have known. What's worse, I think I did know, but I ignored it. I ignored my feelings for you and my lack of desire for Brad. I ignored all of it, because I thought marrying him was what I *should* do. It was what was *right*. So, I'm sorry, but…

"I'm done with *should* and *right*. I'm going to divorce Brad, because I deserve to be happy, or at least to have a chance at happy. And even though you're the reason I've finally figured this out, you haven't done anything wrong. Do you understand?"

Avery nods, tears again filling her eyes. "I understand," she says.

Then, her lips are on mine, and I was wrong before. *This* is the most romantic kiss of my life. Her initiation makes it even more perfect than our last kiss, if perfection could possibly be improved. We're both crying as our mouths connect, drinking in each other's happy tears. I hold her wet face in my hands as she does the same.

"I understand," she repeats against my lips.

My thumbs trace her cheekbones and jaw before trailing down her neck. Though she says she understands, I need to say the words aloud. "It's always been you, Avery."

She deepens the kiss by again wrapping her fingers into my hair and gently tugging. *I love it when she does that.* I want to tell her, but it would require breaking the kiss, and I'm not ready for that. Our tongues collide over and over, striving to become one. I move my hand down farther, knocking the thin spaghetti strap off her shoulder before remembering where we are.

"Let's go for a swim," I whisper in her ear.

She pulls back and looks at me with sultry eyes. "Aren't we wet enough?"

I smirk suggestively, and her hand flies over her mouth as if she's just realized what she said. At the sight of her wide eyes, my smile breaks into a hearty laugh.

She laughs as well. "I meant our *clothes* are already wet. I swear, I'm not trying to talk dirty."

"You're naturally good at it, then?" I tease.

She tilts her head and gives me *a look*. It's enough for me to realize that dirty talk is fun with her, even when unintentional. Whenever Brad had tried in the past, his words had felt off-putting and crude. It made me uncomfortable, whereas now, I find myself craving more.

"What was that other line of yours? About holes or cracks or something?" I ask, still laughing.

Avery crosses her arms and gives me her best fake-annoyed look before caving. "You can't cover your holes with someone else's love; you have to fill them yourself."

"That's the one!" I playfully slap her knee before doubling over with laughter.

"You're the worst," she says. "Keep making fun of me, and you'll be filling all your own holes… and cracks!"

At that, cackles explode from both of our mouths. Tears again stream down my face, and we both laugh as hard as we had the last time we sat on this beach together, back when I'd convinced myself that I only wanted a friendship with Avery. Though it's only been a few short weeks, that feels like a lifetime ago now.

"So… a swim?" Avery asks once we finally stop giggling like a couple of schoolgirls.

"Yes, let's go!" I grab her hand, and we help each other to standing.

As I lead her toward the scene of my enlightenment, Avery says, "You never explained why you went swimming in your clothes. Was it due to this heat?"

"Not quite. I learned something today." Wading into the cool ocean, I turn to face her when the water hits my waist. "Self-love is choosing to enjoy life's unexpected waves."

"Who's Foda now? I like it," Avery says with a laugh before parroting my words back. "Self-love is choosing to enjoy life's unexpected waves."

And so, we do—all afternoon.

"How's the apartment search going?" I ask Brad, once the kids have been tucked away in my bed.

They've opted to sleep with me every night this week, and I can't say I mind. Sometimes, I wish I had a kangaroo's pouch so I could keep them safe and close to me at all times, especially since the fire.

Brad's expression makes it clear he wasn't expecting my question. "Uh, I was hoping we could talk about that. But first, you still haven't explained why you missed our marriage counseling session today."

"I told you. I was at the beach."

Even if I hadn't told him, the fact that I came home covered in seawater and sand would have been evidence enough. I'd then handed off the kids and raced into the shower. Like I always tell the kids: *You haven't been to the beach if you don't come home with sand in your cracks.* I inwardly chuckle at the inside joke Avery and I now have regarding *cracks*, juvenile as it may be.

"What's so funny?" Brad asks.

Apparently, I'd outwardly chuckled. "Nothing," I say.

Brad eyes me suspiciously. "Anyway, being at the beach isn't an explanation for why you didn't leave and come to our session like you were supposed to."

"First off, I don't owe you an explanation for anything." I wag my finger in the air before holding up another. "And secondly, I didn't leave because counseling isn't necessary anymore. I've made my decision."

"Slow down," Brad holds up his hands as if I'm pointing a gun at him. "I'm sorry for everything I've put you through this past year. I would take it all back if I could. Please, can't you find it in yourself to forgive me?"

I take a deep breath to calm my voice. "I *have* forgiven you, Brad. We've both made mistakes, and I love the family we've created…"

"That's great! Then let's…"

"But I don't want to get back together," I finish by cutting him off. "I'm sorry if this sounds harsh, but I've realized some things lately. Back in high school, I was insecure, and you were this popular guy that paid attention to me. It made me feel special. Then once we started dating, and more girls were interested in you, I felt even more special since I was the one you had chosen."

"You *are* special, Jess. I still choose you!"

"Please let me finish. You're missing the point. I was with you because of how our relationship made me feel about *myself*, not because of how I felt about you. Despite your mistakes, you're a good man, Brad, and an especially good father. I will always love you for that, but I don't think I was ever *in love* with you."

Brad steps closer to me. "Babe, you don't mean that. You're just hurting. Because I hurt you, and I am so, so sorry for that."

I step back and push his arms away when he reaches for me. "You're not hearing me. I want a divorce, Brad, and not because you cheated on me. Yes, that betrayal hurt. But now I see that I only thought I loved you because I didn't love myself. I do now, and it's changed what I want."

"No." Brad shakes his head.

"I'm not trying to be hurtful," I say in response to the look on his face.

There's a beat of awkward silence, so I walk over and fluff the *Love Never Fails* pillow to busy myself. It would feel ironic, except that love isn't failing. It was simply misplaced before.

"There's someone else, isn't there?" he asks, having a sudden breakthrough of understanding himself.

"That's not what this is about," I say. "Once I started loving myself, I stopped needing to be *chosen* and realized I should be the one *choosing*."

"And you don't choose me."

There wasn't a question in his statement, but I answer anyway. "No, I don't. I'm sorry if that hurts you, but it's the truth."

Brad lowers himself onto the sofa, a combination of shock and defeat on his face. "What now?"

I push past my emotions and lay things out as logically as I can. "You can still stay here until you find a new apartment, if you want. Though, we should probably set a goal for when that might be. We'll also need to find someone to handle our divorce. Maybe a lawyer or… I have no idea what's standard. Divorce was always a non-option. Yet here we are."

Joining him on the sofa, I laugh to lighten the mood, but there's nothing funny about any of this. My parents flash to mind, their likely disappointment fluttering like butterflies inside me. I won't let it discourage me, though. I can't. My course is set, and I'm sailing toward a life I never imagined but desperately want.

"I never thought I'd ever be divorcing you," Brad finally says, "but I guess that's why I took our marriage for granted. I took you for granted, too. I'm really sorry, Jess."

His apology this time is less a plea for forgiveness and more a statement of finality. *Our marriage is over.*

Chapter 31

The next day at work, anxious energy threatens to bubble out of me like a shaken soda can. It's unusually slow, even for a Thursday, which is making each minute feel like ten. At this pace, the remaining half hour of my shift will be an excruciating three hundred minutes.

Avery had told me she'd be busy today, first with Rome's physical therapy, and then with a full schedule of other patients at the rehab center, but I've been lucky enough to see her a few times, coming and going from the hotel like a short, curly-haired version of Gal Gadot—my personal *Wonder Woman*. I'm truly amazed by her. In the short time she's been helping me, my range of motion is almost back to normal. At the thought, I roll my left shoulder, which, despite being sore from all the swimming yesterday, feels great.

I glance at the time on my computer and sigh. Only two minutes have passed since the last time I checked. *Twenty-eight minutes to go.*

"What's crackin', Smiles?"

The sound of Diego's voice puts a huge smile on my face even before I turn to see him standing behind me. I assume it's why he calls me *Smiles*. I can't help it, though. Being around friends puts me in a good mood, and I'm especially happy he's here now.

"Diego! Please tell me you're on a break. I've been dying for someone to talk to!"

"I'm all yours for the next… nine minutes," he says, looking at his smart watch.

"I'll take it! There's something I have to tell you."

"You and Rome hooked up!"

"No, definitely not, and please lower your voice," I hiss while scanning the lobby. Fortunately, I only see Nessa at the front desk, which reminds me… I still need to thank her for upgrading Avery's room.

Excitement buzzes through my veins like electricity. I've been wanting to tell someone about Avery ever since our incredible night last week. I'd picked up the phone to call Natalie several times but then lost the nerve. Everything feels too fresh, too delicate. But with Diego, my reservations magically disappear.

"There's someone else," I say.

Diego walks around my desk and sits in the chair across from me. "Spill the tea!"

"Okay. I need you to keep this between us for now, but… it's Rome's physical therapist, Avery. We spent the night together."

"Skrrt!" Diego mimics the sound of screeching tires. "What do you mean by 'spent the night?' Imma need details."

My cheeks burn, nuclear-style, holding an explosive smile that can't be contained. "Well… I'm not one to kiss and tell, but we certainly weren't *sleeping* that night."

"Damn, girl! You and the brunette snack, no cap? Are you a top or bottom? No, no, let me guess. I bet you're a power bottom! Have you DTRed yet?"

Top, bottom, DT what? And what's a cap have to do with anything? I have no idea how to respond to him.

After I stare in confusion long enough, Diego sighs and says, "Never mind. Sex, Jessica. Are you two having sex? And DTRed means *defined the relationship*. Do I have to spell out everything?"

"Oh, yes," I say, with cheeks ablaze. "You know I don't speak your Gen Z slang."

"OK boomer," he teases, before crossing and then uncrossing his arms. "Wait, was that 'yes' to the sex or to spelling things out?"

"Both, and I'm not a boomer—thank you very much. I'm technically a millennial, even though Nat says we're more like xennials. You know, digital adults with an analog childhood."

It's apparently his turn to stare at me blankly.

"Somewhere between Gen X and Y," I explain.

"Ah," he says, "you mean geriatric millennials."

"Okay. I'm done sharing."

"No, no, please. I'm sorry!" Diego clasps his hands in mock beggary.

I laugh, unable to act offended. My age is the one thing I openly embrace. *Mid-thirties and proud.* "You're lucky my bestie didn't hear you say that. She's sensitive to such things."

Diego puts on a serious face. "I thought I was your bestie?"

I laugh again, then tilt my head down to look at him over imaginary glasses. "No, honey, you're my work husband. Besides, I thought I could only be your BFF if I dated Rome, which I technically have a few times, but…"

"You what?" Diego exclaims, sounding indignant. "And I'm just hearing of this now! Let me get this straight. You dated Rome a few times, and now you're banging his chick instead?"

"She's not *his* chick, and I wouldn't say *banging*," I whisper-yell, again looking around the lobby to make sure it's clear.

"Didn't you say you were friends with her in high school?"

"Yeah. Sort of."

"Ooh, I love a good friends-to-lovers romance!" Diego steeples his hands and wiggles his fingers. "Are you FWBs or boo'd up now?" He holds up a hand. "*Sorry*, I forgot. That's 'friends with benefits or in a relationship' for elder millennials," he says with an exaggerated eye roll.

"I don't know. We haven't *DTRed*," I say, *seeing* his eye roll and *raising* him one silly face. "But we're meeting for drinks after my shift in… twenty-five minutes. Ugh, time is going so slow!"

Diego leans forward on his elbows. "Can we please back up to you dating Rome? What was *that* like?"

"It was fine," I say, suddenly regretting having mentioned it. I can't let on that it was all a ruse, as that would expose Avery's secret. "We went out for drinks one night, dinner another, and then to the golf range once, but we didn't have a connection."

"Because of your dopplebanger," Diego says matter-of-factly.

"My what?"

"Avery. That's her name, right?"

"Yes…" I say, still confused.

"You two look alike, and you're hooking up, so… dopplebanger." He shrugs. "I'll text you a link to some terms you should know now that you're a baby gay. You do use the internet, right?"

At that, I toss my pen across the desk to hit him in the chest.

"I kid. I kid." His tone turns sincere. "I'm truly happy for you both. She's a ten, but…"

"Stop right there," I interrupt, not wanting to hear anything negative about Avery. *She's a ten. Period.*

"No, hear me out. She's a ten. But you're a ten, too." Diego continues as I shake my head. "You are, Smiles. Anyone would be lucky to be with you. Never forget that."

"Aw, thank you! You're going to make me cry."

My eyes are already wet with tears as my heart swells. I've not only been blessed with the best family, but with the best friends as well. Though I suppose they're one and the same. As my mom always says: *Family is everyone we choose to surround ourselves with, related or not.*

Then suddenly the surge in my heart ebbs, like the tide being pulled back out to sea. *My mom. My family.* I hadn't yet thought of how I would tell them about my divorce… and about Avery. They won't understand, but I know they love me. They'll love me no matter what. Right?

I look across my desk at Diego, and it's as if he's reading my thoughts when he places his hand on top of mine and squeezes it.

"You don't have to tell anyone your truth until you're ready," he says. "I hid my true self for years, keeping my relationships secret from everyone. Until one day, I met someone I didn't want to hide. We were in love… or at least I thought so at the time."

We don't speak for a minute, but then I ask, "How did you tell your parents?"

"I invited them out to dinner with us one night. They'd thought Ryan and I were just friends, but when we arrived holding hands, they learned otherwise." Diego shakes his head. "In hindsight, it wasn't the best way to break the news. My parents had gotten to the restaurant early and were sipping drinks at the bar. When they saw us, my dad dropped the margarita glass in his hand. It shattered on the ground, making a scene. We drew even more attention when my dad yelled at Ryan to take his 'filthy hands' off his son. Ryan was mortified. He turned and ran from the restaurant. I followed him out, and my parents haven't returned my calls ever since."

His hand is still on top of mine, so I cover it with my free hand, giving it a hug.

"Ryan dumped me soon after the incident. He could tell I was upset about not hearing from my parents, and he didn't understand why I would keep trying. I think he was afraid of having to face them again, or, I don't know… maybe the regret I felt once they found out bothered him too much. In either case, we broke up, and I moved to San Diego. A year later, I still leave a voicemail for my parents every Sunday, hoping they'll get over being mad and just talk to me."

I squeeze his now trembling hand once more between both of mine. "I'm so sorry, Diego. And I'm sorry if asking you to tell me the story made it worse."

"No, it's okay," he says. "It is what it is, and I'm happy to help you. My biggest piece of advice, based on my experience, would be to tell them privately—not in front of Avery. That's the one thing I would've done differently."

Grateful for the guidance, I nod and then ask, "But you would have still told them?"

"Absolutely," he says without hesitation. "Even knowing they wouldn't talk to me again, I'd still tell them. I didn't want to live a lie anymore. My dad was always my hero growing up, you know—and he still is. I think that's part of what Ryan couldn't understand. But in my heart, I know heroes always do the right thing… eventually. So, I have faith my dad will come around, and in the meantime, it feels good to no longer be lying to my hero."

I think of my own dad and smile. *He's my hero, too.* "Thank you so much. This has been more helpful than I could possibly express."

"*De nada*, Smiles. Best of luck with your lady friend tonight." Diego winks at me, then stands. "My break is over, unfortunately, but keep me updated."

"Totes," I say, hoping to sound hip.

Diego's scrunched face says I missed the mark. "Please don't ever say that again. Totes is cheugy."

"What's…" I start to ask before Diego cuts me off.

"Internet," he instructs, walking off with a little dance in his step.

Nineteen long minutes later, I clock out, change into a figure-flattering cocktail dress, and rush to the bar. Avery is already there when I arrive, and my breath catches at the sight of her pretty smile. I've come to realize her smiles are rarer than one would hope for, but—like a rainbow in a city that hardly gets rain—it's that much more special when you see one. I'd happily chase the end of every rainbow to put more smiles on her face.

For the next hour, which goes ridiculously faster than those nineteen minutes had, we sit and talk about *everything*. All the awkwardness from before is nonexistent as we fill in the blanks from the years we've been apart. I talk about Lucas and Chloe, and she shares stories of her time in LA and her travels, both in the U.S. and abroad. It's fascinating to hear about the places she's been and the amazing animal advocacy work she's done.

We also reminisce about our high school days, recounting all the lazy afternoons and summers spent at the beach, the bonfires at night, and the many classes we had together those four years—including our favorite drama class with Mrs. Beckett. Avery had been upset when Brad was cast as Romeo in our school play freshmen year, as she had secretly wanted to play the role opposite me but couldn't due to being a girl. As she tells me this, the corners of her mouth dip into a deep frown.

"*Juliet and Juliet* would make for a better modern-day retelling anyway," I say, desperately wanting to bring back her rainbow smile.

"Yeah," she says with a half laugh, "instead of feuding families, they'd have disapproving parents."

I tense at her words, and she notices.

"I'm sorry," she says, "I wasn't thinking."

"There's no need to apologize. You're not wrong." I stare at the near empty drink in my hand, and a beat of silence passes. Then another.

"Have you told anyone yet?" she finally asks.

I slowly shake my head. "Only my co-worker, Diego. He's… Well, his parents haven't talked to him in over a year since they found out."

"I see," Avery says, almost under her breath.

It strikes me that she might be upset or think I'm cowardly. I then think of Ryan, who hadn't understood the importance of Diego's relationship with his parents, and how that had ended things for them. Sickening fear creeps up from my belly, burns through my chest, and grips my throat. I'm not sure what I'm more afraid of: telling my parents about Avery, or losing her if I don't.

The constriction in my throat makes it difficult to speak, but I manage to ask, "What about your family?"

Avery's gaze scans the hotel bar before landing on me. "Damien knows. He's the only family I have left."

Suddenly, my fear pales in comparison to the heartbreak I feel for Avery. My hand flies to her bare shoulder, and I give it a squeeze. "I didn't realize. I'm so sorry."

"It's okay. It's just been Damien and me for a long time now. Speaking of my brother…" Her eyes dart past me, and her rainbow smile returns. "Raldy! You made it."

"Hey, Sis," a deep voice behind me says.

Before I can turn in my chair, Avery stands and wraps her arms around the man I assume is Damien, though I'm not sure why she called him *Raldy*. As I stand and wait to be introduced, I notice the man is tall with hair the same dark hue as Avery's. Based on his side profile, he seems to be handsome—with a straight nose, clean-shaven face, and sharp jawline. His eyes are squeezed shut as he hugs Avery, drawing my attention to his long dark lashes and arched brow.

Once their embrace ends, he immediately turns to me and holds out his hand. "Hi, Jessica. I'm Damien. I've heard nothing but good things about you."

"Aw. Likewise." I take his hand in mine, ready to shake it, then I look into his eyes… and freeze.

Those memorable eyes are unmistakable. They are an intense, bright green—the color of the lime in my drink.

Chapter 32

Nine years ago

What is that awful noise? My head is pounding. My eyelids feel glued shut. When I'm able to crack one open, the room is blurry. Everything is so… gray. The walls are gray. The window shades are gray. The bedspread is gray.

Wait… Both of my eyes pop open. *This isn't my bed! Where am I?*

The whirring continues and is followed by a dripping sound I now recognize as that of coffee brewing. I look down and see the casual sundress I'd been wearing yesterday during my huge fight with Brad. We'd both said hurtful things we didn't mean due to the stress of our fertility challenges. The bitterness of Brad saying he only wanted to have children if it happened "naturally" still stings in my chest. I push through the pain to a seated position.

My wedge sandals and a thin piece of teal fabric—*my thong,* I realize—are on the floor beside the bed. *The bed that is definitely not mine.* Flashes from last night come back to me in fuzzy fragments.

I'd gone to Altitude Sky Lounge for a drink after I'd left the fertility center. I was hoping to see some of the old crew at the rooftop bar I'd worked at after college, but the faces there were all new to me. The unfamiliar bartender earned my attention right away—with his tall build, chiseled features, and dark hair. What stood out the most, though, were his gorgeous green eyes. They were an intense lime green that matched the garnish of the drinks he served.

How can I remember those eyes so vividly and still have no recollection of how I got to… wherever I am?

I grab my thong off the floor, consider putting it back on, and then ball it in my fist instead while scanning the area for my purse. It doesn't appear to be anywhere in this room, which I now see is ridiculously tidy. *Nothing like my bedroom.* I need to get out of here… but where the heck is *here?*

The continued sound of percolating coffee reminds me that "where" is not the only mystery to solve. I'm clearly not alone, and the "who" part of this puzzle suddenly feels much more important. The answers to "why" my panties were on the ground and "what" I may have done last night rank high on the priority list as well. *Think, Jessica. What happened after you sat down at the bar?*

It slowly comes back. I flirted with the cute bartender by asking for a drink that matched the color of his eyes. He laughed, batted his lashes at me teasingly, and then said, "How about one that matches the blue in your dress instead?"

"An Adiós Mother F'er?" I asked, unable to say the popular blue drink's vulgar name in full.

He laughed again. "I was going to suggest a Blue Hawaiian. An Adiós will give you a partial lobotomy."

"I could use one of those after the day I've had," I said, and I meant it. "Adiós me, baby!"

"As you wish," he said with a wink, and my heart leapt—whether from his good looks, the flirtatious wink, or *The Princess Bride* reference, I wasn't sure.

When the strong drink was served, I remember looking down at it and reciting the ingredients in my head: blue curaçao, vodka, rum, tequila, gin, sweet-and-sour mix, and Sprite to top. I'd served plenty of these potent drinks back when I had tended bar, but I'd never once tried one myself…

Until last night. No wonder my memory past that first drink is shotty, at best. I drag myself toward the edge of the bed and reach for my shoes. My stomach, normally iron-clad, churns loudly before I'm hit with a wave of nausea. I clutch my sandals against my gut and double over, willing this awful feeling to pass. How many drinks did I have? And more importantly, how did I end up in this strange bedroom?

"Morning," a deep voice says. "I thought you might want some coffee."

I spring upright, much to my pounding head's misery, and see the handsome bartender from last night, standing in the doorframe. He's wearing athletic pants and a white T-shirt, and he's holding out a steaming mug of coffee. The normally pleasant smell has me covering my mouth and shaking my head. There are so many questions I want to ask him, but when his green eyes lock with mine, all I can manage is, "Do you know where my purse is?"

"Uh… yeah, it's by my front door," he says, looking to his right and pointing to what I can only hope is my way out.

I slide my feet into my wedges, not bothering to buckle the ankle straps before standing. "Thanks."

He takes a step back to clear a path for me as I head toward the door, still clutching my thong in my fist. I want to ask him why I wasn't wearing it this morning. I *should* ask if we had sex last night. But I'm too afraid of the answer. If I don't know for sure, I can pretend it never happened.

Ignoring the aches of my head and stomach, I put one foot in front of the other until I'm standing over my purse. It's on a chair near his front door as he'd said. I shove my underwear inside and then fish out my phone. I open the Uber app, which Brad had recently helped me install. *Brad… I can't believe I've done this to Brad.*

"Are you feeling okay?" the deep voice behind me asks.

I don't turn to face him. I can't. "Mm-hmm. I'm just going to take an Uber back to my car."

"Where's your car? I can take you."

"No, no, that won't be necessary."

"Are you sure you even need an Uber? My place is right across the street from the bar."

At that, I lower the phone in my hand, grip the handles of my bag, and swing open his door. "Great. I'll just walk. Bye!"

I shoot down the hall and don't dare turn around when I hear, "Hey, wait!"

But I can't wait. I need to hurry home, make up with Brad, and forget the last twenty-four hours ever happened.

Chapter 33

Now

I gulp and then gulp again, hoping my shock isn't obvious. "Nice to meet you, Damien."

He tilts his head. "You look familiar. Have we met before?"

"I don't think so," I lie. "I must have one of those faces."

"You were at our high school graduation ceremony, Raldy," Avery says, coming to my rescue. "Jess has also done some community theatre in the past—she's a super talented actress—so maybe you saw her in a local play."

"Oh really?" Damien asks.

"Speaking of which…" Avery turns to me. "Our *Romeo & Juliet* conversation reminded me that I know a director at the La Jolla Playhouse who's looking for someone to play Lady Capulet in his political retelling. Teenagers from far-right and far-left families fall in love, things get ugly—it's supposed to be very 'Hamilton-meets-Shakespeare.' Anyway, I know it's not a lead role, but you mentioned wanting to get back into acting and…"

"The role of Lady Capulet sounds awesome!" I cut in, letting excitement mask my discomfort.

"That's great," she says. "If you're interested, I can get you on the audition schedule and make introductions."

"That would be amazing. Thank you!" My eyes lock with hers, their syrupy sweetness drawing me in like a honeybee. I feel myself leaning in when Damien clears his throat.

"Should we get headed to my place? I've got something special planned for dinner tonight."

Avery steeples her fingers. "Ooh, I like special!"

We planned to have dinner with Damien tonight. Drinks were a way to kill time until he got off work and picked us up from the hotel, since parking can be tough in his neighborhood. The memory hits me like a slap in the face. How could I have forgotten? And more importantly, how can I get out of this?

"Don't you want to have a drink first?" I ask, desperate to at least stall this train wreck of a night.

"I've got wine at my place. Plus, I'm driving. My car's just out front." He motions toward the exit, and Avery leads the charge in that direction.

This is happening.

Much to my relief, Damien no longer lives in the apartment I had woken up in nine years ago. He now owns a condo in the lively neighborhood of Little Italy. With its plethora of restaurants and trendy bars only steps away, I'm surprised he's cooking tonight.

"Don't worry. We can order takeout from *Buon Appetito* if I mess up dinner," Damien says, after leading us to the kitchen. "With as much as Ems travels, I figured she's overdue for a home-cooked meal."

"I told you he does too much for me," Avery says, shooting me a smile and giving her brother a quick hug.

"I'm sure it'll be delicious. What can I do to help?" I ask, looking around the sleek kitchen.

Its stainless-steel appliances pop against a backdrop of black granite countertops and cherry wood cabinets. And it's as ridiculously tidy as I remember his old bedroom being. My already nervous stomach tightens.

Damien shoots me a look before busying himself with food prep. "Nothing, but please make yourself at home. There's an open bottle of red on the counter and white in the fridge."

"I'll grab us some wineglasses," Avery says.

"Just a small pour of red for me, please," I say as Avery begins filling the glasses. The last thing I want to be is drunk in front of her brother… again.

"So, Jess, Ems tells me you're an amazing mother. What are your kids like?"

I know he's only making polite conversation, but my heart nearly stops at Damien's mention of my children.

Avery hands me a wineglass and responds before I can. "They're adorable is what they are. Lucas, in particular, looks just like you, Jess."

"Thanks. He got the Serrano family brown eyes and olive skin," I say with a nervous laugh, before promptly changing the topic.

"Avery tells me you're our new District Attorney. That's impressive!" I say with forced enthusiasm. "Thanks for speaking to my best friend's fiancé, Derek, by the way. He mentioned your advice was really helpful."

Damien glances at me over his shoulder while stirring something on the stove. "*Assistant* District Attorney, and it was my pleasure. He seems like a great guy. It'll be nice to have a future prosecutor in our ranks with such an impressive background in law enforcement."

Avery lifts an eyebrow and smirks. "My dear brother is downplaying his enthusiasm. He called me up, giddy with excitement, right after talking to Derek. This could be the beginning of a very long bromance."

Damien laughs. "In my defense, it's not every day you meet someone as passionate about the same thing as you. Speaking of which, Jessica, I hear you recently adopted a rescue dog. Are you a big animal lover like my sis?"

"What is this? The Spanish Inquisition? You don't have to answer all my brother's nosy questions," Avery says with mock annoyance in his direction.

"Sorry, sorry," he says, moving to rinse a long, purple, squash-looking thing in the sink. "Excuse me for trying to get to know your girlfriend better."

The word *girlfriend* echoes in my head. We hadn't yet *DTR'd*, as Diego would say, but there it is. He called me Avery's girlfriend. And I like it. Even better, she hasn't corrected him.

My smile comes easy. "It's totally fine, and yes, I also love animals, big and small. Actually…" I turn to face Avery. "I've recently given up eating red meat. Yay for the pigs and cows!"

"Cheers to that." Avery taps her wineglass against the one I hold out. "But please don't feel like you need to do that for me, Jess."

"I'm not. I mean, I thought of you when I made the decision, of course, but I'm doing it for me."

"And for the pigs and cows," Damien says.

"And for the pigs and cows," I echo, raising my glass again.

Two glasses of wine later, I'm feeling much more relaxed as we sit to eat dinner. Damien made vegan eggplant "parm" with homemade marinara sauce, and its savory aroma has my mouth watering. The melted white "cheese" crusting the top is still bubbling as he sets it on the table between us.

"Can you explain again how this isn't real cheese?" I ask, wanting to reach out and poke it.

"It is technically cheese, just not made from dairy," Damien says, as if that should make sense.

My confusion must be evident, because Avery quickly chimes in. "The vegan mozzarella is made from coconut oil and other plant-based ingredients, like potato protein."

"And the vegan parmesan is nutritional yeast with ground cashews and garlic powder," Damien adds.

I smile and pretend to understand what *nutritional yeast* is. "Are you vegan too?"

"No, I'm a guilty carnivore," he says with a laugh, "but a friend of mine shared this recipe so I can show off for my little sis."

Avery grins at her brother. "I like this *friend* already. Does she have a name?"

His cheeks blush, *and darn if they aren't the cutest siblings.* "Why does my friend have to be a she?"

Avery crosses her arms and stares as if the answer is obvious.

"It's new," he says. "You'll meet her if it works out."

"Maybe we could double date," I offer without thinking. *No more wine for me.*

"Maybe," Damien says, in a way that implies *probably not*, before raising his wineglass. "*Buon appetito.* To the pigs and cows."

Avery and I both raise our glasses and repeat our new toast of the evening. "To the pigs and cows!"

The vegan cheese tastes better than expected, and before I know it, I'm scraping my plate clean. We politely argue over cleanup duty before Damien starts clearing the table.

"No guests of mine are washing the dishes," he says. "Can I get you something else to drink, Jessica? Coffee or espresso, maybe?"

"No, I'm fine. Thank you." I turn to Avery. "I should get going. I'll just take an Uber back so you two can catch up more."

With a pile of plates in one hand, Damien grabs the glass in front of me and then freezes. "Are you sure we haven't met before? I used to be a bartender at Altitude downtown years ago. Maybe you went there for drinks?"

Taxes. Bloody overdue taxes.

"No, I've never been there before," I outright lie.

"Geez. Lay off, big brother," Avery says with a laugh. "She's not one of your bar hussies. Stop trying to claim her just because you're jealous." Her tone is teasing, and a tad possessive, as she wraps her arm around my shoulders. "Why don't we catch an Uber back to the hotel together?"

"I'd love to, but I need to get home. The kids are still shaken from the fire, and I want to kiss them goodnight before they fall asleep." *Only a partial lie this time.* It's after eight, so the kids are most likely passed out already, but I can't face Avery. Not until I get my thundercloud of emotion under control.

Avery sighs. "It's hard to argue with that. You're such a good mom, Jess. I'll order a car for you and then stick around to give my brother a hard time for scaring you off."

Damien's voice rings out from the kitchen, amid the noise of dishes clanking. "Lucky me."

"It has nothing to do with him. I promise." *Wow. I am on a roll tonight.* "Thanks for the delicious dinner, Damien," I yell into the kitchen.

After a few parting words with her brother, Avery walks me outside to wait for my ride. All the while, Damien's earlier words loop through my head. *You have a familiar face. Have we met before? I used to be a bartender at Altitude downtown years ago. Maybe you went there for drinks?*

Without a doubt, that was my chance to come clean. And I blew it.

Chapter 34

"A threesome? Really?" Natalie asks as I stare at the ceiling in her office.

It's painted a pale blue with white wispy puffs meant to resemble clouds. The overall ambience of this space is soothing, but I'm beyond being soothed after last night's encounter. Even the plushness of this amazing couch, gently hugging my sides, can't calm my nerves.

"Seriously, after everything I've shared in the last hour, that's the part you can't believe?"

"I'm sorry, but… Remember that abstinence club you tried to make me join in high school?"

"It wasn't a *club*. It was a church group."

Natalie dismisses the difference with a wave of her hand. "The point is… I always thought I was the more sexually adventurous one. Clearly, I was wrong. Though, to be fair, sex in a public place is still on my bucket list, but I'm not sure Derek will go for it, being an officer of the law and all."

"As interesting as that is, can we please get back to my problem? How am I going to tell Avery? I can't keep this from her."

Natalie leans back in her chair and steeples her fingers. She's visibly transitioned from my best friend to free therapist, and I couldn't be more grateful.

"What are you thinking?" I ask.

"It's nothing…"

"But?" I prompt. There's always a *but*.

"*But* I find it interesting that you feel the need to confess to Avery, who you've barely started seeing, even though you were never compelled to tell Brad." She smirks when I turn on my side to face her. "Your feelings for her must be pretty strong."

"They are," I admit. "I think that's part of what's been so confusing, though. I'm drawn to Avery like I've never been to anyone else, but besides her, I think I'm only attracted to men."

"Your attraction could be more about the person than their gender. I think that's a thing." Natalie taps her chin with the pen she's holding. "In either case, I'm happy you went for it. And even though I'm officially pissed you didn't tell me until now, I can understand you feeling confused and wanting to wait."

"It doesn't matter now. I'm going to lose her, and I have no one to blame but myself." My stomach clenches at the thought.

"You're being too hard on yourself." Natalie, back in best friend mode, does another dismissive wave with the flip of her wrist. "So, you got drunk after a bad fight with Brad and woke up at her brother's apartment almost a decade ago. You don't even know for sure what happened, and you didn't know he was Avery's brother at the time. I'm sure she'll forgive you."

I glance at the clock on the wall. My shift at the hotel starts in an hour, but I'm nowhere near ready to leave this couch. "There's more to the story. Something much worse I haven't told you yet."

Back in therapist mode, Natalie sits up taller and crosses her hands on her lap, waiting for me to continue.

I take a deep breath, filling and emptying my lungs completely, before drudging up my darkest secret from the depths of my soul. "First off, only me and a priest in Santa Barbara know what I'm about to tell you. It can't leave this room."

Natalie rises from her chair and extends her pinky, which I shake. "A priest in Santa Barbara?" she asks.

"Yes. I drove over eight hours round trip to go to confession up there so my own priest would never know. That's how bad this is."

Natalie sits back down, seeming to understand the seriousness of this conversation. I inhale deeply again and then hold my breath, steeling myself for what I'm about to share. It reminds me of all the times I used to cut my hand to become blood sisters with Natalie. I knew it was going to hurt, but I did it anyway. *Ready, set, cut.*

"Five weeks after I woke up in Damien's apartment, I found out I was pregnant with Lucas."

I close my eyes to avoid seeing Natalie's reaction, and I'm transported back to that day. The two faint lines that formed a plus sign were blurred by my tears. What should have been the happiest moment of my life became tainted by mixed emotions.

"I don't know anything for sure. Like I said, I don't remember that night. And I also had makeup sex with Brad the next morning, so he could still be Lucas' father. But…"

"But," Natalie repeats softly.

Neither of us needs to finish that sentence. Natalie knows how difficult it had been for Brad and me to conceive. I'd often called her while crying, sometimes as late as midnight when she lived in New York. She knows all about his low sperm count, my blocked tube, and how hopeless I had felt.

"The thing is… I don't regret getting pregnant, even if it wasn't by Brad, because I finally got my babies. I know that sounds awful."

"It's not awful, Jess. I know how much your kids mean to you."

Her kind words prompt me to open my eyes. I'm surprised to see that Natalie has moved from her chair to the floor. She's twirling a strand of her long blond hair around her finger, a nervous habit she's had since we were kids.

"Thanks for not judging me," I say, reaching out to touch her arm.

"I would never judge you! You can tell me anything." Hurt radiates from her eyes, and I realize Natalie is right.

"I know I can. The problem is, *I judge me.* Just when I was learning how to love myself, I'm reminded of the biggest reason I hate myself." I sniff back the building pressure in my nose. "When I later found out I was pregnant with Chloe, I was overjoyed for more than the obvious reasons. It proved Brad and I could conceive. But a part of me always believed Lucas' birth is what helped me get pregnant a second time, since it removed the stress of our fertility challenges. Then, when we found out about Chloe's syndrome…"

Natalie cuts me off before I can finish. "Don't even *think* about blaming yourself."

"I don't. And you know I would never change having her, even if I knew she'd be born with Prader Willi. She's my sweet, precious miracle. But I can't help sometimes feeling like…" I gulp down a sob. "Like maybe her pain is my punishment."

The sobs are uncontrollable now. My whole body is convulsing. Natalie must have scooted closer, because I feel the warmth of her hug. She's shushing me in a soothing tone one would use to calm a crying baby. I think she's also telling me I'm wrong, but it's hard to make out her words over my wails. I'm not sure how long we stay like that, but once my tears run dry, I sit up and blow my nose with the tissues Natalie hands me.

"Thanks," I say. "I didn't realize how badly I needed to get that off my chest. I'm sure you understand now why I've never been able to tell Brad, and also why it wasn't hard for me to forgive his cheating. The secret I've kept all these years is much worse."

"I don't know about that," she says, shaking her head. "Your secret certainly doesn't make what Brad did okay. But I guess that doesn't matter anymore. Have you ever thought of getting a paternity test, just to know?"

"No," I say without hesitation. "I've never wanted to know. Brad is Lucas' father, whether by blood or not. He's been his father ever since our first ultrasound, which he framed and hung on our bedroom wall. He was his father when he held Lucas in the delivery room, and when we dropped Lucas off for the first day of kindergarten. He'll be Lucas' father for the rest of their lives, and I don't want anything to ever change that."

Natalie opens her mouth to speak and then closes it, as if thinking better of it.

"What is it?" I ask.

"Nothing," she says.

Nothing is never really nothing with Natalie. I tilt my head down and stare at her until she caves.

"I agree Brad is Lucas' father."

I continue staring at her, waiting for the *but*.

"There's no but," she says. "Brad is his father, regardless of paternity. I'm just trying to figure out how else you could learn what happened that night with Avery's brother. You could ask him outright, although…"

"Although is a fancy *but*," I tease, hoping to lighten the sickening weight in my gut.

She ignores my attempt at humor and twirls her hair again. "Since you were too drunk to consent, you'd essentially be accusing him of rape."

My jaw drops. I hadn't thought of that. All these years I've drowned in guilt over what I might have done that night. Never once did I consider what may have been done *to me.*

"What if I gave my consent, and I just don't remember it?"

"Trust me," Natalie says, "if you were drunk enough to black out, then you were definitely too drunk to give your consent. Derek helped me see that once, and he says all men should see it that way."

My mind races to process everything. Avery loves her brother. If I tell her what I think *might* have happened, she'd be outraged—not only at the idea of her brother and me together, as I initially feared, but also that I would assume the worst of him. Then there's the possibility that Avery could be Lucas' biological aunt…

"What do you plan to say to Avery?" Natalie asks, interrupting my thoughts.

My reply feels like the most honest thing I've said in nine years. "I have absolutely no idea."

The hot sand burns my toes as I again sit on the beach, staring out at the lapping water. I'd called out from work. There was no way I could dole out recommendations to tourists with a wildfire raging through my heart. As difficult as it may be, I know what needs to be done to contain it.

"Hey," a voice says from behind.

I turn to see Avery's pretty, freckled face, and my heart drops. *It's time.* "Hey. Thanks for meeting here."

"Of course. You said you wanted to talk." Her words are hesitant, laced with fear, as she takes a seat next to me on my sunflower embroidered beach towel.

It's usually a bad thing when someone says they want to talk. I want to comfort her, but today is no exception.

I take her hand in mine. "Yes, there's something I need to share with you."

"Do you mind if I go first?" she asks, taking me by surprise.

Happy to delay my news, I give her hand a squeeze. "Be my guest!"

"Thanks. It's going to be pretty heavy, to warn you." She takes a deep breath and locks eyes with me. "My therapist recently told me she has patients who have shared more in seventeen minutes than I have in seventeen years. It got me thinking about how I'm not great at sharing things that matter with the people who matter to me. I'd like to change that... with you."

"I'd like that, too," I say.

Avery's gaze moves to the ocean. "I don't talk about this with anyone, not even Doctor K, but... my mother died during childbirth. She hemorrhaged after delivery, and they couldn't stop the bleeding. There had been other complications, so I almost didn't make it either. I came preterm and spent months in the NICU before going home with my father, who was a wreck after my mother's death."

"That's awful. I'm so sorry," I say.

She continues as if she hadn't heard me. "My Aunt Robin, my mother's sister, came out to help with me and my brother for the first year. Then she left once she thought our father was well enough to care for us. And I suppose he was, on the outside, but his insides were still riddled with grief.

"As I got older and learned why Damien and I didn't have a mother, I started feeling guilty for our father's grief. I assumed he hated me. And I hated myself, too. In my mind, I had murdered my own mother."

I shake my head and some of my heartbreak falls in the form of hot tears. "It wasn't your fault, Avery."

Her gaze stays fixed on the sea. "I did everything in my power to earn my father's love. I never got into trouble, never spoke back. I did all my chores without complaint and received perfect grades. But he was still indifferent toward me. Even becoming the perfect child hadn't helped.

"Damien tried to get our father's attention, too—though his way involved throwing fits and breaking things around the house. So, when I was eight, Damien got sent away to live at a boarding school. My father sat me down the next day and said I was all he had left in this world. Then, for the first time I can remember, my father told me he loved me."

Tears stream down Avery's face, and I wrap my arm around her, but she still doesn't look at me.

"Later that same night, he started kissing and touching me inappropriately. I didn't realize it was sexual abuse until years later. All I knew was my father finally loved me. He said we had a special bond but that it needed to be kept secret; otherwise, it would be broken." Avery pauses to wipe away tears and then flips over her wrist. "It's why I got my *no secrets* tattoo. I'd kept my father's horrible secret, and it cost me everything. When I was twelve, touching turned into sex. And when I was thirteen, I got pregnant."

I'm stunned speechless by the horror of it. My whole body freezes. My lungs stop breathing. Even the tears on my cheeks stop rolling. I can't believe she was violated like that... by her own father.

"It's the reason I can't have children now," Avery says in a surprisingly stoic tone. "My father, the former mayor of our small town, couldn't risk anyone finding out what he'd done to me, so he took matters into his own hands.

"He gave me a tranquilizer he'd gotten from one of his friends who owned a racehorse. When I came to, I was lying on a plastic tarp atop our dining room table. There was blood everywhere. I thought I was bleeding to death, but the blood eventually stopped and everything seemed fine… until about a week later, when I was rushed from school to the hospital with a fever of 104.

"I'd developed an infection in my uterus from the unsanitary and incomplete abortion he'd performed. What's worse, I later found out that my father had told the hospital I did it to myself, saying he found a bloody wire hanger in my bedroom as evidence. But at the time, I was too delirious from the fever to understand what was happening. I kept going in and out of consciousness as they wheeled me into the operating room, where I was given a hysterectomy to save my life."

Avery finally turns to face me. "To this day, the thing that haunts me most about the entire horrendous ordeal—the abuse, the procedure, all of it—is that I didn't have control over what happened to my own body. Every woman deserves to decide whether she will stay pregnant, and, ideally, whether she will get pregnant in the first place. But I suppose that's not the world we live in."

I gulp down the tears filling the back of my throat. My mind goes back to her baby, and her choice, being taken away from her. I'm sick with grief for her.

Avery's gaze returns to the ocean. "My father later told me he terminated the pregnancy because he didn't want me to die the way my mother had. It had made sense at the time, but I now know he was only protecting himself. He could have taken me to a clinic, where the procedure would have been safe, but the doctors there might have asked too many questions. They might have exposed his secret." She curls her hand into a fist near her mouth.

"Anyway, after my surgery, I was recovering at home when my brother came back from boarding school unexpectedly. He was seventeen by then, so he'd left without permission and caught a train home. When he arrived, he found our father on top of me and lost it. Damien beat him senseless, then called the police. Our father was arrested, and we moved to live with our Aunt Robin in San Diego."

"Thank God for Damien." My words come out like a whispered prayer.

"I wasn't as grateful to him as I should have been at first. After everything, I still loved our father and wanted to believe that he had loved me. But time and lots of therapy helped. Now, Damien and I are incredibly close. He's my hero." Avery's tearful brown eyes drift over to mine. "That's why I'm so glad you two met last night. You're both super important to me, and I wanted you to know that."

"You're important to me, too," I say, before my heart drops again.

There's no way I can tell her about my history with Damien now. In fact, there's only one thing I can think to do next. I kiss her.

Unlike our previous kisses, filled with passion, this one is sweet and full of something that feels a lot like love. My yo-yo of a heart races, fueled by warm emotion, as her lips move against mine. I slide my hands down both her arms to take her hands. Our fingers interlace as the kiss deepens, and I'm certain the warm emotion is love. *I love Avery with every cell in my body.*

I'm not sure how long our kiss lasts, as time seems to stand still, but I'm painfully aware when she breaks it.

"Thanks for listening to my long story. What did you want to talk with me about?" she asks.

I stare at her wordlessly and blink a few times.

"You know, when you asked me to meet you here at the beach? You said you had something to share."

"It's not important," I say, leaning in to steal another kiss.

She allows it but then pulls back. "Let me be the judge of that. What is it?"

I panic and say the first thing that comes to mind. "I wanted to invite you to a charity event next weekend. It's for Natalie's foundation, to support the Women's Center. I'll be working the event, so I unfortunately won't be able to spend much time with you there, but…"

"I'd love to go!" Avery cuts in. "Natalie's fiancé, Derek, mentioned the charity gala to Raldy when they spoke last week. My brother asked if I wanted to tag along, but I didn't realize you'd be working the event. That kind of works out perfectly! I'll get to see you, and I can keep Raldy company while you're busy."

The uncharacteristic excitement bubbling out of her has me feeling guilty I hadn't thought to invite her sooner.

"That's great!" I say with forced enthusiasm. Another encounter with Damien is less than ideal, but I suppose I'll need to get used to it. "Why do you call your brother Raldy, by the way?"

"Oh. Sometimes I use his nickname without realizing. It's based on our mother's maiden name, Emerald, which we both took on when we moved here. My brother calls me Ems, and I call him Raldy. It's silly, but I think it helped us bond better… after everything."

"It's not silly. It's awesome." I lean in and hug Avery this time, soaking in her warmth and softness before letting go.

"Thanks," she says, staring down at her wrist again. "I got my tattoo because of what happened with my father, but looking at it actually makes me think of my mother. Her parents, who also unfortunately passed away before I was born, had immigrated here from Syria, so my mother and aunt were both raised speaking Arabic. I think it's why I find the language so comforting, even though I never learned it myself."

I trace my fingers over the foreign letters on her skin, trying not to think about the horrible secret I'm keeping from her. "That's beautiful, Avery. What a great way to remember your mother."

She tilts her head. "Is everything okay? You've seemed a little off since you left my brother's last night. I know his annoying questions come off like the third degree, but he's just protective of me. He has a big heart—a lot like yours."

"Your brother is great. Everything is fine." I clasp my hands, praying for it to be true, while Natalie's earlier words echo in my head: *If you were drunk enough to black out, then you were definitely too drunk to give your consent.*

"Okay… but you could've invited me to the charity gala over the phone. Are you sure that's all you wanted to share?"

My head bobs up and down like a buoy in a sea of guilt. "Yep. That was it."

Chapter 35

The following weekend, I add ice to the towel-wrapped metal vessel and shake it vigorously, counting in my head. *One California, two California, three California.* My goal is thirty long seconds, but I lose count somewhere in the high teens, count to ten Californias once more, and call it good.

"Here you go, sir. One dirty martini, shaken not stirred," I say with a wink, after dropping three olives into the bottom of the glass and filling it. *These rich guys in tuxedos all like to think they're James Bond, so why not play along to make their evening?*

I smile as he thanks me and heads off into the large ballroom. Through the dim haze, I catch the sparkle of fine glassware and porcelain atop each candle-lit table. White floor-length linens serve as a base for diamond-shaped black lace covers, which drape halfway down each round table. The guests, also dressed in black and white attire—some sitting, most standing—are like chess pieces on a checkered board.

"How's it going?" Natalie asks, approaching stealthily from behind. If this were a game of chess, she'd be the queen. Most people who see her probably think she's one of the fancy guests rather than the benefit's organizer.

"Smooth sailing so far," I say.

"Is anything getting low?"

"Um… I'm on the last bottle of red from that case. And the vodka is half gone, but still good for now."

"Okay. More will be coming your way soon."

"What can I get for you, sir?" I ask the next man in line.

"Your best whiskey, neat. That means without ice, sweetheart," he mansplains.

I already knew that, of course, but I smile extra wide anyway. "Coming right up."

Having thought her gone, I'm jolted when Natalie whispers in my ear. "You have way more patience than I do."

"Years of practice," I say, steadying the bottle in my hand before pouring the golden-brown liquid into an empty lowball glass *without ice*.

After I hand the middle-aged man his whiskey neat, I look over my shoulder to find Natalie still hovering in her stylish white silk gown with black lace cutouts. She no doubt bought it to match the beautiful tables.

"How are things going for you?" I ask.

"Hectic but good." She scans the crowd and bites her lip. If her hair were down, it would be twirled deeply around her finger.

"Relax, Nat. This gala is amazing. You've really outdone yourself this time. You should be proud!"

"Thanks. It's not that, though."

Her nervousness is starting to worry me, but I open a Stella Artois and pour a glass of white wine for the next guests in line before asking, "What is it, then?"

She sighs. "Derek invited Damien to the fundraising gala tonight. He just walked in with Avery as his guest. I didn't know ahead of time, or I would have given you a heads up. I'm so sorry if it's awkward!"

I look out toward the ballroom's wide double doors and immediately spot Avery in a long asymmetrical black gown. One side nearly reaches her ankle in a point of fabric, while the other cuts up over her knee. Her curly hair is pulled high in an elegant updo, with loose tendrils framing her soft, angular face. She's absolutely breathtaking.

"No worries," I say, once oxygen returns to my brain. "She told me she was coming with her brother tonight, and she knows I'm bartending for the event. It's all good. We're doing really well, actually."

"What a relief! But now I feel like a crappy best friend for not staying in touch with how your relationship has been going this past week. Let's catch up for sure after tonight. Thank you again for your help!" Natalie rambles her sentences together in one long breath, and I laugh.

"You've been busy. It's fine!" Turning around, I see Natalie has already glided off and is talking with a member of the wait staff, so I pull my focus back to the line in front of me.

I help five more guests with drinks, all the while stealing glances at Avery, moving about the room on the arm of her brother. On the black-and-white chessboard, she's the king—the most important piece—and the one I'd do anything to protect. This past week has been amazing. We've seen each other every day and have spent practically every minute together when not working, including taking Lucas and Chloe back-to-school shoe shopping and to the beach.

The kids don't know she's more than a friend yet, but we privately *DTR'd* a few nights ago in Avery's hotel room. I officially have a girlfriend, which still feels weird to say after having a husband for so many years, but I've never been happier. It has me wondering if I'll be able to call her my wife someday…

It's like I've been given a second chance to cast the right person in the play of my life. I can't count the times I've looked back on the night of Richie Sampson's graduation party, which, in hindsight, had been like a final audition for the most important role: life partner.

And I'd been Hollywood. Instead of choosing the most talented actor, I cast the one who had the "right look." Brad fit the role of *big, strong husband* simply because he was a man, even though he wasn't right for the part.

"And what can I get for you, sir?" I say for the millionth time tonight, finding it both chivalrous and cliché that only the men are ordering drinks for themselves and their dates.

After pouring another whiskey for a handsome young man and a glass of red wine for his absent wife, I'm delighted to see Avery and Damien step up to the bar next. "Hey! It's so good to see you both. You two didn't have to wait in line, though."

Grateful there's no one else behind them, I dash around the bar and give them each a quick hug, holding on a beat longer with Avery. I'm too happy in her presence to feel inferior in my plain black pants, white button-down blouse, and bar apron. Appearance doesn't matter when you're with the right person. I understand that now.

"We just wanted to come over and say hi," Avery says, as candlelight dances in her warm eyes. "How's your night been going?"

"It's been busy, which is good. Tipsy people donate more." I shoot Damien a quick wink and then turn my gaze back to Avery. "What would you like to drink? Grey Goose pear martini?"

Avery smiles, *and oh, that smile*. Rainbows, puppies, and unicorns all wrapped in a big bow on Christmas morning.

"She knows you well, Ems," Damien says, as I head back to my side of the makeshift bar. "I didn't realize you knew how to tend bar, Jessica."

"I told you," Avery responds on my behalf, "she worked at a bar for a few years after college, like you."

"Oh, that's right," he says in a tone that doesn't quite convey he'd forgotten. "What bar did you work at?"

I'm suddenly a cornered pawn. There's nowhere left for me to move, and Damien seems to know it. There was a telling inflection in his voice at the end of his question, which is now reflected in his posture. His crossed arms are leaning on the bar, and his cool stare is one I imagine him using when cross-examining a witness on the stand.

I clear my throat. "I'm not sure it's even still in business."

Another lie, but I can't say I worked at Altitude after lying that I'd never even been there before. "This is why lying is bad," a silent voice whispers in my ear. *My conscious? A guardian angel? The devil?* It doesn't matter whose voice it is, because it speaks the truth. Even the smallest of lies can snowball out of control.

"Even so, I might remember it. What was the name?" he prods, as I mix Avery's drink.

A nervous sweat breaks out down my back and under my arms. I'm tempted to come clean; to rip the Band-Aid off and admit I lied before; to tell Avery and Damien that I worked at Altitude and recognized him from there; but I can't. This is neither the time nor place to do that, even if I were much braver than I am.

"Good times," I say, almost under my breath.

"Good times?" Damien repeats, shattering my hope that he hadn't heard me.

"Yeah, Good Times Bar," I say more confidently.

There's no Good Times Bar, or not that I'm aware of, but now that it's been said aloud several times, I can't help but picture a sleazy strip club.

Damien cocks his eyebrow as if thinking the same thing. "You got me there. I never heard of that one."

"And what can I get you to drink?" I ask him, rushing to change the subject.

"Oh, I don't know…" He strokes his clean-shaven jaw. "How about an Adiós?"

The metal cocktail shaker slips from my hand as I'm pouring Avery's martini. It breaks the glass and then rattles on the bar for a moment before rolling onto the ground with a bang.

"Shoot!" I grab a towel and mop up the vodka and broken glass with a trembling hand.

It sounds like Avery is asking me if I'm okay, but I can't focus on her words amid the distortion in my head. When my eyes finally lift and meet Damien's, it's checkmate.

"It *was* you," he says, delivering a verdict. *Guilty as charged.*

"Is everything okay over here?" The recognizable voice belongs to Natalie. I don't see her, but I feel her arm wrap around my shoulders from behind. "A sub is on his way over. You can use a break, anyway. Careful with that glass," she says, taking the wet towel from my hand.

The rest is a blur. My apron comes off. I'm shuffled away. A new guy stands in my place with a line at least ten people deep. I don't know when the line formed or how I got into the chair I'm currently seated in, two tables over from the bar.

Avery squats down beside me. "How's your hand? Does it hurt?"

I'm confused by her question until I look at my left hand, which is rested on the table and wrapped in another white bar towel. This towel is dry, except for where I see a red spot in the center.

A few seconds later, Derek appears with a first-aid kit. "Natalie sent me over. Let's take a look."

He removes the towel, and there's a small piece of martini glass sticking out of my palm, surrounded by blood. It doesn't hurt, though. I don't feel my hand. I don't feel anything. My entire body is numb.

It was you. Damien's words echo like screams at a carnival, bouncing around curved funhouse mirrors. Derek says something to me, but my ears only hear *it was you.* I assume he's pulled the glass out, because he's now dabbing at my palm with cotton or gauze. I'm grateful for the distraction when my hand finally stings.

Avery's words come into focus. "It wasn't deep, but we should still go get it looked at if you're in pain." A brief pause and then, "Jess?"

"No, no. I'm fine," I say, not caring about my hand at all.

I now realize Avery and I are alone at the table. Derek and his first-aid kit are gone, as is Damien. My voice is hoarse as I ask, "Where's your brother?"

"He said something important came up. He was going to place a few quick bids on items in the silent auction and then head out. I told him I'd catch my own ride back to the hotel. Are you okay, Jess? I'm worried about you."

"There's something I need to tell you," I manage to say.

Natalie's voice blasts through the sound system. "Ladies, gentlemen, and everyone else not captured by those binary labels…" There's a brief pause filled with chuckles and hand-clapping.

My own hand starts to throb as Natalie continues. "Thank you all for coming out tonight to support the Sylvia Porter Foundation and Fresh Start Women's Center. Our mission is to end domestic violence, and your generous donations make it all possible. I'd also like to personally thank the hardworking staff running this event, as well as those who help manage the day-to-day operations at the center. Can all the staff here please stand for a round of applause?"

Avery looks at me, and I shake my head. She keeps looking at me, so I slowly stand to the thunderous sound of many hands clapping. My smile has never been faker as I drown in the unwarranted praise. My only contribution, serving drinks, had resulted in a broken glass, a bloody scene, and someone else covering for me. All because I'm a liar.

An hour later, after convincing Avery to head back to her hotel without me, the Uber driver drops me off in Little Italy. I wasn't feeling well, or so I'd said. *What's a few more snowballs atop an avalanche of deceit?*

It's a quick walk to Damien's front door. I have to know whatever he knows. I'd been grateful for Natalie's interruption after almost spilling the beans to Avery. It doesn't make sense to tell her anything until I know what happened that night, once and for all.

I knock before I lose the nerve. A minute passes. *Maybe he's not home.* I'm turning to leave when the door flies open. Damien crosses his arms in lieu of a greeting. His sharp green eyes bore into me.

"I'm sorry I lied, but…"

"You thought something happened between us and didn't want my sister to know," he says, finishing my sentence with astonishing accuracy.

I'm done lying, so I nod.

He lets out a long sigh and drops his arms to his sides. "For the record, nothing physical happened between us, but we should talk. Do you want to come inside?"

Relief crashes over me like a wave as I ride the undertow into Damien's living room. It's as tidy as I have come to expect from him. As if being staged for an open house or photo shoot, there are zero signs of clutter anywhere. A single set of coasters sits neatly stacked in the center of the coffee table.

"Please have a seat. Can I get you anything to drink?"

"No, thank you." I say, lowering myself into an upholstered chair.

Though I wouldn't have thought twice before, the black leather couch next to me fills my head with images of murdered cows. Its presence is a reminder that Damien is nothing like Avery, and my guard immediately rises.

"I'm glad to hear nothing happened, but I'm still confused why I woke up in your bed at all. I unfortunately don't remember much after ordering my first Adiós. How much did I drink that night?"

Damien grips the back of the couch, choosing to stand rather than sit. "I think only the two Adiós drinks I made you. They hit you hard, though, and I felt awful. I remember trying to get you to eat some food, but you were too far gone by that point."

Too far gone? The horror of the cows is replaced by mental images of me, drunkenly dancing atop the bar like a girl gone wild. "What did I do?"

"It was a long time ago, but you were in no shape to get yourself home. I remember that much. At one point, you were falling asleep on the stool, and my manager asked me to eighty-six you from the bar. I couldn't just kick you out like that, so I walked you across the street to my apartment, got you settled into bed, and then went back to finish my shift."

"So, you left a strange girl in your apartment while you were at work?" I ask, feeling increasingly skeptical.

"Like I said, you were in no shape to go anywhere. It wasn't like I thought you'd rob me or anything. Besides, we had chatted quite a bit at the bar before you got drunk. You were... friendly enough."

"Friendly enough," I repeat in his same hesitant tone. "Okay, so then what happened?"

"Well, when I got home a couple of hours later, I found you sitting on the ground in my bathroom. You had gotten sick—multiple times, from what it looked like—miraculously, all in the toilet."

On instinct, my non-injured hand flies to my stomach. "Ugh. I'm sorry you had to see that."

"It was fine. Anyway, I made sure you were okay and helped you back into bed. Then I slept on the couch. In the morning, you ran out of there so fast I didn't get a chance to talk to you. I knew you were married, and from the guilty expression you had on your face, I could tell right away that you thought something had happened between us. I looked for you for weeks, hoping to clear the air, but our paths never crossed again."

"Until now." I blow out a breath.

"Until now," he echoes.

"Well, the reason I thought something *might* have happened..." I clear my throat to pluck up courage and then continue. "My underwear was on the ground when I woke up. Do you have any idea why that was the case?"

Damien's green eyes widen with apparent shock. "No idea. I swear. I didn't touch them... or you."

Another wave of relief crashes over me as I realize *I believe him.* All this time, all these years, I thought I'd cheated on my husband. I thought Lucas could have been…

"Maybe you took them off to be more comfortable," Damien says, interrupting my thoughts. "I kind of remember you kicking off your shoes and saying how uncomfortable you were. It was so long ago, though. My memory has faded."

"Your memory is much better than mine, and that makes sense," I say. "Thank you for taking care of my embarrassingly drunk self that night."

"It was no problem. But like I said, I was worried you had the wrong idea, and I tried to find you sooner. I told all my co-workers about you, hoping someone would know who you were, but no one did, so you became the *Adiós Girl* to everyone. Even Avery heard all about the *Adiós Girl.*"

I gulp at the mention of Avery. "Does she know it was me?"

Damien shakes his head. "I haven't said anything to her yet, but I think you should."

"I will. I promise I will."

"Good." Damien finally relaxes his grip on the back of the couch. "So, all these years you've thought…"

"That I was a horrible human being?" I finish. "Yep. Pretty much."

"Well, if something had happened, I would be the one who was a horrible human being, not you."

The tension I didn't realize I was carrying eases, and my shoulders relax. "That's what my best friend Natalie said recently, and I didn't want to accuse you of anything, but I needed to know the truth. I've felt awful for years, thinking I might have been unfaithful—which is not like me at all, by the way! And then I got pregnant with my son, and…"

"Wait a minute," Damien says, "you thought I might have gotten you pregnant? And you never came back to tell me?"

The heat in his voice matches the rising panic in my chest. I hadn't meant to let that detail slip, but it seems irrelevant now. "Nothing happened between us, so it doesn't matter."

"It matters to me!" His face, now red, contorts as he throws his hands in the air. "Holy crap! If I had given in to your advances, I could've been a father without even knowing it."

"My advances?" I ask, confused.

"Yes, your advances. You had been flirting and throwing yourself at me that entire night. I was trying to spare you the embarrassment before. But what kind of person lies about the paternity of their child?"

"I didn't lie. My husband is his father, not you. Nothing happened between us."

"But you didn't know that. And your husband? Present tense? I thought you were divorced?" he asks in a lawyer-like manner.

I cross my arms to match his posture. "We're separated, and we'll be getting divorced soon."

"So, as far as you knew, you had kept a secret from your husband all these years that he might not be the biological father of your son. Is that correct?"

"Technically, but…"

"But nothing," he says, cutting me off. "I wonder what else you've been keeping from my sister. She's been through enough. She doesn't need some liar like you breaking her heart."

I open my mouth to defend myself, then close it. My mountain of lies is too huge to deny. I have lied in so many ways, for so many years. I've lied to all the people I care about. I've even lied to myself.

"I should go," I say, feeling dejected.

Damien points toward the door. "Good idea. I'll walk you out."

Chapter 36

The next day is a particularly hectic Sunday. Besides the normal routine of getting everyone fed, dressed, and out the door to church, it's also moving day for Brad. As of tonight, he will no longer be a resident of our old couch.

In my usual fashion, I'm a bundle of mixed emotions, feeling both grateful and sad to see him go. As Monica from *Friends* said best: *It's the end of an era.*

"You should take the couch," I say, while slipping on my dress sandals.

"What? No, you loved that couch when we got it."

"You lost everything in the fire, Brad. Please take it. I've been thinking about getting a new couch anyway."

Brad nods once, probably feeling a lot like the couch. My heart aches for a second, but then I scratch at a small stain on the armrest and remember how overdue this all is. My love life and living room both need an overhaul.

"I don't have much else to move, so I should be out of here before you and the kids get back," he says.

I grab my purse. "Why don't you walk us out? You can say goodbye to the kids at the car."

After church, I do something I've never done before: I skip our family barbecue. It's an important tradition, but talking with Avery is my top priority today. I leave my kids with my parents, drive to the hotel, and before I know it, I'm standing outside her door taking deep breaths. I'm about to knock when my cell phone pings with a text.

> ***Avery, 11:24 AM:*** *Just got your message about coming over to talk. That's not a good idea. I've heard enough from Damien.*

Story of my life: I'm too late. My chest deflates. I knew Damien was mad, but I'd thought he'd at least give me twenty-four hours to break the news myself. It's hard to be mad, though, when he's only protecting his baby sister. I can't say I wouldn't have done the same.

I knock on the door and wait a minute before replying by text.

> ***Me, 11:25 AM:*** *I'm outside your door. Please let me explain.*

My foot taps on its own accord, and I bite my nails, despite trying to break the habit. There's no sound on the other side of the door. Three dots appear at the bottom of our chat, indicating she's texting, and then they vanish. They appear once more… and then disappear again. I lean against the wall opposite her door and wait. I'll wait forever if I have to.

> ***Avery, 11:32 AM:*** *I'm not there.*

Like a balloon losing helium, I slide along the wall until I'm a heap on the ground. Checking the time stamps, I see that it's been seven minutes. Seven minutes of text, stop, text, stop, and all I get is a statement of the obvious. A three-word reply.

What's more troubling is everything that's said by her non-words. They say: *I don't want to talk to you. What you did is unforgivable. Please leave me alone.*

I can't leave, though. Not until I tell her how I feel—about her, about what I did, about everything. My heart has become an anchor, and I'm moored to this hallway. Any of my co-workers could walk by and see me on the floor right now, but I don't care. My hand shakes as I type out my four-word reply.

> **Me, 11:34 AM:** *I'll wait for you.*

> **Avery, 11:36AM:** *I need time to process everything,*
>
> *Jess.*

This feels like progress. Six words, plus my name. It no longer screams *leave me alone.* She just needs time. I can give her time.

> **Me, 11:37 AM:** *I'll wait for you, Avery.*

And then I drag myself off the ground and leave.

Part IV: We only have Now

"Where there is love there is life."

–Mahatma Gandhi

Chapter 37 - Avery

When I see Rome slip out the revolving door, I follow a safe distance behind, grateful for the distraction. Rome claims to have a tee time at Torrey Pines this morning, but Cam, who books all of his golf games, has told me that's a lie. It's alarming how utterly normal it feels to be surrounded by liars. I've come to expect dishonesty from most people, even Raldy when it suits him, but never Jess. I never expected to be lied to by Jess.

At least she finished her physical therapy sessions last week. There's no way I could see her today and not fall apart. When she'd shown up outside my hotel room yesterday, I'd held my breath until I heard her leave. It had felt wrong saying I wasn't there when I was, but apparently our relationship is based on lies.

As I track Rome's rental car using the app on my phone, I try to push all thoughts of Jess aside. I focus on merging onto the freeway, avoiding the erratic drivers, holding my speed, staying within the lines… but it's useless. My brain does those things without thought, freeing up capacity to instead dwell on all the ups and downs of my feelings for Jess.

The endless rollercoaster of emotions started nearly twenty years ago with *the fall*—that exhilarating plummet toward earth, where unrestrained adrenaline conquers all fear, resulting in an out-of-body experience while also grounding us in what matters most. Love.

Then came the long hopeless ascent, higher and higher into the clouds, which lasted for years. My fear grew with each click upward, hoping my harness was secure. I didn't know if or when I'd ever reach the drop again. I was terrified I might not, and even more fearful that I would. What if I couldn't survive a second fall?

As it turns out, I was in a constant state of free fall. There was no second drop to be reached, just a continuation of the never-ending ride. The night I ended my sexual moratorium with Jess was pure elation, a double loop with an in-line twist. I was flying high on the outside of the rails, the beautiful world at my purview. But in a split second, it was over, and fear returned.

Next came disappointment when she fled my hotel room and didn't call for days. Then a corkscrew of guilt when I saw her happy family at church and considered myself an obstacle. Joy returned when she'd said I'd always been the one for her. The next week and a half was the longest stretch of happiness in my entire life, which I suppose is depressing, but I'd do anything to relive those days.

We'd spent every free minute together. We'd made our relationship official during a tender moment alone. I'd gotten to know her kids better, and I'd *thought* I'd gotten to know Jess better as well. Then came the betrayal segment of the rollercoaster. I now wonder if you can ever really know someone.

Rome's rental car pulls up in front of the familiar, deceptively innocent-looking house, and my suspicions are confirmed. I park four houses down and pull out my camera with the extra-long zoom lens. Through it, I see a middle-aged blond woman greet him at the door. Anabelle Rose of *Rose's Golden Doodles.*

It could be wishful thinking, but a Monday morning visit seems significant. If I'm ever going to expose their evil web of lies, I need to get some concrete evidence fast. And today, I'm hopeful. For the sake of the poor dogs, I pray I'm right.

I snap a picture of Rome right as he heads inside and out of my sight. Then I wait. What for, I have no idea, but I'll know it when I see it. In the meantime, I steady my breath and do my best to clear my mind of all thoughts of Jess. The puppies are what matter right now.

It's not long before a black cargo van pulls up in front of the house. It has a California license plate, which I immediately photograph. My heart jumps into my throat when the rear doors to the van swing open and three large men hop out the back with urgency. Two of them, who appear to be Hispanic, are carrying either end of a large wooden crate. My trigger finger is going crazy, clicking pictures as fast as it can without bothering to focus in on anything in particular.

After many close-ups, I force myself to zoom out and survey the larger area. That's when I see Rome exit the house and walk toward the men who've arrived. *This is good.* I take a bunch of shots with all four men in the frame, and then I freeze. Only my pounding heart is still moving, pumping blood loudly through my ears and back to its position outside my chest.

The third man is directing the other two carrying the crate toward the house. He looks Caucasian, with sandy brown hair that's overgrown, a full beard, and a jagged scar down the left side of his face. He's waving the other two men on with his right hand, while his left hand rests near his hip… on a gun. *The third man has a gun.* I quickly scan the waistbands of the other men, zooming in with the camera as needed, and sure enough, they have concealed weapons as well. *Why the hell do they all have guns?*

My brain is too panicked to know what to do next, but luckily, my trigger finger starts snapping photos again on its own. Through the lens of the camera, I follow the men toward the house, but rather than going inside, they go through a side fence into the backyard. I can't see anything beyond the tall, wooden boards of the fence, so without thinking, I hop out of my car and rush toward the neighbor's house.

If I can get into the neighbor's backyard, I should be able to peek through the fence to see what's going on, hopefully undetected. My heart is pounding even harder as I step onto the next-door neighbor's front lawn. The side gate to Anabelle Rose's backyard swings outward again, and the third gunman steps out, closing the door behind him and standing with his back to the fence like he's guarding it. No, not *like*. He *is* guarding it.

His gun is no longer at his hip. It's in his hand, which is crossed in front of his chest. This is alarming on so many levels. We are in a suburban neighborhood, not some rural farmland in the Ozarks. There's a swing set two houses over, meaning children live on this block. And then there's the fact that I'm standing less than a hundred feet away in plain sight.

My brain kicks into gear, and I duck behind the hedge separating the two properties. I don't think he saw me, but I can't be sure. The good news is, only Rome would recognize me, and he's in the backyard with the other two men. *The other two men with guns.* Rome didn't appear to have a gun, and now I'm conflicted over feeling worried for him and furious at the same time.

Whatever the hell he's involved in seems a lot more dangerous than puppy smuggling. *Oh God, are they stuffing drugs inside the poor dogs?* Or maybe the crate is full of weapons. I've admittedly seen far too many crime dramas, but I need to know what's in that crate. My curiosity has me inching along the shrubs toward the neighbor's backyard, even though the siren in my brain is blaring: *Run! Run away while you still can!*

Chapter 38 – Jessica

It's universally known that Monday mornings suck. I agree, and I don't even work at the hotel on Mondays. Thursdays are technically my Mondays, and yet I don't mind Thursdays at all. In fact, until yesterday, I used to look forward to them. Thursdays meant a night without the kids, which—as much as I love them—also meant an opportunity to spend quality time with Avery.

My lies have slammed that door shut, and while I pray a window will soon open, I spend the whole morning pretending my heart isn't broken in two. *For the sake of my children.* They deserve a mother who is happy, regardless of her current situation. I have to remind myself of that several times after getting out of bed with great effort. Then I slap on my usual cheery smile the way others get dressed in the morning.

Thankfully, the kids seem to be in high spirits as well, despite this being their first morning without their dad in over two weeks. We get through breakfast, morning routines, and a long walk around our neighborhood with Prince Petey, all without my smile faltering. I even laugh with the kids when we "all fall down" after a few rounds of "Ring Around the Rosie," right before ushering them and their backpacks into the car.

And now I'm exhausted. Since showers are a time luxury I couldn't afford today, my greasy hair is pulled up into a quick bun. I'm wearing no makeup or jewelry, and there's an orange juice stain on my white T-shirt when I park in front of my parents' house, but

I don't care. My smile is gone. I felt it fall off my face the second I dropped the kids off at school.

I let myself into my childhood home and startle when Noelle looks up at me from her seated position on the chaise lounge. She's holding a book.

"You don't read," I blurt out of surprise.

She rolls her eyes at me the way only little sisters can. "I'm young, Sissy. I can have new hobbies."

I ignore the implication that I'm too old for new hobbies, not only because it's false, but because I know Noelle didn't mean it like that. Despite being self-centered and oblivious at times, her heart is pure gold.

When I continue staring at her, waiting for a better explanation, she sighs and says, "I've already seen, like, every single rom-com movie ever made, so I figured I'd start reading them instead. Did you know there are, like, *way more* books than movies in the world?"

"Amazing," I say, unable to feign enthusiasm today.

"Plus, I'm an influencer now," she continues. "I normally post about fashion and things like picking out the perfect Christmas tree, but I've recently discovered a lot of untapped crossover potential with the popular Bookstagram and BookTok communities. Check out this idea…

"Step one: read a rom-com novel." She wiggles the book in her hand, which I now see is Christmas themed despite it being summer. "Step two: design a full clothing wardrobe for each of the main characters based on their personalities, dressing them much better than whatever frumpy outfit the author described… if they even bothered. I'm telling you, so far, it doesn't seem like writers care about fashion at all. *Enter, me.*"

She lost me at *influencer.*

"Where are Mom and Dad?" I ask.

"They're both in the backyard. Gardening. Together! I know, right?" she asks as if I'd had any reaction at all. "Mom and Dad are so flippin' cute. They should be characters in a rom-com book. Ooh, maybe I should write one myself!"

"Yeah, I'm sure that would be easy for you," I say with unintentional snark.

"Someone's grumpy today." Noelle tilts her head while looking at me. "Time of the month?"

And now I wish I had something in my hands to throw at my bratty baby sister, because—*period cramps*, I silently curse—it coincidentally *is* my time of the month, but that's not why I'm in a bad mood. "I have something I need to tell you all. Remember? It's why I texted you to come here."

"You're welcome, by the way. It's not like I had *nothing* to do today," she says with attitude, before her hands fly up to her mouth with a gasp. "Oh Saint Nick! Are you dying? Please say you're not dying."

"I'm not dying."

"Good." My sister places a hand over her heart. "Well, since you have some more time among the living, can we please do something about this look you've got going on?" Her other hand points up and down my body, making me wish I'd let her think I was dying.

"Not now," I say. "Let's go get Mom and Dad."

Chapter 39 - Avery

My heart is racing as I lift my leg over the neighbor's chain-link fence. Luckily, it's much shorter and easier to climb than the tall wooden one next to it—the one belonging to *Rose's Golden Doodles*. I'm dressed like I was going into the rehab center today—in simple khaki slacks and a short-sleeved ruffled blouse—which is good for scaling a fence, but not so good for being undercover. I'm not wearing my usual wide-brimmed hat or oversized sunglasses, and my hair is pulled back into a low ponytail, exposing my entire face. If Rome catches even a glimpse of me here, I'll be made in an instant.

Getting recognized is the least of my problems right now, though. *"They have guns!"* my useless brain screams as my body continues over the fence. When my shoes sink into the moist grass on the other side, it dawns on me that this stranger's backyard might contain a dog. And while I've never met an animal who didn't like me, even the friendliest bark would alert three armed men, plus Rome, to my presence. I freeze and wait for it to happen.

I've always considered myself an intelligent person. My actions in the last five minutes have me reevaluating that belief. I turn on my heels and consider getting the hell out of here when I hear a loud *thwack*. I freeze again. Another *thwack*. It takes a second to register the sound of splitting wood. *They're breaking open the crate.*

I run along the fence until I spot a section with a one-inch gap between the slats. With my head tilted ninety degrees, I peer in and see one of the men—who I mentally name Gunman Number

One—holding a crowbar the way one would a golf club. I'm reminded of Jessica's intel and decide he must be Rome's business partner, the Mexican professional golfer. He takes a swing at the top edge of the crate, presumably trying to loosen the cover enough to pry it off, and I remember the camera hanging from my neck.

I time my snapshots to the loud bangs of metal against wood, taking both close-ups and zoomed out photos of the entire scene. Rome and Gunman Number Two stand with their arms crossed as Gunman Number One swings the crowbar yet again at the large wooden crate in the center of the backyard. The large wooden crate without any air holes. *Oh, dear God, I pray there aren't any puppies in there!*

Anabelle Rose and her existing puppies for sale are nowhere to be seen, so I assume she must have taken them inside the house. There's a split in the wood, and Gunman Number One is now using the crowbar in the proper fashion to pry off the lid. It takes him a few attempts to get the right leverage, but then *pop*, the crate is open. My eyes go wide behind the camera lens as I zoom in on the contents.

The particular shade of minted green—covered in black ink, with a portrait of Benjamin Franklin in the middle—is undeniable. The crate is filled with hundred-dollar bills, rows and rows of them. *Countless stacks of cold, hard cash.*

I'm not aware of my trigger finger snapping away until I hear the commotion. The two gunmen seem to be yelling something in Spanish to each other, then there's the squeak of the hinged fence opening. I drop the camera. Its strap tugs on the back of my neck as it dangles near my chest. When I peer through the crack with my bare eyes once more, I see Gunman Number Three, who has re-entered the backyard. His gun, still in hand, is being brandished in Rome's direction.

I follow the point of his weapon across the yard and stop when I land on Rome's face. Two steely blue eyes are wide with surprise… and locked with mine.

Chapter 40 – Jessica

I'm sitting at the kitchen table, across from my mom and sister. My dad, who insisted on standing, is leaning against the beam that separates the small kitchen from the living room. They're all looking at me, waiting for me to tell them whatever it is I called them together for. As odd as the timing is, I find myself biting back a laugh.

It's almost comical, really, how I once thought telling my family about Avery would be the biggest challenge our relationship would face. Now, I'd give anything for things to be so simple. I think of Avery's *no secrets* tattoo, and then the easy part begins.

I tell my family everything.

Brad and I are getting a divorce. Our marriage was flawed from the start. I've had feelings for Avery since high school—romantic feelings—but it wasn't until recently that I understood what those feelings meant. Avery is much more than a friend to me, and until yesterday, we were in a beautiful new relationship.

"What happened yesterday, sweetie?"

I'm busy wiping away tears, so it takes me a second to register that my mom has asked me a question. It's the first thing anyone has said since my info-dump.

"Um," I say, organizing my thoughts, "Avery found out that I lied to her. I'd been hiding a horrible secret involving her brother."

Noelle, already paying more attention than I've ever seen her give to a conversation in her life, leans forward on her elbows. "Her brother?"

"Ay, Dios mío," my dad says, pulling a fourth chair from the table but not yet sitting in it.

"Nothing happened with her brother," I quickly explain, my cheeks set aflame. "The short version is: Nine years ago, Avery's brother helped take care of me after I drank way too much one night, but I couldn't remember anything the next day, so I assumed the worst. Then, when Avery introduced us recently, he recognized me, but I lied and said we'd never met. Then I kept lying to cover up my lies until it all caught up with me… and now Avery doesn't want to talk to me, and who could blame her?"

"I think we need to hear the long version to judge that properly," my sister says.

"Noelle," my mom scolds.

"What? The juicy details might be good for the book I want to write someday."

"Would you like some popcorn for the long version, too?" I ask.

My dad, finally sitting, clears his throat. "I would be okay hearing no version of it, but I'm sorry you're upset, Kissin' Bug."

My mom fans her face while looking up at the ceiling. "And I'm even sorrier that you felt the need to keep any of this from us until now. I thought we raised you to know that you could tell us anything. Well, tell *me* anything," my mom corrects after a short grunt from my dad.

Fighting back tears myself, I stand to grab a nearby box of tissues.

"You did, and I'm sorry. It's just…" I sigh and decide to tackle the unspoken elephant in the room. "You also raised me in The Catholic Church, Mom. I know how you feel about divorce, and I wasn't sure you'd understand about Avery."

My mother, hypersensitive Deedee Serrano, has never looked more offended. She drops the tissue I'd handed her and straightens her back. "First of all, it doesn't matter what I understand or don't understand. I am your mother, and I love you no matter what. Don't you girls ever forget that!" She looks from me to Noelle, then back to me. "Secondly, these are modern times. I know divorce is sometimes necessary and people love who they love. Please don't treat me like I'm some stubborn mule."

Out of the corner of my eye, I see my dad tiptoeing out of the kitchen. "I'm sorry, Mom. I didn't mean to insult you. I guess I was confused—or maybe I made an incorrect assumption—about why you encouraged me to go to marriage counseling with Brad."

Deedee's fury, as my dad calls it, subsides as quickly as it had risen. I believe my father's exact phrase is: *Hell hath no fury like Deedee's.* My emotional range was most certainly inherited from my mother.

Her shoulders, which had been pulled up near her ears, relax. "To be honest, I was hoping you'd decide to divorce Brad. I never liked him for you, and after he cheated…"

"You never liked Brad?" I interrupt, astonished by this very new information.

My mom shrugs as if this isn't the huge revelation it is. "He was always so smug. Even back when you two were in high school, it bothered me how he acted like you were lucky to be in his presence, when we all knew it was the other way around. But I didn't want to be a meddling mother…"

Noelle releases a sudden hiss of air from her lips, no doubt unintentionally, earning her a sharp glare.

"Anyway," our mother continues, "I encouraged marriage counseling because the decision to divorce Brad needed to be yours, and because I didn't want you to have any regret. I figured if you went to counseling and it didn't work out, then you'd at least know you tried your best. And your best has always been good enough, honey." Her hand covers mine as I reach for another tissue.

"Ugh, you both need to stop this now," Noelle says, stacking both of her hands on top of ours, "or else I'll start crying, too."

Mom playfully pinches Noelle with her free hand and then adds it to the pile. I place my remaining hand on top, and we've built a six-hand sandwich on the table.

Right then, my dad reappears in the kitchen, randomly whistling the melody from "Bad Boys" by Inner Circle, as if we hadn't been having a serious conversation all morning. It's classic Carlos Serrano, and I absolutely love him for it. We all start laughing, and before I know it, we're singing the chorus together.

"Bad boys, bad boys, whatcha gonna do…"

Chapter 41 - Avery

All he saw were my eyes through a gap in the fence. He doesn't know it's me, not for sure. I'm mentally reassuring myself as I sprint across Anabelle Rose's neighbor's backyard. I feel like a caged animal, sure to be headed for slaughter if I don't get out. My brain, which has been mostly ignored up to this point, screams: *Call nine-one-one!*

I pat my pockets as I continue running to the far back corner of the yard. Leaving the same way I came in isn't an option. They'll see me if I cut across the front yard. *And shoot me.* I gulp down fear and keep feeling for my phone, but, of course, I left it in the car.

My car is three houses over. I just need to get to my car, and everything will be okay.

The adjacent neighbor's yard also has a tall wooden fence—similar to that of the yard filled with gunmen, cash, and surprisingly no puppies—so I'm boxed in on both sides and can't go out the front. That leaves only the back of the fence, which I climb as if my life depends upon it—since it very well may—all the while telling myself: *It will all be fine.*

A belt loop on my pants somehow snags on the top of the chain-link fence once I get my second leg over, but I attempt to jump down anyway, hoping the force will be enough to rip the material free. And maybe if I bought my pants at one of the many popular brands that still use child labor to stitch their clothing in places like Bangladesh or Sri Lanka, then gravity would have been enough. But no, I paid twice as much for sustainably sourced, cruelty-free, organic cotton *freaking khaki pants* that are apparently so well made my hundred-and-twenty pounds dangling from a metal fence is not enough to tear them.

So now I'm thrashing like an animal caught in a snare, my feet mere inches above the ground, praying these stupid pants are also bulletproof. Ironically, I'm a lot like one of *Rose's Golden Doodles'* socially conscious buyers—plagued by good intentions with results that backfire.

My mind wanders back to the load of cash sitting one yard over. It's much more money than could ever be made by puppy sales alone. Have I stumbled upon a money laundering operation? Rome had mentioned a cash-back guarantee for unhappy puppy buyers, so maybe that's how they cycle the dirty bills. Okay, maybe I've binged one too many episodes of *Ozark*, but I still think it's plausible as I continue to twist and turn my body.

A rip of fabric, and then—thank God—my feet hit solid ground and I immediately start running. I hear shouting now but don't dare turn back.

This neighbor's house has a dog, but it's trapped inside, barking at me through the sliding glass door. I don't fault the dog for barking. I'm an intruder, and the large mixed-breed is doing his job, but it makes me wonder if his humans are home. My second thought is to wonder if that would make my situation better or worse. On the one hand, I could ask them to call the police. On the other, it would delay me getting to my car and potentially put them in danger, too.

A moot point, as I'm over the other side of the fence already and now running across their neighbor's front lawn. I'm no longer on the block where my car is parked, but I'll have to deal with that once I get farther away from the men with guns. At the thought, I finally look back over my shoulder, half expecting to see a gun pointed at me, but no one seems to be chasing me. Not yet, at least.

I run across two more lawns, passing the home with a swing set, and stop in front of the house that aligns with where my car is parked, one block over. This house is surrounded by a short, white picket fence, like the one Jess has around her home. *Nope. No time for…*

I freeze, needing to assess my options but feeling stuck. Like a sputtering engine deprived of fuel, my brain has stalled out. *Think, Avery. Think.* The most direct route would be to cut across this backyard and the one behind it, but that could be risky. Or I could run to the end of this block, which I can't see beyond the curve in the road, and then double-back on the block where my car is parked. Or… *What would Jess do?*

The mental question comes out of nowhere and conjures images of my old bracelet embroidered with the letters WWJD. It was standard issue from the all-girls' Catholic school I'd attended before moving to San Diego. Once my crush on Jess had bloomed, I remember often asking myself what she would do in various situations, usually ones involving an awkward social setting, as it was natural for me to shy away from large groups of people.

People. Jess would reach out to people. Without further hesitation, I run to the front door of the house with the white picket fence and knock loudly, pressing the doorbell a few times as well for good measure. A moment later, the door swings inward, and a middle-aged woman greets me with a puzzled face.

"Ma'am, I'm so sorry for the intrusion," I say, "but there are dangerous men nearby, and I need to use your phone to call the police. Please."

"Of course. Of course. Come in!" She ushers me inside, and I've never felt more grateful.

Chapter 42 – Jessica

"I'm so grateful for this family," I say, hugging my mom and sister tightly.

Noelle pulls back from the hug. "Brainstorm time. What can we do to get Avery talking to you again?"

"I don't know," I say with a sigh. "She said she needed time to process everything, and I want to give her that, but I'm not sure what I'll even say once she's ready to speak to me. Saying *I'm sorry* is not enough."

"You could get it tattooed on your forehead," my sister jokes.

"Noelle, don't be silly. She gets that from your father," Mom quips to me while leaning to get a view of Dad outside in the garden. He'd gone back to pulling weeds after his musical interruption, giving us free rein for girl talk.

"No… That could actually work," I say, an idea forming in my head.

Deedee throws her hands up in the air. "Great! I've raised two crazy daughters."

"It's different from Noelle's idea," I say to calm her, "but her idea gave me an even better one."

"You're welcome," Noelle says with a curtsy.

"Grab your purses," I tell them. "We're going on a field trip."

The next morning, I drop the kids off at school again and then head to my audition—the one Avery helped me get. I almost canceled, but then I realized I deserve this. Acting has always made me happy, and I deserve to be happy, regardless of the lies I've told.

I'm a ball of nerves when I step onto the stage. It's a musical retelling of *Romeo & Juliet*—and my singing voice is rusty at best—but luckily, Lady Capulet doesn't have a solo song. From what I've been told, the director wants to focus on the emotional depth of the characters in this slightly darker, political version of the original play.

Emotional range, don't fail me now. When the lines I'd memorized start falling out of my mouth, the world stops spinning. I'm no longer Jessica Serrano-Clark, soon-to-be divorced mother-of-two with a mountain of guilt and a girlfriend who won't talk to her. No. I'm *First Lady Capulet*, ambitious wife of a pig-headed President, and mother to a young girl who doesn't know what's best for her. I'm seen as timid and selfish, but I'm misunderstood and strong— and I've got this.

After a few parting words with the director, I exit the theatre feeling invigorated. Even if I don't get the role, I'm happy I auditioned. I've finally put myself back out there after all these years, and it feels amazing—like an adrenaline rush after a good workout, which makes you question why you put off exercising for so long.

At the thought, I call Noelle. "Hey, want to go for a run on the beach with me?"

"Who are you, and what have you done with my sister?" she replies.

"Ha ha. I'm serious. I'm in a good mood and want to get a workout in. Are you in or out?"

"Out," Noelle says, "but I have a better proposition. I'm dog-sitting at a McMansion in La Jolla right now, and they have a lap pool if you insist on exercise. You should come over here."

"How'd you get that gig?"

"You know the yoga class I teach on Wednesdays?"

"Sure," I say, even though it's impossible to keep up with her long list of jobs.

"Well, a woman who takes the class needed someone to watch her adorable Shih Tzu while she was away on business this week. And before you give me a hard time, she said I can invite a few people over if I want. So, are you in or out?"

"It is tempting, but…"

"She also has extra bathing suits for guests in the pool house," Noelle says, anticipating my concern. "I'm telling you… this place is unreal."

"Okay. Text me the address."

Ten minutes later, I pull up in front of a grand palace with white stone walls and a terracotta roof. After pushing the intercom button at the front gate, my gaze lands on the incredible ocean view just beyond the house. I'm imagining what it would be like to wake up to that view every morning when my sister's voice comes through.

"It's open."

A buzz and a click later, the gate slides to the right, revealing an amazing tiled courtyard, complete with an elegant fountain and circular drive. I pull in next to my sister's forest-green Volkswagen and then startle when the speakers on my SUV blare with an incoming call. The name on the screen has my heart racing.

"Avery! Hey. I'm so glad you called."

"Hey," she says.

A beat of awkward silence passes before I work up the courage to ask, "Can I come see you… so we can talk in person?"

"That's not…" She stops and takes an audible breath. "Jess, I'm calling to let you know that I'm leaving San Diego. My flight is in a few hours."

"What? How can you be leaving?"

"It's a long story, but Rome has been arrested for suspected money laundering, among other charges. That means I no longer have a job here."

"Money laundering? I thought he was involved in puppy smuggling?"

"The investigation is ongoing, and probably will be for some time, but I was following Rome yesterday and stumbled upon a large delivery of cash by three men with guns."

"Oh my gosh!"

"Yeah, it was crazy, but I ran to a neighbor's house and called the police. I had thought Rome saw me peering through the fence, but he must not have, because the men were all still there in Annabelle Rose's backyard when the authorities arrived. They think the dog breeder is likely one of several cover businesses they're using to filter the cash through, paying expenses in dirty cash and then collecting legitimate money from customers. It's still unclear where the puppies were coming from, but the good news is their operation is shut down now."

I take a few breaths to absorb the information. Avery was in a dangerous situation. She could have been hurt, but she instead succeeded in her mission of stopping the questionable breeder.

"Jess, are you still there?"

"Yeah, sorry. Thank God you're okay! You are okay, right?"

"Yes, I'm fine. I was a bit shaken up yesterday, but now I'm focused on what will happen to the puppies that were on the property. The police are currently holding them as evidence, but I want to make sure they get placed in loving homes. That's part of why I'm leaving. Rome's assistant, Cam, who is also now unemployed, has reached out to the animal advocacy group and wants me to join him at their shelter in Denver. From there, we'll work to get things sorted out."

My head is spinning. *Denver?* Why does she need to go to Denver to sort things out? And selfishly, what about us? I jolt at the knock outside my window and look to see Noelle waving at me. Having completely forgotten why I came here, I hold up a finger to buy more time.

"Can't you help the puppies better from here?" I ask, hopeful my logic will persuade her to stay.

"Possibly, but I need Cam's help, and I think the trip will be good for me. I need to get my head on straight… about everything."

"I see. You'll be coming back, though, right?"

The dead silence on the other end sinks my heart.

"When do you think you'll be back?" I ask, determined not to give up on us.

"I'm still figuring things out, Jess." Her tone is soft, and a little sad. "I've got to go now. I just wanted you to know what happened."

"Thank you," I say, unsure what else there is to say.

When the call ends, without as much as a goodbye, hot tears stream down my face. There's another rap on my window. This time, my sister is giving me a concerned look and motioning me to roll the window down. I wipe my cheeks dry and do as she suggests.

"What's going on?" Noelle asks.

I unlock my doors. "Get in the car. I'll catch you up on the drive."

In usual baby sister fashion, Noelle crosses her arms. "Tell me where we're going first."

Since I don't have time to argue, I tell her. "First, we're picking up Mom and Dad for moral support. Then, we're headed to the airport. I need to see Avery before she boards her plane."

Noelle hops in my SUV and slaps the dashboard. "What are we waiting for? Go, go, go!"

I do as instructed and floor the pedal. My tires squeal on the tiled courtyard as I round the driveway and then race down the street.

My sister squeals louder than the tires had. "This is so exciting! It's like the big gesture at the end of a nineties rom-com, except you won't be able to catch her at the gate. You need to stop her before she gets through security."

With that, I depress the pedal even further. *Towanda.*

Chapter 43 - Avery

The last two years on the road have taught me to travel light. My entire world fits within a twenty-one-inch carry-on, plus one personal item: my trusty canvas bag full of surveillance equipment. I suppose I won't need that stuff anymore, but you never know with Cam. He has a knack for finding potential animal cruelty situations that require further research, and I'll happily welcome any distraction.

After a farewell hug from my brother, I turn on my heels and roll my luggage toward the check-in kiosk. While I'm excited to see my friend and get his help, my heart still aches to be with Jess. It's an all-too-familiar ache, only this time, I wish it would stop. I used to think all I needed was for Jess to return my feelings. But when Damien told me about the secret she'd been keeping for years, it was like the opening in my heart—the one that has forever sought to be filled—caved in on itself.

I understand the destructive power of secrets far too well. I can even understand why Jess felt the need to keep one, but her words have lost all meaning. Love without trust is a Hollywood mansion built on an unstable cliff. I can't possibly know if her stated feelings are real, or merely lies that suit her current desire. And when it shifts like a capricious wind, where will that leave me? Heartbroken and alone, as usual.

Worse than that, the hope that has kept me going all these years will be crushed. I can't let that happen. I won't. Denver will give me the distance I need to seal off the hole in my heart once and for all. My brain is in the driver's seat for a change, and this is how it needs to be.

With my printed boarding pass in hand, I head toward airport security. People with luggage are moving in a zig-zag fashion through line barriers in an enclosed area, while the end of the line stretches outside and around the corner. My eyes are searching for the TSA pre-check signage when I spot…

It can't be. My not-yet-closed heart must be playing tricks. Jess is looking right at me, and she's not alone. Deedee and Carlos Serrano stand on either side of her, as does a younger woman I assume is her sister. I don't even realize I've stopped walking until Jess is running in my direction.

She stops a couple of feet in front of me and holds up a hand. "I know you said you needed time, and I respect that. Please, take all the time you need. But before you get on that plane, I just need you to know…" Jess grasps my free hand in both of hers. "I'll never stop fighting for you. *For us.* Because I love you, Avery. I love you so deeply; I feel it in my bones."

Her words, which I know I shouldn't trust, cause an immediate fissure in my heart. Rendered speechless, I'm desperately rebuilding my walls when she continues.

"But another reason I won't stop fighting for us is because *I also love me.* You once said I deserve to be on my own list of loved ones, and above all else, I want my loved ones to be happy. And guess what? Being with you, near you, even breathing the same air as you—it makes me happy. *You make me happy, Avery.* I sound like a broken record right now, but I don't care. Happy, happy, happy." Jess laughs and sniffs back tears. "So, to recap: I love you, I also love me, and I want us both to be happy. Of course, I'd love it if we could be happy together, but that's entirely up to you."

My brain attempts to regain control, but it's spinning. I look beyond Jess and see Deedee Serrano waving at me. "I'm confused… Your family is here."

"They're here for support. Regardless of what you decide, I wanted them to know about us. Because I'm done with secrets, Avery." Her soft brown eyes lock with mine, and the fissure deepens. "I never should have lied to you. *Sorry* doesn't begin to express how horrible I feel about that. I know my words are probably hard for you to trust right now, but I'm hoping this will help."

Jess turns over her wrist, and for the second time in five minutes, I don't believe what I'm seeing. Familiar Arabic letters in black ink stare back at me: لا اسرار

"No secrets," she says, translating her markings to English. "Never again, and definitely not from you."

I'm shell-shocked. "You… got a tattoo? For me?"

Her hopeful expression shifts to one of panic. "My sister thought the idea was crazy, but…"

"*Psycho* was the word I used," a female voice interrupts.

"Thanks for that, Sis." Jess throws a look over her shoulder, and I notice her entire family has moved closer and is now observing our conversation.

"Anyway," Jess continues, "I wanted to show you how serious I am, but I hope you don't mind that I copied your…"

"It's perfect," I croak, holding back a barrage of tears. The fissure has officially torn my heart open wide, but it no longer aches, as love pours in to fill every available space.

"I love you too, Jess. I always have. That's a secret I've kept for way too long. But I'm done with secrets too… for real this time." I hold up the tattoo on the inside of my wrist to face hers, a mirror image and symbol of our commitment to each other.

Tears flood my eyes, and I'm soon wrapped in a tight hug. I can feel the love in it transfer to me as easily as heat. I could live forever in this embrace. All of my fears are washed away, swept out to sea by a healing wave of love. And just like that, trust is no longer an issue.

Words may not always be honest, but actions and feelings never lie. My foundational trust is solid. I feel loved, therefore I am loved.

I'm wiping away tears when the embrace tightens all around me. A few beats pass before I realize what's happening. I'm encircled by Jess' family in my first ever group hug. In another life, I'd think this was weird, but it feels oddly wonderful.

I am loved. I am accepted. I am healed.

Epilogue – Jessica

Two months later

Sometimes, the hardest person to love is still yourself. But when you practice self-love and surround yourself with the right people, you find it's not as hard as you once thought.

I step forward in my pantsuit as First Lady Capulet, holding hands with Mr. President and First Daughter Juliet as we join the entire cast at the front of the stage. We all raise our clasped hands high before taking a bow. Once upright, my eyes immediately lock onto Avery, who stands with her brother and the rest of my family as they all cheer and applaud. The whole audience, in fact, appears to be giving us a standing ovation.

The external validation feels great, as it always has, but I no longer need it. Even without their praise, I know I gave a stellar performance tonight. Because I gave it my best, and my best is enough.

After changing into street clothes, my theatre family and I, along with our loved ones, all head to a local diner for celebratory pancakes. I'm surrounded by family—all the people who matter the most, related or not—and I've never been happier.

"Cheers to a successful opening night!" our director shouts, a fork of fluffy buttermilks lifted in the air.

We all cheer, and I clink my mug of vegan hot cocoa with Avery's before stealing a quick kiss.

Avery smiles and says, "The play was great tonight. You were amazing. Correction: You *are* amazing."

"Thank you, and thank you for helping me get the role in the first place."

"No, no. I only helped you get the audition. Getting the role was all you."

"In either case, it feels great to be acting again," I beam, taking in the joyous event.

A few of my co-stars are hugging and singing. The Montague crew stands near the diner counter, and the actor playing Mercutio, barely twenty-one himself, yells, "A round of mimosas, please! Hold the juice."

"Make my coffee Irish!" another actor hollers in jest.

Natalie approaches with Derek by her side. "Congrats again on an outstanding performance, bestie! This looks like a fun group, but the *mister* and I unfortunately need to get headed home."

"The mister!" I laugh while giving her a hug goodbye. "I still can't believe you two got married at the courthouse."

"Believe it, chica. You both were witnesses," Natalie says, referring to Avery and me.

"I know. But no big party or dancing?"

"Actually… Derek and I discussed it, and we plan to donate all the money we would have spent on a big wedding to the next charity gala for Fresh Start. We figure we can announce our recent marriage there to the other donors, and maybe even steal ourselves a first dance," she says with a wink. "You'll both have to be there, of course, as guests of honor. No bartending this time."

"Done!" I shout, hugging Derek goodbye next.

"That sounds lovely, Natalie. Thank you," Avery says.

Natalie turns to leave. "Oh, and I apologize in advance, but I think my mom plans to stay here a while longer tonight. She drove herself, and she's currently talking your mom's ear off, no doubt about her latest boy toy."

I laugh again. "No worries. I love your mom, and I'm sure mine doesn't mind."

Across the room, I see Linda saying something to my mom, whose cheeks immediately blush. My dad sits nearby, occupied with Lucas and Chloe, who are listening intently to some story he's telling with lots of hand gestures. Noelle sits across from them and is looking at her phone. The whole scene is wonderfully classic.

After Natalie and Derek leave, I turn my full attention back to the classic beauty by my side. "I love you, Avery. Have I said that yet today?"

"A few times with your words; countless times with your actions. But don't stop on my behalf. There's no limit," she says with a rainbow smile.

"In that case, I love you infinity." I lean in for another sweet kiss, gratefully uninhibited by any fears or doubts of the past.

"I love you, too," she says. "By the way, Damien wanted me to congratulate you on his behalf. He loved the show but couldn't join us for pancakes due to an early morning. He'll see us again on Sunday for the family barbecue."

My heart smiles at how comfortably Avery has settled into this family, knowing it was once a sensitive topic for her. Just last week, Lucas asked if he could start calling Avery "mom" too, and I worried it might weird her out. Instead, her eyes had filled with joyous tears. We told both kids they can call Avery whatever they want—she's family now, regardless of the title—and "mom" seems to have stuck. I'm still "mommy" to Chloe, and hope I always will be, but her sweet use of the word "mom" when she reaches for Avery's hand melts my insides every time.

Damien and I made our peace, not long after Avery and I reconciled, and he's become a brother to me as well. We are both passionate about the same thing: protecting our loved ones.

"Are you okay?" Avery asks, and I realize a tear is sliding down my cheek.

"Better than okay. These are happy tears," I say, wiping them away before taking Avery's hands. "I love our family so much."

All is right in the world as I look into Avery's sugary brown eyes. As it did all those years ago, our eye contact tells me everything I need to know. We are good. Life is good. Once my divorce is final, we can make things legal. Until then—and always—I'll give her my best, and my best is enough.

Noelle's voice jolts me from the tender moment. "I want that."

I turn to see her staring at us, only a few feet away, and I tilt my head in confusion. "Want what?"

"That. What you have." My sister's cheeks blush when I point at Avery. "Well, not *exactly* what you have, but the love part. I'm ready to find my happily ever after."

"That's great, Sissy! I'm sure you will."

"I'm done with San Diego guys, like Hayden, who only want one thing," she continues, "and that's why I thought you should know… I'm moving."

"What?" Avery and I both ask in unison.

"Don't be silly. You don't have to move to find love," I say.

"Oh, yes, I do," Noelle says, taking a defensive stance. "If my holiday romances have taught me anything, it's that all I need to do is move to a small town, take on some project where I need help from a handsome stranger, and then… *Bam!* We'll be in love by Christmas."

I shoot Avery a skeptical glance, then face my sister. "You can't be serious. Those are *fictional* stories, Noelle."

She places her balled-fists on her hips. "I'm as serious as presents."

"She takes gift-giving very seriously," I explain to Avery, still not believing my baby sister's insanity.

"*She* also has already found the perfect small town," Noelle says, referring to herself in the third-person. "Get this, it's called Holiday Pines! How perfect is that?"

Her enthusiasm, and the fact that she is serious enough to have a town in mind, forces me to take a seat. My voice cracks when I ask, "You're really leaving San Diego?"

"Don't get all emotional on me, Drama Queen," Noelle teases. "Holiday Pines is only about an hour's drive away. It's in our local mountains!"

"How have I never heard of it before, then?" I ask.

"Two words: small town." Noelle's smirk grows, then fades. "Look, I know this sounds crazy, but I'm sick of sitting around and waiting for love *to find me*. It's time to take charge and make things happen for myself."

Avery adorably gnaws on her bottom lip before saying, "No offense, but I don't think love works that way."

"Maybe not, but I've got a good feeling about this plan. It'll be like my own *Christmas tree farm of dreams*: you build the right conditions, and love will come! You'll see."

Noelle's contagious excitement pops me to my feet, and I give her a hug. "Well, in that case, I'm happy for you!"

"Thanks. I'm happy for you, too! Both of you." Noelle gives me an extra squeeze before hugging Avery next. "I better head home and start packing. Christmas is only a few months away!"

Once my sister scurries off like an eager elf, I again take Avery's hands. "Well… I guess we'll see how it goes."

Stay tuned for Book Three of the Fresh Start Series, ***When Love Holidays: A Christmas Rom-Com!*** Noelle has the perfect plan to find love during the holidays as the star of her own small-town romance. What could go wrong?

P.S. If you enjoyed this book, please leave a review! Amazon, Goodreads, social media, and other online book sites are all great options. Thank you in advance for your support! XOXO

Acknowledgments

There are so many people to thank, but first, I'd like to acknowledge a special young man named Landon and his amazing mother, Marisa. Landon is a Prader-Willi syndrome (PWS) warrior, who I've had the pleasure of watching grow from an adorable baby to the sweetest teenager. He mastered Uno at a young age, loves to dance, and brings joy to all around him. If not for Landon, I wouldn't know PWS even existed, which is why I hope to help spread awareness to readers. (To learn more, visit https://www.pwsausa.org)

To Marisa, thank you for taking time out of your hectic schedule to answer questions about raising a child with Prader-Willi syndrome. The candid sharing of your personal experience and emotions greatly contributed to this story, even though I'm sure the real-life challenges are far from captured here. All that you have done—and continue to do—as a working single mother is astounding. You should be very proud.

To my "blood sister" and bestie, Janet, thank you for always being one of my biggest cheerleaders and for letting me be a part of your fun-loving family. The larger-than-life personalities in your clan definitely inspired some of the lovable characters and banter in this book. (Donna, if you're reading this, thank you for being a second mother to me… and for teaching me that a girl can never have too much jewelry.)

To my good friend and fellow romance book lover, Sarah, thank you for reading (and re-reading) the drafts of all my books and providing valuable feedback. Having you in my corner means more than you know! Thank you for also nudging me out of my comfort zone by suggesting we attend an in-person romance book conference… I can't wait!

To Steph, Olivia, Kristina, and many other friends who have supported my newfound passion of writing by celebrating my book releases and letting me blab on about my stories, you are all my family. Thank you!

They'd be playing the music to boot me offstage by now if this were the Oscar's, but it's not, so I'd also like to thank my husband for supporting my decision to take a "break" from my day job, which enabled me to finish this novel a lot faster than the first one. And even though he'll never read this or anything I've written, because he doesn't like to read books—Blasphemy! I know—he still tolerates me talking about my books and book ideas *all the time* and supports me pursuing what makes me happy: writing emotional stories with entertainment value.

I'd also like to thank Colleen Hoover, not because we're friends or have interacted at all—a girl can dream—but because I'm a huge fan of her work. Like many others, I "discovered" her books through social media, read one, got hooked, and then read them all. The emotions she is able to elicit with words alone… mind blowing. Fangirling aside, #CoHo is an inspiration to a no-name indie author like me, as she started out as a self-published newbie too, and now her books are uber popular. It gives me hope for *maybe someday*. #IYKYK

Last, but certainly not least, I'd like to thank all of my advance readers and author friends, many of whom I've met through the wonder of #bookstagram and social media. You are such an amazing community of readers and writers (often both) who have helped me tremendously on my journey. Fun fact: The "S" in my pen name stands for my real first name, Sheena. So, if any book influencers out there want to be the first to start the #SheGre phenomenon, or something like that, I would not be opposed. Kidding, but not kidding. I love you all!

About the Author

S. J. Greene lives in San Diego, California with her husband and adorable rescue dog, both of whom are the loves of her life. She enjoys spending time in nature and, of course, reading romance novels! Her passion for writing evolved from a creative outlet—needed to balance out her overly analytical mind—to two published novels, with more in the works.

Though romance is at the heart of all her stories, S. J. Greene likes to color outside the lines when it comes to genres. In her *Fresh Start* standalone series, *When Love Hurts* (Book 1) is a romantic suspense novel with women's fiction and crime elements, whereas *When Love Heals* (Book 2) falls under contemporary women's fiction with romance and LGBTQ elements. *When Love Holidays* (Book 3) will be in the romantic comedy category. She also has plans for another rom-com, a psychological thriller, and a fantasy novel… Be sure to follow her on Amazon, Goodreads, and social media to stay updated on what comes next!

https://linktr.ee/author.sjgreene